LAIR OF THE WITCH

"Fool! If thou wilt not take what is offered thee, become what thou art—the lowest of the low!" Her hands snapped out, Magnus felt her will compelling his own as her eyes seemed to swell, swallowing him, dragging him into the dreadful, bloodshot, yellow gleam, and he felt himself dwindling, growing slack, falling to his knees, till he writhed on the floor.

"Be the serpent thou art," she hissed, malicious satisfaction in her eyes, "and shalt be evermore."

A hundred yards from her tower, he felt his body drift to the ground at the foot of a huge old oak—and, suddenly, whip itself about, curving against the bark.

"There shalt thou stay," the hag grated, "warding that tree from harm, till death take thee—and thy bones shall assure all who come nigh that they must do the bidding of the Hag of the Tower!"

Warlock and Son

WARLOCK AND SON

CHRISTOPHER STASHEFF

ACE BOOKS, NEW YORK

This book is an Ace original edition,
and has never been previously published.

WARLOCK AND SON

An Ace Book / published by arrangement with
the author

PRINTING HISTORY
Ace edition / October 1991

ISBN: 0-441-87314-6

Ace Books are published by The Berkley Publishing Group,
200 Madison Avenue, New York, New York 10016.
The name "ACE" and the "A" logo
are trademarks belonging to Charter Communications, Inc.

PRINTED IN THE UNITED STATES OF AMERICA

10 9 8 7 6 5 4 3 2 1

Several of the chapters in this book are based on the following traditional ballads:

"Allison Gross"
"Matty Groves"
"True Thomas"

Another chapter is based on Keats's *La Belle Dame Sans Merci*.

I would like to thank the members of the singing group Clam Chowder, whose performances reminded me of the richness of this source.

1

"By your leave, my father, I cannot agree," Magnus said.

Rod stared, a morsel of meat halfway to his mouth on the tip of his knife. "Agree? What's there to agree about? The Duke of Loguire is building up his army! That's a matter of fact, not opinion!"

"Aye." Geoffrey laid down his spoon, scowling at his brother. "Dost say the King's agent lie? Then hie thee to the South thyself and witness with thine own eyes!"

"I do not doubt the report," Magnus said. "I cannot agree that 'tis a threat."

Rod frowned. "Why?" He ignored the alarm and warning plea in his wife's eyes and pressed on. "You know Duke Anselm fronted as the figurehead in a rebellion twenty-five years ago. Frankly, I think his brother was a fool to let him inherit when their father died, even if Tuan is king."

"Surely that was for Their Majesties to decide, not thyself."

"Unfortunately, yes—and I think my worries are proving true. Anselm's planning to rebel again."

"That," Magnus said, "is opinion—and 'tis there that I cannot agree."

1

"Why, thou great loon!" Geoffrey erupted. "Dost think he gathers soldiers only to play with them?"

"Frankly," Magnus said, "yes. And thou, younger brother, art ill-equipped to judge the workings of a man's mind."

"Save in matters of war!"

"But not in matters of play," brother Gregory pointed out. "In that, I think Magnus hath insight in a fashion—for this Duke Anselm hath ever sought to make his daydreams gain substance by warping the real world into their semblance, hath he not?"

It still unnerved Rod to hear such perceptive comments coming from one so young, even though Gregory had crossed the border into adolescence, being thirteen. He tried to think up something to say that would take the sting out of his son's precociousness, but he wasn't having much luck.

Neither was Geoffrey. He stared, startled speechless, but Cordelia said, "Thou art right in that, Gregory—but Geoffrey is right to be wary, for Duke Anselm ever hath been eaten within by the worm of Envy, from all that Mother and Father have said of him. Whiles his father lived, he burned to become Duke—and now that he hath the title, he doth choke on his own gall at seeing his younger brother in place above him, on the throne. Nay, he may indeed seek to take what his brother hath, by force of arms."

"Why, how is this?" Magnus turned on her. "Thou, too? I had thought the lass of quick compassion would see more to pity, and less to fear, in this man."

"Why, so I do," Cordelia said, "but if I have a gift for reading the hearts of people, I have also the gift of seeing their curdled bitterness."

"I think we may leave him to his royal brother," Gwen began, but Rod shook his head. "Tuan has a good heart, but he always assumes the best of people. That's why he's always so surprised when they turn nasty—especially his own brother."

"Yet Queen Catharine surely can see the malice within him," Magnus protested.

"Does she ever see anything else?" Rod held up a hand to forestall protest. "No, I take that back. I'm sure she does see the occasional virtue—but I highly doubt that her royal spouse will listen to her."

"As some husbands ought," Gwen said darkly. "Yet he cannot act without her concurrence, Magnus."

"Right." Rod stabbed the air with his knife for emphasis. "Which nicely paralyzes the Crown while Anselm builds up his forces."

"But he may not intend war!" Magnus protested. "Must thou hang him for murder ere he hath lifted a dagger?"

"He shall hang himself, soon enough," Geoffrey assured him.

"I doubt not that he will show sign of his intent," Gregory qualified. "He is small of mind and heart, and will be guided by his counsellors."

"And they are more eaten by envy than he," Cordelia said. "They burn to plunge our world into chaos."

"Why, thou art all leagued against me!" Magnus shot to his feet, sending his chair clattering. "Thou wilt not so much as hear me out, wilt thou? Very well, have delight in thy converse, then—the dissenting voice will be silent as its owner doth depart!" And he strode out of the chamber.

The family stared at one another in shock as his boots rang on the flagstones, fading. A servant's voice rose in query, but Magnus virtually snarled in answer, and the door of the keep boomed shut behind him.

Then Gwen and Cordelia were on their feet. "Quickly! We must to him, ere he hath passed out 'neath the portcullis!" Gwen stopped, staring at her husband. "Wilt thou not go!"

"No." Rod's eyes had taken on a faraway look. "I think not."

"But his soul is in turmoil, Father!" Cordelia protested.

"Turmoil indeed." Gregory looked up at Rod, frowning. "Whence cometh such an outburst, Papa?"

"Why, for that his younger siblings have spoken back at him," Geoffrey said, with a hint of contempt.

"No," Rod mused, "I think it goes a bit deeper than that."

"Then since thou art the fount of wisdom in such matters, thou must needs go to calm him!" Gwen said, exasperated. "Dost thou say this is a young man's heartache? And wilt thou not then follow him to assuage it?"

"Yes," Rod said, "but not right away. He needs a little while to cool off. If I came after him right now, he'd snarl at me and head for the tall timber."

"Doth he not do so already?" Cordelia countered.

"Yes," Rod said, "but he'll come back. If I go after him before he's ready to talk, he might go and stay."

Geoffrey looked up at him, frowning. "Why, how is this, my father? What malaise of the soul hath stricken my brother?"

"One that I remember all too well," Rod answered. "It has something to do with being ready to take on the world on your own, but not seeing your way clear to leaving home to take a try at it."

"Thou wilt not tell him to leave!" Gwen cried in alarm.

"No," Rod said, "but I'm not going to tell him he has to stay, either." He picked up his knife again and cut another gobbet of meat. "One way or another, I think I have time to finish my dinner."

He had a notion it might be a while before he saw another one.

• • •

He found his son by the bank of the river, beneath a gilded canopy of autumn leaves, his mount tethered nearby. Rod reined in Fess and muttered to the robot-horse, "Stay near, okay?" Fess only nodded by way of answer, honoring Magnus's mood with silence. Rod dismounted and stepped quietly over to his son, who was staring into the swirling eddies and watching the fallen leaves drift away.

"Feeling like one of those leaves yourself?" Rod asked softly.

Magnus looked up, startled. Then he relaxed a little, into a brooding wariness, but confessed, "Aye. My life is like to that, is it not? Bearing me where it will, the stream of events carrying me along to a destination I wot not of, and would not choose if I did."

"Maybe," Rod said slowly, daring to sit on the fallen log beside him. "But you need to be able to control your progress in that stream, don't you? Or at least be able to choose your own river."

Magnus looked up, surprised. "Thou hast stood in my shoes before, hast thou not?"

"Yes, but for just the reverse reasons. I'm the second son of a second son, so I had no place in the world I was reared in—but I couldn't get away, either."

"Whereas I cannot get away *because* I am the heir," Magnus said with bitterness.

"No," Rod said. "That doesn't have to bind you. You won't do any good in my office if you don't believe in it and want it. Besides, you have two brothers to take up the burden if you don't want its privileges."

Magnus stared at him, shocked and, yes, hurt. "Dost thou cast me out, then?"

Rod sighed; the boy was in one of those moods where you couldn't say anything right to him. And, yes, still very much a boy in his heart, though he was a man in his body and skills and mind. Twenty-one was old enough to be grown, too young to be mature.

At least, it was since he'd been held at home all this time. A peasant of his age would have had a wife and two babies already—and the responsibilities that went with them. He might be tied down, but he'd have taken those first vital steps toward real maturity.

"No," Rod said, "I'm not saying you should go—and I'd rather you stayed here, much rather. But that's for my sake, not yours. I'm only saying you can go if you feel the need."

Magnus answered with a sardonic smile. "Why, surely, sir. And could you not say the same for yourself?"

Rod bit back the automatic answer—that it was Magnus himself who held his father to Gramarye, along with his sister and brothers and, most of all, his mother.

His mother, whose beauty and sweetness made Rod want to stay, even now as she passed fifty, and who made the allure of the rest of the galaxy seem trivial by comparison. He studied his son's face, debating what his response should be . . .

. . . and it came to him in a flash of inspiration. "You've got a point there." He rose. "I *can* go, can't I?" His teeth showed in a slow, wolfish smile. "I can go kiyodling off wherever I want, if I feel the need. Thanks, son—I think I will."

He turned away to Fess, mounted, and rode off into the night while Magnus stared after him, thunderstruck.

Then anger surged, and the younger man thrust himself to his feet, mouthing imprecations, and hurried off after his father. He didn't doubt for a second that the old man knew exactly what he had done, or what he was doing.

• • •

They rode through a dark evergreen forest, dimmed even further by the lowering thunderheads over the treetops, and by the dying of the day. Magnus rode behind, unable to hear the conversation between his father and the robot-horse he rode, since they communicated by radio waves, not telepathy. Rod had a microphone implanted in his upper jaw, just above his front teeth, and an earphone behind his ear, in his mastoid process. Fess's transmission gear, of course, was built in.

Then, too, they might not be saying anything—and Magnus didn't *really* think they were chuckling over the way he was following after them. Even so, he seethed inside. There was a great deal of resentment within him, and Magnus didn't try to pretend it wasn't there. What right did his father have, to go dragging him off at a moment's notice?

Of course, Magnus hadn't really been giving up much—he hadn't had any interesting projects going. In fact, he'd been half out of his mind with boredom and frustration, feeling that his whole life was going to be wasted in the back of beyond, with no great deeds to do nor any great loves to win. He still felt that way—but it was annoying to have his father pull him along in his wake, anyway. It was his duty as the eldest son to ride after his father and watch over him— not to mention anyone else he might encounter.

For a moment, it occurred to Magnus that perhaps only he knew this was his duty, that maybe no one else thought it was, and that it might in fact not be, that he could just sit back and let his father wander off on his own, this time.

As Dad probably would have preferred.

Magnus shoved the thought aside and hunched his shoulders, leaning angrily into the breeze that was freshening into a gale. No matter whose idea it was, he was stuck with it.

Even if he was only a self-appointed guardian, the job still needed to be done.

Didn't it?

Rod risked a glance behind, and stifled a chuckle. "He's still coming, Fess."

"I gather he has not taken the point, Rod."

"Oh, yes he has—on the surface level. But then, he always has known his responsibilities to the rest of the family. What he doesn't realize is that he's old enough to lay those aside for a while."

"How long do you think it will take him to realize he is free to go if he wants to, Rod?"

"A long time, Fess. My boy is nothing if not determined."

"Did you say 'stubborn,' Rod?"

"Now, now, let's not season the conversational serial with synonyms. But I expect it to take him an even longer while to admit to himself that he really does want to go."

"He certainly seems to be of such a mind right now, Rod."

"Yes, but he hasn't really started thinking about it seriously yet."

A blast of wind slapped across Rod's face. He looked up, surprised that the day had grown dark. "When did it start to rain?"

"Several hours ago, Rod, though never with great force. There are still only occasional raindrops."

"Gusts of sleet, you mean." Rod shivered. "Next time I go stalking off in high dudgeon, remind me to wait for good weather. How bad is it outside those pine boughs above us, Fess?"

"A steady rain, I should say, from the sound—and not much more light than we have here, under the canopy."

"Better make camp, then, while I can still see a little." Rod pulled off the trail and dismounted. The ground was even, carpeted with last year's needles—there wasn't much undergrowth in the pine forest; the dense canopy overhead kept out the sunlight that would have encouraged scrub. Rod rotated his shoulders to ease the stiffness, heaved a sigh, and plodded off into the night to look for stones. He came back carrying two large rocks, and saw Magnus rolling stones up to make a fire circle.

Rod stood a moment, taking the chance to watch his son unaware. It was still something of a surprise to see Magnus's face atop that tall frame with all the muscles—a sight that startled, but also filled Rod with pride. The boy had turned out well, though darker in both mood and feature than Rod would ever have guessed, from his bouncing blond baby. He stood six foot seven in his stocking feet, and might still be growing. His black hair surmounted a face long and lantern-jawed, broad across the cheekbones but tapering sharply to a square chin, with a wide, thin-lipped mouth and large, widely spaced, deepset indigo eyes. To look at him looming, tall and wide, in the dusk, gave the stranger a chill of wariness—until he saw the quirk of humor about the lips, the readiness to sympathize. Not an ogre, no, but a gentle giant, whom no good person had any cause to fear. Rod smiled, warmed by the thought, and looked directly into his son's eyes as the young man looked up at him, taken unawares— and Rod saw a smoldering resentment, dimmed now by surprise.

That jolted Rod. When had his boy become bitter? At what? Who had hurt him? For a moment, the old anger shot through Rod; he would cheerfully have converted his son's tormentor into spare parts and musical instruments, if he could just have found him—but there was the old, secret dread that he might have been looking for himself.

He choked the emotion down; it was probably groundless,

anyway. "You don't have to do that, son—I can still do my own hauling."

"Canst thou indeed?" Magnus favored him with a sardonic glower. "And am I any the less bound to haul for thee? I, too, wish fire quickly!"

"Well, that's good sense, anyway." Rod set the stones down and straightened, frowning. "But as to your being bound—no, you're not. You can pay the price of waiting a few more minutes for a fire, but you don't *have* to help. Don't have to follow me, for that matter, either."

"Oh, do I not?"

"No, as a matter of fact, you don't." Rod scowled, stung by Magnus's sarcasm. "It was your choice to ride after me."

"Choice!" Magnus spat the word out as though it were an obscenity. "What choice have I, when all's said and done? I am the eldest; if thou dost sally forth, I must follow."

"Oh?" Rod pounced on it. "Who told you that?" And, before Magnus could answer, he added, "Your mother?"

Magnus reddened, but also looked away. "She said no such word today."

"What—she gave you standing orders? A little old for it, aren't you?"

That stung; he could see the anger flare in Magnus's eyes. "A little old to be biding at home, am I not? To still cling to her skirts—or thy house!"

"So go." Rod spread a hand toward the forest. "Nobody says you have to stay. The whole country's open to you."

Magnus stared at him, dismayed and hurt. Instantly, Rod regretted the sharpness of his tongue, realizing he'd pushed it too far—but before he could think of anything that might cancel what he'd said, Magnus snapped, "Well enough, then, an thou wilt! If thou wouldst not bide at home, wherefore ought I? Nay, thou hast loosed me, thou hast unfettered me!" Then he recovered himself long enough to give Rod a mocking bow. "I depart, obedient to my sire! And I wish thee joy of thy leisure!" He turned and strode away into the forest, leading his horse.

Anger whipped Rod, but so did dread and guilt. Frantically, he reminded himself that his son was a boy no longer, but a man grown, and fully capable of dealing with any menace that might greet him.

Or so he thought. Rod bit back the stormy words that came unbidden to his lips, and turned to set his foot in the stirrup. He mounted, muttering, "Pushed that a little too hard, didn't I?"

"Not if you were deliberately trying to send him away, Rod."

Did the robot's tones imply censure, or was Rod only imagining it? "No, I just wanted to make him feel free to do as he wanted. I didn't mean to make it be real."

"Then it was only an error in judgement." The robot's tone was neutral.

Rod frowned at the horse's head. "All right, mentor—if you think I flunked the exam, say so."

Fess hesitated just long enough to let Rod know how close he had come to the point, then said, "Perhaps it would be more accurate to say that you should have spoken only as your emotions dictated, Rod."

Rod shook his head. "You know a parent can't do that, Fess, or the race would have died out from rebellions and outrage long since. We have to do what's right for our kids, not just what we want to do." He shrugged. "Maybe I just don't have the right instincts."

"Or perhaps you should have been more honest."

"Yes, perhaps I should have." Rod sighed. "But the fat's in the flames now, and I'd better go hunting for a fire extinguisher. Follow him, Fess—but at a distance. We can't let him know."

"He is old enough to care for himself," Fess protested. "You spoke rashly and foolishly, yes, but you must not let your guilt push you into intruding upon him."

"I won't intrude—but I want to be close enough to come if he calls."

"There is no need . . ."

"Oh, yes there is—because the father may not be the son's responsibility, you see, but the son is the father's."

"I have never understood that attitude, Rod—but your father evinced it, and his father before him."

"Grandpa." Rod's determination hardened at the memory. "Yes, Magnus still is my responsibility—he always will be."

"But *why*, Rod?"

"Because I brought him into the world," Rod explained. "If I hadn't, he wouldn't be in any danger at all—and he certainly wouldn't be so unhappy." He shook his head. "My son, my duty—and if anything happened to him, I'd go berserk."

"He is his own man, Rod, or is trying to be. You must let him go."

"I know." Rod nodded. "So don't follow very closely, all right? Just in his general direction. After all, I wasn't going any place in particular, was I? And his direction is as good as any."

"Do not overtake him, though," Fess advised.

Rod shook his head. "Wouldn't think of it—and if I do, it'll be a total coincidence. Right, Fess?"

"Right, of course." Fess sighed. "As you will, Rod." And he moved off into the night.

2

Magnus rode into the deepening gloom, seething with anger, hurt and bewildered. His father didn't want him? Well, he didn't want his father! For a moment, he was sorely tempted to go back, to go home—after all, Dad had given him leave.

Not that he needed it. He was a man grown, and should have been living by himself now, not still at home. Most of the young men of his age were already married, with their own homesteads and their own children. Only the romantic failures, the old bachelors whom no one wanted, still lived at home with their parents.

At twenty-one, to be an old bachelor!

And, of course, in a medieval society, there was no alternative, no third choice—except the army, or the monastery. You lived at home with your parents until you married. Or went for a soldier. Or to the cloister. For a moment, Magnus wondered how many young men married simply to escape their parents' houses and become masters of their own homes. . . .

Though some of them were anything but masters. Magnus had seen quite a few who had escaped their parents' authority only to find they had become henpecked husbands, or if not actually subject to their wives, at least forever contending with a nagging termagant. More than a few, from what Magnus had seen. He shuddered at the thought of such a life with no escape in sight, then shuddered again at what it must do to the children. Though most of the marriages he had seen seemed happy enough—the husbands didn't expect much, and the wives expected less, so neither was disappointed.

Was that the limit of his choices?

To be fair, he reflected, calming, he had never known the other young men of his generation very well—noblemen's children did not become intimate with commoners, and children who had no psionic talents seemed to avoid witchkinder in any case. The young espers, the ones who had answered the call to the Queen's Magic Corps twenty years before, had wed each other and had children, to the delight of his father and the Order of St. Vidicon, both having a vested interest in increasing the number of operant espers— but by the time the younger generation had generated offspring, Magnus had been ten. Even his little brother Gregory was a year or two older than the other young magic-folk. It had been a pretty lonely childhood, he supposed, though he and his siblings hadn't really noticed—they'd had each other's company, and that had usually been enough. Friends their own age had been a huge treat—Their Majesties' sons, Alain and Diarmid—but only a treat. They hadn't been a necessity. What contact he had had with other young men his age had been fleeting, and frequently hostile. He hadn't missed the company—till now.

A scream tore through the treetops. Magnus looked up, suddenly alert, blood pounding at the thought of danger—a fight would be an almost welcome diversion now. Then a gust flapped his cloak, and he realized it had just been a sudden blast of wind.

Looking down, he saw a man standing before him.

Magnus started, shocked. Then he scowled, anger rushing. "Who art thou, who dost come so unmannerly in silence?"

It was a good question, he saw—for the man was like nothing he had ever encountered on Gramarye. He wore a top hat and a Victorian caped coat, trousers, and Wellington boots—but all very tattered. His staff was ornately carved, and he wore mutton-chop whiskers. They were tattered, too.

"*What* art thou?" Magnus demanded again, hand going to his sword.

"Thine evil genius, Magnus," said the apparition.

Magnus's eyes narrowed. "How knowest thou my name?"

"Do not all in Gramarye know the name of the High Warlock's son?"

That stung—the implication that he could not be known for himself. Magnus shifted the subject. "I ha' ne'er seen garb like to thine. . . ."

"Thou hast," the stranger interrupted, "in thine history books."

"Save there." Magnus tossed his head in impatience, though dread lurked within him. What did this stranger know of his books? "*Whence* comest thou?"

"From the London of thy books," the stranger answered. "I am one who doth pick and sort among the rags and tags of other people's thoughts for that which might be of interest or value to me. That which I cannot take, I buy—and that which I tire of and find to be of no worth, I give to others. I have a present for thee."

"I want it not!"

"I think thou wilt, for 'tis a spell of invulnerability."

"To make my body impervious to weapons?" Magnus's lip twisted in a sneer. "There is no such thing, only illusion!"

"Thou art poorly suited to speak of things that cannot be," the ragpicker said softly. "Yet 'tis not thy body I would make immune to harm, but thine heart."

That gave Magnus pause. There had been enough young women in his life who had feigned love, but really wanted only to exploit him in one way or another, that he already realized the value of the spell the ragpicker spoke of. "And what shouldst thou gain thereby? What would I give to thee?"

"Why, naught," the ragpicker said softly, but with too great an air of innocence. " 'Tis only as I've said— a rag of no great use to me, and therefore do I give it."

"I trust not one who doth profess to give in altruism," Magnus grunted, "and surely not one who doth seem alien to this time and place, while knowing too much of me. I'll have naught to do with thee! Avaunt!"

The ragpicker shrugged and smiled. "Thou wilt change thy mind presently. I'll visit thee anon, when thou hast greater cause to know this present's value." He swept a hand between them in a gesture, and disappeared.

Magnus stared at the spot where he'd been.

Then he turned to ride on, more shaken than he was willing to admit to himself. He strove for composure, regulated his breathing—and, in a short while, calmed enough to begin to become aware of his surroundings again. The ground had risen beneath him; his horse had followed the deer track automatically, and Magnus realized that he had absolutely no idea of where he was.

Which was just fine.

Somewhere in the middle of the Forest Gellorn, of course—the largest wilderness in the land, its depths as much unknown as the Carboniferous Period mainland—and in the foothills of the mountains along its northern edge, at a guess. More than that, he didn't know. More than that, he had no wish to know.

Magnus realized he was shivering with the chill. He pulled up, surprised to see that he was soaked through. He had to find someplace dry, where he could build a fire, or he would have to teleport himself and his horse back to civilization—and he wasn't quite ready to deal with other people, yet. Morose and melancholy, he was nonetheless enjoying the solitude, and wanted to make it last a bit longer. He listened carefully, probing the night with psionic senses as well as hearing . . .

. . . and heard the dull, repetitious thrumming of a music-rock, somewhere not too far distant. They virtually infested Gramarye now: The crafter Ari, who had been deceived into flooding Gramarye with rocks that made music leading young people to be victimized, had tried to correct his misdeeds by making more and ever more rocks that chanted music pleading for kindness and consideration. But lesser crafters, once shown that the trick could be done, had begun making music-rocks of their own, though the tunes were rarely as compelling as Ari's.

This one, however, was the exception. Frowning, Magnus made out the words:

> The Hag o' the Tower—she must be
> The ugliest witch in the North Country—
> Has trysted me all day in her bower,
> And many a fair speech she made to me.
>
> She stroked my head, and she combed my hair,
> And she set me down softly on her knee,
> Saying, "If you will be my leman so true,
> So many braw things I would you gie . . ."

"Away, away, ye ugly witch,
  Hold for away, and let me be;
I never will be your leman so true,
  And I wish I were out of your company!"

She's turned her right and round about,
  And thrice she blew on a grass-green horn,
And she swore by the moon and stars above,
  That she'd make me rue the day I was born!

Interesting notion. Magnus's attention strayed from the song as he found himself wondering if this was the work of some local crafter seeking revenge on a milkmaid who had turned him away—or if there might actually be some danger from some sour old witch who had a grudge against people in general.

If so, the fight would be welcome. Magnus was in the mood for mayhem, and looking for an excuse. Magical or physical, a good, brisk fight was just what he needed.

Unfortunately, no antagonist appeared. Drenched, chilled, and shivering, Magnus looked around for shelter. He reflected that animal trails usually led somewhere, and that even deer knew where to find a roof. He clucked to his horse and moved through the night, along the track.

It was only a rocky overhang, not even a cave—but there was dry ground beneath it, and even some dead leaves and small branches blown against the rock face. The deer had departed long since—at a guess, a doe had only used it to shelter her fawns last spring, and it was late autumn now. Magnus gathered the leaves, piled twigs on top of them, and stared at the little pyramid, thinking of the molecules in the leaves at the center, thinking of their random, erratic movement, of that motion speeding up, growing faster and faster. . . .

A coal glowed to life in the center of the pyramid.

The young warlock smiled. It was always reassuring, knowing that his skills were still sharp. Practice made perfect, after all; he had to keep doing the little things, in case he should have sudden need of the big ones. He fed the fire kindling, and once it was a true blaze, went off and brought back some thick, wet branches, broke them into smaller lengths, and set them around his fire to dry off, draping his cloak over them. That done, he unsaddled his horse, rubbed it down as well as he could, looped a nose bag of oats over its head, and dug into the saddlebags. Hardtack, cheese, and sausage made a Spartan meal, but they suited his mood. He washed it down with plain water from a skin, took the nose bag off the horse and splashed some drinking water into a hollow for the the animal, then stripped and set his clothes to dry while he wrapped himself in the warmth of the cloak. He unrolled his blanket, sitting down and winding it about his lower body, then took the small harp from his saddlebag and tuned it.

He plucked a few chords, letting himself fall into a reverie, dissolving the disappointment and anger, letting his mind drift where it would.

It moved with the longing that he usually kept hidden away. Now, though, contemplation freed it to rise up, as young men's spirits will, into thoughts of the consolation and companionship of a woman he had not met. Somewhere, she was waiting for him, or so the stories said—somewhere, he would find her; his sister believed this with religious conviction, their mother had sung to them of it when they were small, and he had never questioned it—only wondered, as he did now, what she would be like, when he would find her. He did not wonder what it would be like to be with her—he knew that, from the tales and the songs and the poems: it would be bliss.

He had never had much experience with women his own age, for the same reasons that he had known so few of his male peers: the common people did not associate closely with the nobility, nor the non-espers with the esper "witchfolk," and the psionic babies of his own generation were ten years younger than himself.

Of course, noblemen did have quite a bit of association with peasant women, though none of it official—but Magnus had been raised by Church and Book, and with a strong sense of responsibility; he had frankly never thought of seducing a peasant lass—it would have been a violation of his obligations as a nobleman, to take advantage of a woman he had no intention of wedding . . .

Or was not in love with.

Because, of course, love was the magic spell that brooked no resistance. If love came, and you turned away from it, you might never find it again, and live lonely all your days. The songs warned of that; the stories cautioned against it—and all promised the bliss that came of following true love, whenever it came and wherever it led, regardless of rank, wealth, or prudence.

Parents, of course, advised quite the contrary—once you were old enough to understand. But by that time, the dream of True Love had taken hold, far more deeply than any mere warning could do. Magnus longed for the bliss of that love, though he would never have admitted it—and yearned for the sexual satisfaction that was promised with it.

There had been hints of sexuality in his life—from older women, peasant girls. But always there had been the knowledge that they were his father's enemies, and his king's, seeking to use him for their own purposes—or, if not enemies, that they somehow sought to take advantage of him, even as they were letting him take advantage of them; so he had resisted them all, turned away from them. What they offered was not True Love. If a woman was really in love with you, she wasn't trying to use you, wasn't trying to gain anything by binding herself to you—she only wanted to be happy with you, and therefore make you happy.

As he would wish to delight her, in every way he could.

So far, though, it was all just a daydream. Magnus plucked a final chord and tucked the harp away. He put more wood on the fire, then checked his garments and found them still damp, except for his smallclothes. He girded his loins, set a saddlebag for a pillow, wrapped himself in cloak and blanket, and lay down to sleep.

In the night, he dreamed—of a beautiful maiden, smiling at him like the sun, swaying close to him and closer, removing her clothing piece by piece, all the while beaming up at him without the slightest hint of duplicity, open and giving, wanting only him, yearning to make him happy, thus finding her own joy. His heart swelled with delight, knowing this was True Love as she swayed closer to him, naked body a vision of delight, and he was about to embrace both her and the rare ecstasy that came in such dreams, when . . .

He woke.

And she was still there, heavy-lidded and smiling with invitation, but fully clothed and beckoning.

Magnus stared, started to sit up, then halted in embarassment; he was hardly in condition for a woman to see him. But she beckoned further, making soft sounds in her throat and reaching down to catch his hand. . . .

At the touch of her fingers, all doubt, all reservations, all concerns of modesty left him. He rose, transfixed by her gaze, aware only of her eyes, feeling as though they pulled him, as though he were falling into them. . . .

She led him away from the campfire, off into the night. Charmed in more ways than one, he followed, oblivious to the rain and the chill, aware only of her.

• • •

Rod had camped not too far from his son, and slept when Magnus slept. Fess, always vigilant, noted by radar when the young man left his campsite, though not why; he waked Rod.

"What?" Rod craned his neck, squinting around at the darkness. "What did I have—a two-hour nap?"

"One, Rod."

"An hour! What did you wake me for?"

"I thought you might not wish to wait for breakfast, Rod. Magnus has left his campsite."

"Left! In the middle of the night? Why?"

"There is no indication, Rod—but radar shows that he did not take his horse."

Rod lay still, letting the implications sink in and fuel the worst aspects of his imagination. Then he pushed himself up and started rolling his sleeping bag. "We'll collect the beast, then. Start following."

But even with Fess's infrared night-sight, it went slowly. He didn't know the trail.

The dream-wench did, though.

High up she led Magnus, to a tower atop the high hill, and within it, and up a spiral staircase. At the top, they came out into a chamber hung with tapestries and furnished with damask pillows and a huge feather bed, all glowing with the light of a fire against one wall. Then, slowly, swaying, she began to disrobe, eyes never leaving his, smile wide and inviting.

But some niggling doubt at the back of his mind still pressed; some childhood fear of the unknown, perhaps, weakened his concentration, expanded his awareness just a little, and he realized that the tapestries showed writhing figures engaged in sexual foreplay—then going on to the act itself, pictured more realistically than he had ever seen. But beyond that simple coupling were other images, more exotic posturings, even bizarre, even . . .

Cruel.

At the edges of his vision there were scenes involving whips and chains, of bound men and masked women, and the dissonance rocked Magnus, the juxtaposition of the postures of cruelty with the actions of love shocking him to his core—and the shock of the pictures jarred him back to his senses. Not completely, but enough for him to realize that he, the warlock, was enchanted, bound within the spell of an expert. He was shaken by the thought of such expertise, for he knew himself to be the most powerful esper of his generation. Who was this woman, who could befuddle his senses and draw him by a glamour, an attractive illusion, so complete that he did not even think to resist?

Or was it a woman?

The thought was like a slap in the face, and Magnus bent his will to dispelling the glamour, to seeing things as they truly were. For a moment, he saw bare walls decked with old spiderwebs, a floor strewn with refuse about a rotting straw pallet—and the most hideous crone he could ever have imagined. Only a few white hairs strayed over a nearly bald and liver-spotted scalp; a huge bent nose protruded from a mass of warts with two malevolent yellow eyes; the skin sagged, almost hiding a gash of mouth that opened, showing two rotting teeth and crooning, in a voice like a rusty gate, "Nay, dream . . . dream . . . forget this nightmare vision, for there is naught of the real about it. . . . Come back to the truth, to the actual, to the vision of my pleasures, my treasure. . . ."

The rusty gate was suddenly transformed into a thrush's song, low and melodious, husky and thick with desire, and the beautiful woman was back, the tapestries glowing behind her, writhing as they enacted the pleasures they showed, and she was stripped to the waist, a vision of earthly delights, beginning to unfasten her skirt as she crooned, "Oh, I love thee! Oh, I ache for thee! Come, caress me, my treasure!"

But Magnus, with the sensitivity of a lifetime's training, was aware of a mind sliding around his own, seeking the entry he had given it, then denied it, probing, finding the crack of desire in his shield, pressing against it, pushing and tickling at his mind. He was breathless for a moment, amazed at the skill it revealed, for he could tell that her mind was no match for his own in sheer power—

But far greater than his, in dexterity, born of long practice.

How many young men had she bent to her will, to have become so proficient at it?

What did she want of him?

"Only the pleasure that you seek to give me." The skirt came away; there was no other garment beneath it, and her body swayed against his. "Come, my love. I am open to thee; I ache for thee! Come!"

"Nay," Magnus grated, and with a wrench of his will, he saw the room as it really was again, saw the naked, filthy hag who pressed against him, and recoiled from her in revulsion.

Then the enchanted room was back, and the woman was young, beautiful, and sensuous once more. There was sunlight behind her now, from a window high above, turning her silken hair into a flame of gold. "Come," she breathed, eyes devouring his, fingers plucking at his breeches. "Have at me!" And her head tilted back, eyes closing, lips parting. . . .

A flash of memory of that slash of mouth, with its rotten teeth, made Magnus recoil again . . . but the memory was quickly smothered with the sight of her, proud and glorious and longing, standing full in a sunbeam, and his body clamored for her with an intensity that was sickening. She smiled, beckoning, and almost against his will, he felt himself stepping toward her with slow, dragging steps, reaching out to touch her perfect skin, head bending over hers, lips parting. . . .

He forced out the single syllable, thwarted longing shaping it to a groan: "No!"

"Thou canst not mean *no*." Tears filled those huge, wondrous, violet eyes, filled and overflowed; the beautiful head bowed, shoulders heaving with sobs. "Oh, thou wilt not leave me forlorn!"

Guilt seized him, and shame at making a woman weep; pity filled him, and he reached out to gather her close, to comfort her, to press her to him in the golden rays of the setting sun that seemed to set both of them aflame with desire, gilding the huge expanse of snowy feather bed, and he felt his need for her rising, filling him, a physical pain within him.

But the thought of pain reminded him of the tapestries. Out of the corner of his eye he glanced at them, and recoiled with a gasp of horror.

Suddenly, the tapestries were gone, and the cobwebbed walls were all that were there behind the naked hag who stood before him, screaming, "Fool!" Oblivious of her nudity, she howled, "Villain! Vile miscreant! Travesty of a man! If thou wilt not take what is offered thee, become what thou art—the lowest of the low!" Her hands snapped out; he felt her will compelling his own as her eyes seemed to swell, swallowing him, dragging him into the dreadful, blood-shot, yellow gleam, and he felt himself dwindling, growing slack, falling to his knees, till he writhed on the floor.

"Be the serpent thou art," she hissed, malicious satisfaction in her eyes, "and shalt be evermore."

He strained against the compulsion, but again, the touch of an expert had bound him, constrained him; he knew she had only convinced him he was a snake, that physically he was still every bit the man he had been—but his subconcious knew differently. It was now convinced of his snakehood as completely as it had once been certain of his humanity; she had bound him within his own skull, far more expertly than anyone he had ever met, and he could no more throw off that conviction than he could leap to the moon unaided.

"Away," she hissed, lips curving with cruel satisfaction, and he felt himself rising, lifting, up off the floor and to the stairwell. He writhed and strained against the compulsion— but only felt his body whipping about like a snake's. She crowed with delight, and followed him down the spiral stair—down, down, and down, then out into the dusk, for night was falling again.

A hundred yards from her tower, he felt his body drift to the ground at the foot of a huge old oak—and, suddenly, whip itself about, curving against the bark.

"There shalt thou stay," the hag grated, "warding that tree from harm, till death take thee—and thy bones shall assure all who come nigh that they must do the bidding of the Hag of the Tower!"

She turned away, and Magnus stared after, at the sagging, mottled flesh and gaunt shanks, realizing that the music-rock's song had been a warning, that he should have heeded it more closely. . . .

How had it ended?

He strove to remember, but had only a fleeting notion that the youth had escaped the fate the witch had bound him to— and he had the vagrant dread that if he looked, he might find the skeletons of other young men bound around tree trunks nearby. The music, he thought desperately—maybe the song would tell him the means of escape! He listened, yearning, but the only sound was the wind. Even the birds would not sing so close to the witch's lair; no doubt they shied away from the miasma of her malice. And certainly the music-rocks had been stilled by her rage.

Magnus slithered against the bark of the tree, knowing for the first time in his life what was meant by the word "despair."

At sunset, Rod came to a village in a small valley. Smoke from cook-fires drifted up into a clear sky; peasant men were making their way out into the fields, sickles in their hands, to gather in the last of the crop.

It was very quiet.

Rod frowned; this was wrong. Peasant farm laborers should have been singing as they went out to the fields, as they did in the rest of Gramarye. Granted, it was chill in autumn; their breath steamed, and they wore heavy woolen tunics; but even so, the peasants of Gramarye laughed and jested as they went to their work, and sang as they reaped. Their wives sang, too, as they went about their work—and the children chanted rhymes over their games.

But no one sang in this town.

Rod looked up at the sun, and saw the silhouette of a dark tower against it, at the top of a ridge. The local lordling? A tyrant, crueler than most? Could that be the cause of the silence?

One way to find out. He rode down into the town.

The peasants drew back at sight of him, and the whisper ran. "A knight! A knight!"

Rod frowned. Was a knight so strange a sight here?

Well, he'd have to ask. But as he rode toward a housewife, she looked up in alarm, called her children to her, and shooed them into the house.

Well! Rod had heard of peasant mothers telling their nubile daughters to turn their faces to the wall when the gentlemen passed by—but not their toddlers! He turned to an old man who was shuffling along the single street. "Good day, gaffer!"

The man looked up at him warily. "What wouldst thou wi' me, sir knight?"

"Am I so strange a sight? Are knights so rare here?"

The old man launched into a windy and elaborate answer obviously disguised to hide the facts, but Rod was adept at extracting sense from circumlocutions, and ascertained that yes, knights were that rare—even the local baron visited only once a year, with all his men. Otherwise, he stayed away, for fear of the witch in the tower, and his bailiff came with a very strong guard only once a month. Other than that, there were never any knights who came this way, except for the very occasional wanderer who rode on up the trail to the tower—and was never seen again.

Rod frowned. "What's so bad about this witch? Is she that cruel?"

The old man explained that, yes, she was, and went on in some detail. When he was done, Rod rode on up the trail in his own turn, face set in very grim lines, resolved to rid the peasants of the hag's tyranny—and very much afraid for his son.

3

What do you do when you're a snake?

Of course, Magnus's options were rather limited—he was bound to the tree by the same sort of subconscious compulsion that had him convinced he was a serpent. If he tried to slither away, he found himself moving counterclockwise, around the base of the trunk—and if he wanted to move clockwise, he had to squirm backwards. It struck him as ominous that the only direction he could go, forward, was widdershins, opposite to the direction of the sun's path; surely that was strengthening the spell, driving it deeper into his subconscious by use of a direction associated with magic.

In a word, he was stuck. What had he done to deserve it? Nothing, except dream about women—and refuse the blandishments of a female. He had taken no action to hurt her; he had only preserved his own integrity, and kept himself from being used and eventually degraded (if the tapestry was any guide to her future plans) by saying "no."

How to escape?

He couldn't think of any way out except—and it galled him to admit it—to call for help. If anyone could help him, which for some reason, he doubted. Probably a subconscious command the witch had left—but there it was.

Still, it was worth a try. Who could he call? His mother and father, of course, but he winced at the indignity of calling on his mother at his age. And it would be just as bad calling his teenaged brothers, and Cordelia would be impossible; he could do without their laughter, thank you.

Which left Dad.

That, he definitely did not want to do—not after having quarreled with him, and been told to get lost. But there was no alternative—Dad was better than his mother or siblings.

Of course, there was Fess.

But where Fess went, Dad would go—after all, he was riding the robot-horse.

Rod rode uphill through the gathering gloom. He could no longer see the squat tower, but he knew it was there. Weariness tugged at every fiber, but he fought it off and kept riding. "He could be anywhere around here—if he's here at all. Any sign of him, Fess?"

"There is a trail off to our right, Rod."

"You mean the footpath? The one that virtually screams, 'Look here to discover intruders'? That footpath?"

"The very same, Rod. The one you decided to avoid."

"I noticed you didn't disagree. Why? You see some sign of Magnus there?"

"Unfortunately not—but we might, if we went closer."

"No need—we're coming out on top of the ridge, now." Rod tensed. "Odds are the trail leads there, too—to the tower." He loosened his sword in its sheath.

Fess stopped, looking downward.

"What's the holdup?" Rod frowned.

"There is a skeleton, Rod."

Rod froze, then looked down.

Sure enough, it was a skeleton, wrapped around the base of the tree as though it had died out of devotion to the forest. Rod felt his scalp prickling. "Odd posture, wouldn't you say?"

"I would, Rod. It is indicative of ritual slaying."

"Or someone with a bizarre sense of humor." Rod was far less charitable than his robot. "A someone with a very twisted mind—and a cavity where his heart should be."

"There are others," Fess reported, surveying the hillside with infrared eyes. "A dozen at least, that I can see from this location."

"The townsfolk did say something about the witch taking young men, didn't they?" Rod scowled. "And something about very few of them ever coming back."

"Surely you are not saying that this is what she did to them when she became bored with them!"

"I've heard of worse—I suppose. Come on, Rust Rider. Let's see what we can find around the other trees."

"Rod, I resent . . ."

"Okay, okay! You're a Stainless Steel Steed. Up and out of the trees now, okay?"

Moving slowly, Fess stepped out of the scrub and into the shadow of the last tree, a huge old oak with the scars of broken limbs, rough bark, and . . .

Something pale at the base.

Rod stared down, transfixed, not even able to speak.

A snake lay coiled around the roots—a pale snake with his son's head. Magnus opened his mouth—and hissed.

Fury struck, anger at the witch who had mangled his son. The world about him dimmed as Rod concentrated on the spell, the compulsion imposed on his son, which had twisted his perceptions into seeing himself as a snake, and made him project his own delusion into other people's minds—with all the titanic strength of the hybrid esper he was.

Rod tore at that compulsion, pushing it away with all the strength of his mind; for a moment, he saw Magnus as he really was, naked and curled around the base of the oak. But only for a moment; then the young man's mind forced the delusion back into Rod's, and he realized just how much more powerful his son's mind was than his own. Rod withdrew shaken and reeling. Awe and dread pooled within him, but he let them pass, holding on to Fess's mane and waiting for the dizziness to subside, for pride to rise in its stead—and found that the anger was still there, glowing hot, but controlled now, energy to be directed, not tearing loose. He looked down into his son's shrunken face. "Who did it, Magnus? Tell me her name. Just think it. Show me her face—and where she is."

The snake's face creased with desperation; the mouth opened, but all that came out was a strained hiss. Magnus's mind, though, flashed through the answers to Rod's questions—the name "Hag of the Tower," the song drifting through the dusk, the dream-girl, the long, long tug of wills between seduction and truth. . . .

"Got it." Rod nodded. "In the tower." He turned to look up at the stone pile, the image of the foul old witch still vivid in his mind, and sent out a telepathic summons, immediate and commanding, brooking no delay. He felt Magnus's mind writhe in a panic of shame and embarrassment at the thought of the help he was calling in, but Rod quelled it with a stern admonition, a pure-thought equivalent of "This is no time for vanity." Of course, it was scarcely "vanity" when the "help" would see you coiled around a tree trunk—but there wasn't much option, either. Aloud, he said, "You stay there for a few minutes," and turned Fess's head away toward the tower. Behind him, Magnus gave a last hiss, as much of exasperation as of despair—but Rod felt the young man's mind melding with his own, subordinating its strength to his direction. Rod smiled tightly, solace and warmth almost making him forget his anger for a moment.

Then he came to the portal.

The door to the Hag's tower was ten feet high, of stout old hardwood planks, weathered past gray into darkness, and polished at head-height by use. Something glinted in the moonlight; Rod looked up. He saw a scythe blade with its tip broken off. It hung from a rusty chain, and attached to that chain were old horseshoes, broken bolts, cracked pots—a complete collection of junk metal—framing the portal. Above it hung another chain, stretching off around the tower with more junk attached.

Lousy housekeeping—but all Cold Iron. That explained why the Little People hadn't done anything about the witch.

Rod was glad the door wasn't anything that looked to be worth saving. He narrowed his eyes, directing Magnus's ferocious raw emotional power at it. . . .

With a blast like that of a cannon, the door flew apart, splinters flying in all directions. An unseen field deflected them as Fess leaped ahead, carrying Rod into the darkness of the witch's lair.

It was infested.

All around the curve of the walls stood great earthenware urns, unglazed terra cotta, sealed across their mouths—but as Rod rode in, those seals broke, the jars cracked; a foul ichor began to ooze out, and strange bloated beings struggled through the openings. They leaped down, fully formed and instantly alert, and came at him from all sides, hairless rats the size of Doberman Pinschers, glowing yellow-green teeth dripping ichor, running on two feet, front paws stretching out to claw.

Rod was in no mood for subtlety. He pointed both forefingers, thinking of machine guns and laser cannon, and streaks of ruby light sliced through the rats. Supersonic screams tore at his head as the rats split in half, twitching, tops and bottoms both still struggling toward him, then in half again as the ruby beams came back, and back once more, till they were struggling, heaving blobs of protoplasm. Then, suddenly, they subsided into mounds of gray fungus. Rod nodded; it had been an open question, whether they had been constructs, or just illusions. In either case, light had dispelled them.

He turned to the spiral staircase. "Think you can manage them, Fess?"

"This body has its limits, Rod, but that helix does not surpass them." The horse started up the steps.

As he passed the first turn, a huge hissing filled the stairwell. Rod scowled, eyes trying to pierce the darkness. "What's coming, Fess?"

"I hear a rapid scraping, Rod, but I do not see . . ."

Two yellow eyes glowed in the darkness above them, small but wide apart, and the hiss filled the whole stairway, beating at Rod's ears. Enough, he decided, and thought of molecules racing faster and faster, closer and closer together. . . .

A spark glowed in midair, growing and growing, shedding a dim light on the scene. . . .

Enough for Rod to see a monster snake, gliding down the stair toward him. Its body was at least three feet thick; its mouth opened a foot wide, and that was just enough to let out the hiss. The pits beneath its eyes were minor caves—but it seemed to have been waked in mid-molt. Shreds of skin hung from it, some showing muscle and blood underneath; a rotting crest waved atop its head; wattles hung down from its jaws. There wasn't enough light to tell colors, really, but it seemed to be the grayish-blue of a dead fish's belly.

The anger surged back, forestalling both panic and nausea. What kind of depraved maniac kept pets like this around the house? Rod drew his sword, trying to think of something a little more effective.

"Hold fast, Rod." Fess half-reared, striking out with a hoof.

The snake almost sneered—until the steel hoof caught it sharply in the face with a soggy crunch. The serpent reared back, hiss rising almost to a shriek, then struck in rage.

But Fess had given Rod just time enough to think up the appropriate response. He wasn't the world's best crafter, but he could manage something simple, and had: he had pulled together the witch-moss at the bottom of the stairs. It now shot toward him, powered by his son's telekinesis—a twenty-foot trident with tines eighteen inches apart. It arced down, catching the snake just behind the head, slamming it down against the stone of the stair. It couldn't pierce the rock—there was a limit to the hardness witch-moss could be formed to—and the center tine bent against the serpent's scales; but the top of the handle bent, too, against the ceiling, pushing like a living thing, and the snake thrashed about, hissing in fury but unable to lift its head against the force of the spear. The whole stairwell resounded with the noise of the giant's thrashing—but it could do no damage; the walls of the spiral held it too closely.

Now that it was immobilized, Rod could devote himself to its demise. The stairwell itself seemed to become dim, the snake brighter, as he concentrated all his attention on it, thinking of it as just a huge doughy mass. He felt another mind warring with his, striving to keep the snake in its current form, but he had expected that, and bore down all the harder—with the strength of two minds, one distinct and alien from the Gramarye gene pool and mindset, the other a hybrid with ferocious strength. The witch's power crumbled, and so did the snake; it softened more and more, losing its color and becoming the grayish-pink amorphous mass that was witch-moss in its natural form.

Not enough. Rod knew that if he left it raw, the witch could easily re-craft it into the snake, or something even more dangerous, as soon as he and Magnus stopped paying attention to it. He thought of something small and harmless, lots of somethings—and the doughy mass separated into thousands of small curly objects that lightened in color as they hardened. Rod rode on up the stair, through drifts of macaroni that lined both walls. Stray bits of pasta crunched under Fess's hooves, but didn't impede him at all.

"Not too slippery, is it?" Rod asked.

"Not when it is uncooked, Rod, no." The robot-horse climbed on up the stair and out into the chamber at the top—

A chamber hung with scarlet brocades and filled with cushions, downy, tempting—and the most voluptuous wench Rod had ever seen, sloe-eyed and full-lipped, clad only in a swath of gauze about her hips, accentuating that which it concealed. Golden hair tumbled down over her shoulders, parted in the middle to reveal the high curves of full, naked breasts. The houri gave him a heavy-lidded, inviting smile, and murmured in a husky voice, "Dally with me, brave stalwart."

"No, thanks. I've got a wife at home." Suddenly, Rod was more glad than ever that he had married Gwen; even without being there, she protected him. "And she looks good even without projecting illusions." He glared at the houri, and her outline began to shimmer.

"Nay!" she screeched, and a bolt of pure energy, hatred whetted by anger and fear, stabbed out at Rod.

An answering bolt shot out from him, sped not by himself, but by Magnus; Rod kept concentrating on seeing the woman as she really was. The two bolts met in the air with an explosion that made his ears ring, and distracted the witch

just long enough for Rod to finish locking her mind into seeing only what was truly there. She screamed in anguish,
arms coming up to cover her nakedness, body curving in on
itself in shame; then she uncoiled, hate stronger in her than
any other emotion, and leaped at Rod, fingers hooked to
claw.

He was amazed how high she could jump—her fingers
nearly touched his eyes before he stiff-armed her, jarring her
aside but catching one wrist and hauling up on it. Her feet hit
the floor, but the single arm was still outstretched. She
screamed, more in rage than in pain, and flailed about with
her free arm, but Rod held her with her back to Fess's side.
She twisted, trying to get at his leg and groin, but her arm
wouldn't turn that far, and she howled in pain. Rod slipped
down off the horse to catch her other hand and pulled it behind her back, pinning her forearms together with one hand
while he reached in his saddlebag and brought out rope. He
bound her wrists together with three quick loops, braced
himself against her thrashing as he tied the knot, then let go
and shoved her away. She fell sprawling, an obscene,
scrawny lump of naked flesh, screaming curses. Rod caught
up a silk scarf from among the cushions and bound it around
her head. She still screamed into the gag, but at least he
couldn't make out the words—not that he needed to; the images her mind was projecting were enough to make him
shudder.

He yanked her to her feet and shoved her before him.
"You can walk down those steps, or you can roll—but down
them you go."

She balked at the top, but felt the rage within him that was
at least equal to her own, and stumbled away down the steps,
still screaming into her gag. Beside them, heaps of macaroni
stirred and softened, but Rod locked them into their own
forms again, and she gave up the attempt. Instead, she tried

to fill his mind with pornographic visions. When she found him immune, she unleashed lurid imaginings of the tortures she would have loved to visit on him.

"Not bad," Rod grunted. "I'll have to try that on somebody sometime. On the other hand, why put it off?"

The visions stopped.

The witch stumbled out of the tower door and fell rolling in the grass.

"Not far enough," Rod snapped. He yanked on the rope, just enough to remind her that he still held her leash. The strands bit into her wrists, and she screamed in rage, but scrambled to her feet and stumbled away in front of him.

He brought her to a halt before the tree where Magnus lay. "Remove the spell, hag! Turn him back into a man!"

The witch slowly lifted her head, venomous eyes seeking his, malice twisting her features. The vicious thoughts reeking from her were clear: this much she could still deny him, this much pain she could still cause—and she would. Then a picture opened in Rod's mind, of Magnus standing beside him, restored to his proper form as the witch strode away free, and the two of them turned to leave her.

"No deal," Rod snapped. "If you won't do it the easy way, I have someone who will." He focused his thoughts, sending out a single, sharp appeal.

A rush of wind, a stir of whispering overhead, and a graceful figure drifted down in the moonlight, poised on a broomstick, to land directly in front of Rod. The maiden hopped off, frowning at the witch, then turned to Rod with sudden anger. "How now, my father! Hast thou taken to shaming and binding helpless old women in thine age?"

Rod had been braced for anything; still, he found it in him to resent the crack about age. But he stifled it and said, "She's helpless only because Magnus and I have bound her mind as well as her hands, Cordelia. Before we did, though, she played games with your brother." He nodded toward the tree.

Cordelia turned, and the snake shrank back, but not before she had seen its face. Instantly, she was all compassion. "Oh, Magnus! What hath she done to thee!" She dropped to her knees by the snake, hands outstretched—but her brother shrank back farther, looking up at her wild-eyed. Cordelia looked into his eyes, and stilled.

Then she whirled, up to her feet and at the crone. "Thou hag, thou monster! Thou hast maimed his soul as well as his mind! 'Tis his heart thou hast bound, as much as his body!" Her eyes narrowed.

The witch screamed, going rigid, eyes wide, staring back at the maiden—but Cordelia advanced, face cold, hands rising, nails glinting in the moonlight. The witch thrashed, trying to break free, but Rod held her—until suddenly, her eyes rolled up, and her head lolled. Cordelia nodded with grim satisfaction. "I know the manner of it now, how she bent his mind."

"I think you may have hurt her a little," Rod pointed out. "I take it she didn't want to let you know."

"Nay, but I did not wait upon her humor—and if she hath taken some pain from it, I fear I am not contrite." She turned away to her brother.

Rod smiled after her, watching her kneel by the snake, pride upwelling.

Cordelia lifted a hand, but the snake coiled away from her. "Why, how is this, my brother?" she asked, her voice soft, gentle. "I am as I ever was—only thy little sister, thy playfellow of childhood days."

Magnus looked a little reassured, but he glanced at her from toe to head, and stayed back.

"Ah, she hath maimed thee indeed!" Cordelia cried. "But gaze into mine eyes, brother, and try to trust! I love thee, for thou art of the same bone and blood as I. Thou hast done naught to regret, though thou wert sorely tempted, and the only blame that could attach to thee is that thou didst not tear that witch asunder when first thou didst see her!"

Magnus thawed enough to answer, mind to mind. *I could not, without proof of wrongdoing.*

"And indeed I should have been wroth with thee an thou hadst! But now I am not wroth, but proud! Nay, I see thy fear—but thou dost know me, and know I will be as good as my word! None shall know of this night's doings by my lips, brother; I shall never speak a word of thy misadventure, nor of the warping that the old witch wrought. Trust a little, brother, only a little, and ope thy mind to me for moments!"

The snake was still; then, slowly, he brought his head forward.

Cordelia touched his forehead, lightly as a feather, and her eyes glazed as her mind worked with his. Then, as Rod watched, the snake uncoiled, slithered away from the tree, and lifted its head until it hung poised two feet off the ground. Its form fluxed and flowed—and Magnus sat there cross-legged, naked but whole, his face ashen.

"Thou art restored!" Cordelia whirled up to her feet again, modestly turning her back on her naked brother. "Father, thy mantle!"

Rod whipped his cloak off, letting the witch fall, and reached down to help his son to his feet. Magnus towered over him, so the cloak was very short as Rod reached up to settle it around his shoulders—but it came to mid-thigh, and had slits for his arms.

Cordelia whirled back, throwing her arms around him. "Praise Heaven thou art come back to us!" Then she shuddered, and began to cry.

Magnus stood immobile a moment, then reached an arm around her shoulders and pressed his sister against his chest.

Another minute, and he found his voice. "I am well, sister, I am well—thanks to thee. Nay, I praise all the saints that thou wert born a sister to me!"

"Yet thou art not fully healed." Cordelia looked up at him, eyes filled with tears. "There are scars there yet, brother— and thou hadst not given me leave, so I did not linger to mend. Nay, I know not if I could have, so deeply did she wound thee."

"Peace, sister—'twas not her alone, but many, and in many bouts."

"But these are wounds that only women give!" Cordelia's tears dried instantly under the heat of anger and indignation. "Nay, how could they have used thee so!"

"Thou hast seen some among them," Magnus said softly. "The milkmaid who sought to entrap us, when Mother and Father were gone—the maids of the floating world, when we followed the sounding rocks . . ."

"Aye, I remember." The anger was gone, and Cordelia lifted a hesitant hand to her brother's cheek. "But I did not guess they had hurt thee so. Ah, Magnus! Have I misjudged thee all these years, then? Is there so tender a heart as that, under this warrior's hide?"

Magnus blushed, and let her go. "Thou hast given thy word thou wilt not reveal what thou hast learned this night. . . ."

"And most surely I will not! Oh, my poor brother!" Cordelia flung her arms about him protectively, though her head scarcely came to his breastbone. "Would I could undo the hurt so many lasses have given, that I could give such grace as to o'erbalance their cruelty—for I am a woman, too!"

" 'Tis not thy place." Magnus's arm came up again, embracing, comforting. "I must heal myself, must I not? Nay, sister, 'twas not thy doing, and thou must not hurt for me."

"How can I do otherwise!"

"Why, by being the bright and bonny lass of sunlight and good cheer that thou hast ever been." Magnus's lips touched her forehead briefly, vagrant as a wind. "Only be thyself, and thou shalt do as much as any can to heal me, and more." He held her away from himself and smiled down. "God willing, I shall do as much for thee as thou hast for me, though my province is warding, not healing."

Cordelia looked up in alarm.

Magnus laughed softly and squeezed her shoulder. "Nay, fear not, good sister—I'll not ward thee so closely as that! Nay, I shall not defend unless thou dost ask."

She smiled again, and joined his laughter.

Rod smiled too, and stepped forth. "If you two don't mind, I really don't think we should hang around."

Cordelia looked up, saw the witch unconscious on the grass, and nodded. "But what shall we do with her?"

"I think we might leave her to natural forces." Rod turned to the trees and called out:

> By oak and ash,
> By earth and flood!
> Come forth, all
> Who live by wood!

The night was still a moment, and the witch's eyes flew open wide, flicking from one side to the other. The whites showed all around her irises, bloodshot. She began to tremble.

Then the long grass stirred, and a foot-high figure stepped forth. Another joined it; more came from the underbrush. Then a branch moved aside, and an eighteen-inch figure stepped out, broad-shouldered and large-headed. Its face tilted up to the light, and it grinned. "I had thought if thou hadst come this way, there might be summat of a stir."

The witch moaned.

"Right as always." Rod smiled slowly. "How nice to see you, Puck."

"Is it truly? What hast thou in store for me?"

Rod nodded toward the lump of flesh on the grass. "Know anything about this one?"

The hag moaned.

Puck's eyes glinted in the moonlight like chips of ice. "Aye, we know of her. When she hath come forth, she hath used her magic to strike at the Wee Folk who dwell nearby. She hath hurled old nails to fend us off, and hath injured many and slain two."

Rod nodded. "We'll leave her to you, then." He turned away, catching Magnus's and Cordelia's arms and moving toward the forest path. Cordelia stepped aside to catch up her broomstick before she came along—not quite quickly enough to escape hearing the hag scream with terror, a scream that was cut off in the middle. Cordelia shuddered and hurried on under the shelter of the bare branches. "Father . . ."

"They're merciful, in their way," Rod said firmly. "You can be sure she won't have even a fraction of the pain she's given others."

"Yet without trial . . ." Magnus said.

Rod looked up, startled. "Don't tell me you think she could be innocent!"

"Why, certes not!"

"Well, then." Rod nodded. "Don't worry—the elves have their own form of due process. They won't even need you two as witnesses. And, son—the Wee Folk don't generally spread gossip. At least, not to mortal people."

Magnus nodded, relaxing a little more. "Thou wilt say naught of this to my brothers?"

"Of course not—nor to your mother, either."

"Unless she doth ask," Magnus qualified.

"Well, yes. But don't worry—she can keep a secret, too."

"As to that—" Cordelia frowned. "Wherefore didst thou summon me, and not Mama?"

Rod shook his head. "I don't 'summon' your mother, Cordelia. I call for help, maybe, but I don't 'summon.' And this is probably the last time I'll be able to call you that way."

Cordelia studied him, pensive. "And 'tis therefore thou didst summon me, not her?"

"Why, no." Rod looked up, surprised. "I called you because you're the best at healing, daughter. Your mother has trained you very well, and even though she may have more experience, you have so much talent that you've surpassed her—in that one area at least. Or so she says. Didn't you know?"

4

Cordelia flew off into the mists of false dawn after once more promising to tell no one of the night's adventures. Rod and Magnus managed to retrace the young man's trail and find his horse and clothing. Now, once more dressed and mounted, Magnus was recovering his self-confidence.

They came down out of the trees as the sun was rising—and the other son was remembering that he was supposed to be feeling aggrieved. "Thou didst follow me, didst thou not?"

Rod started to answer, then caught himself with the denial still on his tongue. He had tried never to lie to his children, though there were times when he'd felt he'd had to. This wasn't one of them, however. "Yes, son, I did."

"Why? Didst thou fear I was not equal to whate'er might rise against me? Dost thou think me yet a child?"

"No," Rod said, relieved that it had been a double question. Answering the one of his choice, he said, "I know quite well that you're a man grown."

"How, then, didst thou hap upon me when I was in such dire need?"

"Because the peasants asked me." Rod gestured at the village. "Ask them, if you don't believe me."

But there was no need to. The peasant men were coming out to their fields; they saw Rod and froze. Then they dropped their hoes and ran forward with glad cries.

" 'Tis the stranger-knight returned!"

"He doth live! He hath prevailed!"

"Praise Heaven thou art well, sir knight!"

"I do." Rod smiled down at them. "I assure you, I do."

The men cast apprehensive looks at Magnus, but turned back to Rod.

"Didst thou escape the witch, then?"

"Didst thou not find her?"

"I found her," Rod said quietly. "Oh, yes, I found her—didn't we, son?"

Magnus clamped his jaw shut, and managed a grim nod.

The men looked up, startled, glancing covertly from father to son and back again, realizing that there was a resemblance after all. "And thy son?"

"I couldn't have defeated her without his strength," Rod assured them.

"Then thou hast triumphed!"

"The witch is dead?"

"The Wee Folk have taken her," Rod replied.

"They did not seem overly fond of her," Magnus added. "I doubt me not that if she is not dead, she doth wish she were."

The peasants muttered to one another in fright, making the sign of the Cross—whether at the mention of the Wee Folk, or of the hag, Rod didn't know. Certainly the combination would be enough to make a saint take precautions.

The women came running up then, children in tow, and the men had to turn to give them the news while the wives tried to shush the babes. Magnus took advantage of the interruption to lean over to Rod and mutter, "Neatly done, Dad. Thou didst not lie."

"No, but I sure made one hell of a false impression, eh? Well, that happens. Thanks for your help, son."

Magnus started to answer, then remembered his own prevarication, and had the grace to blush.

One of the older peasants turned back to Rod. "We can only thank thee from the bottoms of our hearts, sir knight. The witch hath beset us, long and sorely."

"Why, how is this?" Magnus demanded, suddenly alert. "Have you no lord to protect you?"

"From a witch like to her?" The peasant shook his head with a grim frown. "Even he did fear this vile hag, young sir, as did his father before him. He came once each year to show himself, so that we might know he was our lord, and his bailiff came but once a month, with armed men behind him, to take his tax. Yet sin that they would do no more, the hag too required tax of us—tribute, she called it, in cloth, grain, meat, and other goods."

"Money, too," said another man. "When we had it."

Magnus frowned. "And if thou didst not pay?"

"Then would she make our cows go dry, keep the rain from our crops . . ."

"Or bring far too much of it," another peasant said. "In truth, she hath brought flood."

Or taken the credit for it, Rod reflected sourly. "I can see that would be reason enough to pay."

"Oh, there were better!" cried a wife. "She would make the men no longer wish to lie with their wives, or would make us women barren."

Several men reddened with embarrassment and looked daggers at her, but she was staring up at Rod in righteous indignation and didn't notice. Rod nodded; he could believe that these events, at least, were really the hag's doing.

"Her worst deeds thou hast seen, I doubt not," the first peasant said grimly, "and she would do it, whether or not we paid our tribute."

The woman nodded. "Our sons."

"Now and again," another peasant said, "she would beguile away some young man to use as a toy. Whene'er one of our youths failed to come home at day's end, 'twas cause for mourning, for we knew we'd not see him again."

Magnus scowled. "She let none go free when she had done with them?"

"There were one or two. Elber, dost thou hear?" Another woman elbowed a middle-aged man who stood among them but seemed not to be paying attention. He jumped at the contact, turned to her, and said, "Eh?" His face was completely vacant.

"Thus would they come home," the woman said with contempt, "those few that were seen again. Not the lad himself, but his hollow husk."

Magnus stared at the man's empty gaze, and shuddered.

"Well, she won't bother you again," Rod said firmly. "You might consider cutting down the Cold Iron that's hanging over her doorway, so the Little People can get in and decontaminate the tower. You'll find she doesn't demand tribute again, and I doubt you'll ever find any trace of her."

The peasants cheered, and the woman in front called, "Bless thee, valiant knight!"

"I can use it," Rod returned. "Don't forget, though—your baron will probably be paying much closer attention to you now. His taxes will still need to be paid."

They looked at one another, startled; they hadn't thought it through that far. Magnus stared, too, then began to look angry.

Time for a quick exit. "Make the best of it," Rod advised. "Good luck." He turned Fess away toward the forest.

A unanimous cry of protest rose from the crowd, and they ran after him. "Wilt thou not stay, that we may honor thee?" the headman cried.

"Thanks, but I have other tasks to see to." Rod smiled and waved. Magnus glanced at him, then at the peasants, back to Rod, then back at the peasants again. He forced a smile and waved, too, then rode after Rod.

As the leaves closed about them, he demanded, "Wherefore didst thou not stay? I am a-hungered, and bone weary. Art thou not, also?"

"I am," Rod agreed, "but we can camp in the forest."

"Wherefore, when we could have soft hay upon which to spread our cloaks, and hot food for the asking?"

"Because it would come with a price tag," Rod said.

" 'Tis a price we have already paid!"

"Yes, but I saw the looks on some of their faces—calculating looks. I wouldn't put it past them to ask us to get rid of the local lord."

"Well . . . mayhap we should!" Magnus said stoutly. "These folk do but exchange one tyrant for another!"

"How do you know their baron is a tyrant?"

Magnus tossed his head in impatience. "What matter? He could be—and if he could, their form of government is wrong! Thou didst teach me—thou, and Fess in the classroom—that folk should be free to choose their own ruler, and the manner of his ruling!"

"Self-determination. Did you teach him that, Fess?"

"Yes, Rod, as per your instructions."

"Which I learned from your curriculum in the first place." Rod managed a sardonic smile. "Kind of ironic, when you think about it—a bunch of aristocrats, all diehard liberals, and all totally convinced the people should rule themselves. Maybe that's because there weren't any 'people.' "

"Aye—thou hast said thy home, Maxima, had naught but aristocrats."

"Well, that's what they called themselves. After five hundred years, I suppose they had the right to—but when there's nobody there to rule, the term kind of loses meaning."

"They were, at least, noble."

"I'd have to agree," Rod said judiciously, "or that their ancestors were. Of course, they chose their own form of government—and it was, at least functionally, a democracy."

"The House of Lords, ruling none but lords?" Magnus smiled, without mirth. "Yet an thy folk could choose their own form of government, wherefore ought not these peasants?"

"They do have that right. Enforcing it is another matter. And remember—their right of self-determination is limited by their interaction with their neighbors. If the next village chooses a different form of government, and the two systems clash and disrupt one another, both have to remember the other's rights."

"They would have to agree together." Magnus frowned. "And where we must think of one village, we must think of a dozen."

Rod nodded. "Or a hundred, or a thousand—or the whole Isle of Gramarye."

"Why not say 'the whole of the Terran Sphere'?"

"Because they don't have much contact with the other planets yet—and what little they do have, they're not aware of."

"But when the day comes that they do, what then?"

"By then, if all goes as I'm planning, they should have a functioning democracy, in place and well oiled by at least a hundred years of experience. They'll be ready to become part of the larger democracy that governs the Terran Sphere."

"The Decentralized Democratic Tribunal." Magnus frowned. "Thy life's work—preparing them for their place in it. For my countrymen could wreak havoc untold on the rest of the human worlds, could they not?"

"Oh, yes," Rod said softly. "The only collection of espers in the known galaxy? You bet they could."

"And who art thou to tell us we must not gain dominion where we may?"

Rod turned to stare at his son. How had Magnus worked it around so he and his father were on opposite sides? "I'm the one who seems to remember the concept of individual rights. Or do you think Gramarye's right to rule should wipe out the rest of humanity's right to self-determination?"

"Nay." Magnus frowned, wondering in his turn how his father had turned the argument back on *him*. "Yet by seeking to foster democracy among us, thou dost impose thy will. The folk of Gramarye should be free to choose what form of government they may."

"True. Do you honestly think those people back there would really choose anything other than an effective democracy?"

Magnus turned thoughtful, running over possibilities. "It may be," he said slowly. "The history books Fess gave me to read told of a case or two of folk wishing to be ruled by another."

"Biblical Israel shifting from judges to monarchy." Rod nodded. "Any of the other cases, though, are just stage-dressing for a power grab—like the Roman proletariat offering a crown to Julius Caesar."

"Naetheless, thou wilt not deny 'tis possible!"

Rod shrugged. "Anything is possible. That doesn't mean

it's good. I'm just naturally wary of any form of government that doesn't guarantee the basic human rights."

"I could subscribe to that," Magnus said slowly.

"Then you'll find you're supporting a democracy of some kind, son, though it may work differently from the ones you've studied. Asserting the rights of the individual always leads to self-government of one sort or another."

"I can think of other forms."

"Yeah, but will they really be democracies hiding under another name? If they're not, are they really enforcing human rights, or just claiming to? Either way, you also have to ask how they're affecting their neighbors. You may have a local tyranny that's really part of a larger democracy, and it's the bigger government that's really guaranteeing those rights."

Magnus thought that over, frowning. "Dost thou say no government, no society, can exist in isolation from others?"

"Well, it's possible," Rod admitted, "though interstellar travel and FTL communication have made sure that even the separate planets are affecting each other all the time, and very deeply, though that isn't always apparent. If it can happen anywhere, son, it'll be right here in the Forest Gellorn."

Magnus looked up in surprise. "Why, how dost thou mean? Even that little village has a lord!"

"Yes, but it was right near the edge of the wildwood. As we go deeper in, I think we'll find villages set up by escaped peasants, outlaws, malcontents—or even just people who became lost. There'll be some traffic between them, but not a lot—this is a very big, thick forest, with lots of wild animals. . . ."

"Some of which may be quite strange," Magnus grunted, "due to witch-moss, and the projective esper who knoweth not what she—or he—may be."

"Or what effects he's having. But isn't that true of all of

us? Anyway," Rod rushed on, "if there's any place on Gram-arye where a pocket society can exist free of outside govern-ment, it'll be here. Shall we take a little detour to see what kinds of government we may find?"

"This whole excursion is a detour," Magnus pointed out, "and one government that the people welcome, but is not a democracy, will be enough to prove my case."

"So my holiday from marital obligations and daily routine becomes a quest. Why not? But for now, I'm tired, and we're far enough from that village so that I don't think they'll find us. Let's pitch camp, son. I could use some sleep."

They slept the clock around, woke at dawn, and broke their fasts. Feeling largely restored, they broke camp, drowned and buried the fire, and rode off into the morning.

A few hours later they heard a bell tolling.

Rod frowned. "Kind of jarring, considering what a bright and peaceful morning it is."

"And somewhat late for Mass," Magnus agreed. "Of course, 'tis naught of our affair."

"Exactly. So we're going to go look, right?"

"Certes." Magnus smiled. "For what else have we come?"

They rode down the path that led through the trees, since it seemed to be going in the right direction. Sure enough, the bell's tones became louder—then the forest ended abruptly, and they came out into a large cleared area, a square mile or so of land so flat they could see the thin dark line of trees on the other side. Strips of farmland lay all about in a crazy-quilt pattern, divided by hedges. People had hewn them-selves farms out of the midst of the forest.

A hill rose at the eastern side of the clearing, and a village of wattle-and-daub houses clustered around it. Up near the top stood a fieldstone church—square and blocky, but with a recognizable steeple—and all about it, the grass was dotted with tombstones.

But the procession that threaded its way through the fields wasn't winding up toward that churchyard—it was coming toward Rod and Magnus, and a newly dug grave a hundred yards off to their left. The mourners didn't seem to see them—for mourners they were, peasant folk dressed in dark clothing, the first six bearing a coffin on their shoulders, following a man in a black robe, wearing a bishop's mitre—a high, bulbous, pointed hat—and carrying a crozier, the ornate shepherd's crook. But he wasn't wearing a priest's chasuble, or even a cassock—only a long robe, like a memory of a baron's leisure clothing. Certainly the huge cross that adorned a priest's chasuble was missing.

Magnus scowled. "Why, how is this? There is only the Abbot of the Monastery in Gramarye, and the new abbot of the Runnymede chapter of the Order."

"Apparently neither of them has heard about his rival here," Rod noted. "Of course, you can't be a bishop if you don't have a priest or two under you—but he seems to have taken care of that."

Behind the bishop came three acolytes in black robes with short white tunics over them—again, like distorted echoes of the garb of Catholic altar boys. One was a teenager, his face set and solemn; the other two were younger, perhaps eight and twelve, both looking rather scared. Behind them strode a priest, very young, also wearing a black robe, with two black-cloaked women behind him, their hair hidden under white bonnets. If they hadn't been with the clergy, Rod would have taken them for peasant wives—but their presence behind the priest made him wonder.

Then came the pallbearers, and the coffin; and behind it strode a short, stocky peasant, his square face lined with grief, his grizzled hair, his smock and leggings the color of old barn wood. Behind him came a few dozen people, young and old, parents and children, all but the babes in arms chanting a slow and mournful dirge.

They came to the grave; the bishop turned and gestured, and the pallbearers lowered the coffin to the rope slings, then down into the grave. At another gesture, the congregation ceased its chant.

"He lies here in sin!" the bishop cried. "In the one sin that cannot be shriven, for when a young man dies by his own hand, he condemns himself to hellfire eternal! When the spirit leaves the body, 'tis too late for remorse; the dead cannot confess! We may only hope and pray that ere the light of consciousness faded, he knew the wrong he had done, and repented of it—for even in the moment of our death, God can forgive!"

"Praise be to God," the priest and—were they nuns?— murmured.

"Yet we must knock upon the door if it is to be opened to us!" the bishop cried. "We must confess if we are to be forgiven! Ranulf did not!"

"This isn't going to be a whole great help to his family," Rod growled.

"He must say what is true," Magnus murmured.

"Only if he's asked."

"He must warn the others of his flock away from the road to Hell."

"Now is neither the time nor the place. Is he doing this for their good, or to buttress his own power?"

Magnus turned to him, frowning. "Why, how would this increase his power?"

"They have to do what he tells them to," Rod explained, "or they rot in Hell."

"Ranulf died alone," the bishop orated, "without a priest nearby! Let us pray that God will have mercy upon his soul—but since we cannot know that, we must believe he died in mortal sin, and cannot therefore be buried in consecrated ground. He will lie here, hard by the wilderness that was in his soul."

"So be it," the crowd murmured.

"So be it indeed!" the bishop cried. "Yet for the father who reared him to discontent and intemperance, to irreverence and impiety, for the misbegotten parent who encouraged his endless, impertinent, blasphemous questioning, the penance must be great, and lifelong!"

The stocky gray man lifted his eyes to the bishop, eyes stony, face impassive.

"Down on thy knees, recreant!" the bishop thundered, suddenly red-faced. "Pray for forgiveness to the God who made thee, forgiveness for having led astray the soul He entrusted to thy care!"

"This is consolation?" Rod murmured, aghast.

Slowly, the father shook his head. "It was not I who led him astray, but they who preach humility, yet practice arrogance."

"Sinner! Recreant!" the bishop bellowed. "How darest thou speak so against those who give their lives to the service of others! Purge the Devil who doth lurk in thy soul, till thou hast learned the very humility of which thou dost speak!" He turned back to the congregation at large. "Henceforth let none in our village of Wealdbinde speak to this man Roble, under pain of sin! Let all shun him, let all turn away from him, lest he spread this contagion of faithlessness among us all!"

The people muttered and backed away from Ranulf's father.

"Let him walk in silence, till he doth learn the error of his ways!" the bishop cried. "If he should seek to speak with you, turn a deaf ear! If he should ask thine aid, turn away thine eyes, see him not! In his pride, he doth set himself apart from God. . . ."

"Not from God!" the father roared. "Thou liest, rogue, and dost know thine own lie!"

"Smite him to silence!" the bishop howled, and a peasant near the father leaped to pin his hands while another struck him across the mouth.

"Never speak again!" the bishop bellowed, finger spearing out at Roble. "For if thou dost, none shall hear thy words of seduction and temptation! Begone, to thy living death!" He turned to the congregation. "Dearly beloved, let us resume our daily life, resolved never to let one soul of this village of Wealdbinde stray as this Ranulf has strayed! Let our compassion be shown by exhorting and admonishing our weaker bretheren! Let us return now to our homes and our fields, resolved to keep them secure against the assaults of the Devil!" And he strode away toward the village, taking up the dirge again. The altar boys, priest, and nuns hurried to follow him, and the congregation turned to fall in line. They strode away quickly, leaving the grim-faced father standing alone by the mound of broken earth that hid what was left of his son. The sound of the chanting faded and died away.

Magnus started to speak, but Rod silenced him with a touch on the arm. The gray man stood alone with no consolation but the wind, gazing at the grave, speaking softly at first, then louder.

"Here ye lie, my son, hard by the wilderness to which thou didst long to go—if for naught but to be away from them, with their everlasting questioning and searching of thy life, their blaming and their harrowing. They're all done now, lad, and they can't hurt thee anymore. They're all done, and they've mangled what's left of the memory of thee, and made it a caution for children—but never thought it should be a caution to themselves. Nay, they're all done now, and thy suffering's done, too, and thy torment is ended."

For a moment, anger showed. "May His Grace, the good bishop, be hanged! For if that's what goodness is, I'd liefer be evil! To torment the young with visions of hellfire, to bind them fast within rules of his own devising, to roar at them and and tell 'em they were born evil, and must strap every last bit o' life out o' themselves, then turn and preach to 'em of the virtues of charity! To tell them that Faith is a gift, then condemn 'em for not having it yet! To tell 'em nothing can be good except what he tells 'em to do! Nay, surely I ought not have let 'em do it to thee! Surely I should have stood against thy mother, taken thee, and fled to the forest! Surely I should have taken thee from the nuns ere they beat out of thee thy regard for thyself, afore they ground thy soul down, making thee to think thyself vile for being male! Nay, and surely, when the priest did thunder at thee that thou must needs take a wife and rear up bairns, whether any lass did suit thee or no, then surely I should have ta'en thee and gone, the two of us together 'gainst the wild beasts of the forest— for better the wolves of the greenwood than the jackals in black robes, who prey upon souls!" Tears glistened on his cheeks. "Nay, they can't hurt thee anymore, lad, though God knows I'll miss thee shrewdly! At the least, thy suffering's done! Nay, I did wrong to marry me! I did wrong to father thee!"

That was too much; Rod winced and took Magnus's arm, turning him away and back to the horses. "We're eavesdropping on something intensely personal. Let the poor man alone in his grief."

Magnus gave him a peculiar look, but turned away and mounted, then brought his horse alongside Rod's, riding beside him—but from the abstracted look on his face, and his conspicuous silence, Rod suspected he was still listening mentally to the bereaved father. He was about to rebuke his son when he remembered that Magnus was a man grown now, presumably with a fully formed conscience. Either that conscience was lacking, in which case it was too late for Rod to do anything about it, or that conscience was sound, in which case Magnus had detected something in the man's thoughts that Rod hadn't been aware of.

Such as wanting everyone to know what he felt the priests had done to his son?

Then why not have shouted it aloud at the funeral?

Because he was afraid.

Afraid? Of priests and nuns? Of people devoted to goodness and charity?

It seemed highly unlikely, but Rod remembered the Spanish Inquisition, the crusade against the Albigenses, and the fires of Smithfield. He reserved judgement. Then, too, these clergy had a distinctly homemade look about them; there was no guarantee that their dogma bore any resemblance to his own. Now that he thought of it, he hadn't heard the "bishop" mention the name of Christ at all.

Of course, there would have been no point in Roble's shouting charges to the faithful, who were unshakeable in their beliefs.

But to outsiders?

Rod glanced up at his son's faraway gaze, and decided not to interrupt.

5

Rod reined in with a sigh. "I don't think we'll ever agree on that one, son," he said, finally breaking the silence.

"But they *do* have the right to be governed as they wish!" Magnus exclaimed. "And if they desire to have a tyrant like that priest bellow and rail at them, if they wish to have him enforce their will with ostracism, who are we to tell them nay?"

"The sane ones, that's who."

Magnus started to say something, then caught himself— but Rod had intercepted the split-second burst of thought that gave rise to the words, and reddened. "I'm a fine one to talk, is that it? If you'll excuse me, son, I think I'd better ride apart for a while. You don't need me to chaperone you, after all."

"I did not mean . . ." Magnus began, but broke off, seeing his father disappear off the trail and into the woods. Resentment burgeoned within him at his father's rejection. Then he smiled, as he realized he could agree with Rod on one thing—he didn't need a parent watching over him like a hawk.

Savoring that thought, he turned away—but he still felt a little guilty at having offended his father.

"There be no need to feel remorse when thou hast done right, young warlock."

Magnus looked up, startled. By the side of the road, gunnysack slung over his shoulder, stood the ragpicker. Magnus firmed his resolve and narrowed his eyes. "What dost thou here? Begone!"

"I but seek to offer thee that which will be of value to thee." The ragpicker swung the bag off his shoulder, reached in, and pulled out a golden chain with a bauble on the end. "Invulnerability, for thine heart! That no wench may ever capture it, to twist and torment it!"

Magnus squinted, trying to make out what the bauble was, but it twisted and turned in a patch of sunlight that made its form seem to blur. "What should I pay thee with?" Magnus demanded. "My soul?"

"Oh, nay! I shall take no pay. I exist but to aid those who are in need—or who will be."

"I trust not those who profess to offer much and ask little."

"Yet thou hast," the ragpicker called after him, "for thou hast acted from that same principle thyself, time and again."

That rocked Magnus a little; he liked to think of himself as motivated by healthy self-interest, though he was aware that it came in many disguises. Still, he realized the comment was just a barb to hook him into further argument and possible exploitation, so he ignored it and rode on.

The trail curved, hiding the ragpicker from view. Magnus was tempted to go back to make sure the man had disappeared, but steeled himself against the impulse.

He rode on as dawn turned into morning, sending dapples of sunlight through the leaves of the forest. The ground began to slope upward, and the trees thinned out. Magnus crested the rise, broke through a final screen of scrub, and saw another village below him in the morning mist. The sunlight struck through the clouds, and sent a shaft down to highlight the collection of huts. Magnus halted, charmed by the sight— and realized that glistening in the shaft of light were the whitewashed boards of a church steeple. With an uncomfortable pang of conscience, he remembered that it was Sunday.

The church bell began to toll.

Magnus sighed and shook the reins. "Come, good mount. I must needs go forth to the chapel, some holy words to hear."

He rode down into the valley, following the dirt road, softened now with the autumn rains, and came up to the church as the last few parishioners were filing in. But he was not quite late—a lady on a white palfrey, flanked by four men-at-arms, was riding down an adjoining road, coming behind him.

Magnus dismounted, tying his horse's reins to a tree limb. He strode up to the church door, then glanced back to make sure his horse had grass to eat . . .

And saw the lady watching him, with a gleam in her eye.

Something about her regard made Magnus uncomfortable. He turned back to the church door, doing his best to ignore her. . . .

"Hold, sirrah!"

Magnus whirled about, instantly seething at the demeaning term—the more so when he saw it was a guardsman who had spoken it. Didn't he know Magnus's rank without having to be told? Even coated with dust and in his travelling clothes, his garb was clearly that of a nobleman, or at the very least, a squire.

But the guardsman wasn't entering—he was holding the door wide, and his fellows had stationed themselves behind the lady, who was marching toward the door. She looked up at Magnus, and her glance seemed to pierce him. He stood numbed by surprise, and she smiled, with newly moistened lips. "Art thou so hot to enter then, young man?"

"Young man!" Magnus took refuge in outrage. "Thou art not so much older than I, milady—and thy servants want rebuke! Thou must needs teach them to know their betters!"

"What!" the guardsman cried, and his halberd swung down.

Magnus dropped his hand to his sword. "School him, lady, or I'll do it for thee."

The three other men instantly lowered their halberds.

Magnus stood poised, hand still on his sword, and locked gazes with her.

Her eyes seemed to swell; her lips parted.

Magnus felt a current pass through him, leaving him shaken. He hoped he looked like a frozen statue.

The lady's lips curved into a lazy smile, and her eyelids drooped. She turned to the guardsmen. "Wherefore dost thou stand here idle, good fellows? Get thee in, to hear the holy man. Nay, get thee all within!"

"But my lady . . ." The guard was clearly taken aback. "Thy safety . . . thine husband . . ."

"Mine husband is my concern." Her voice sharpened. "And this stranger is no brigand; couldst thou not tell his quality, by the look of him?"

The guardsman gave Magnus a doubtful glance that as much as said that he knew exactly of what quality Magnus was, and the young man's grip tightened on his sword; but the lady snapped, "Go!" and the four guardsmen filed into the church, with wary glances behind.

Magnus watched them go, his face stony, his hand relaxing from his sword hilt—and suddenly very wary of turning to look behind him.

"Hast thou no taste for aught but steel?" the lady said, her voice throaty. "No desire to sheathe thy blade in a proper scabbard?"

"Why, so I do." Magnus slammed the blade back by his

side and turned to give the lady a cold bow. "Naked steel must not be borne within the church. By thy leave, milady, I'll step within."

"Art thou so eager to hear a sermon?" There was a faint sneer in her voice. "Nay, belike thou art a very cleric of a warrior, who dost live by the Church and the Book."

That stung, but Magnus knew at least the name of the game, if not its strategies, and retorted, "I am a man for the Book and the Law indeed. Good morn to thee, lady."

"Why, then, speed thee to God." Her lips smiled, but her tone was contemptuous. "And I had thought to bid thee home to dine, to slake thine appetite of me."

The thrill that passed through him was nothing he could control; Magnus had to remind himself that there was no sin in feeling desire, only in giving in to it. " 'Tis not seemly for a lady to entertain a gentleman other than her husband."

"Mine husband is off to the wars," she said instantly, "or to attend upon his suzerain at a conference of lords, regarding their rights in opposition to the Crown, which must surely be much the same as a battle—and will detain him for some weeks yet."

"What knight is this?" Magnus demanded. "Tell me thy husband's name." He could feel himself slipping, and hoped that personifying the man might make him lose interest in the wife.

She frowned, realizing the gambit; but protocol, and regard for her own status, prohibited a refusal to answer. "He is Sir Spenser Dole, and I grow lonely in his absence."

"Then thou art fortunate in having so many brave servitors to accompany thee." Knowing the man's name didn't lessen the tide of hot blood flowing through Magnus's veins, but it did explain the situation—Sir Spenser Dole was a knight advanced in middle age, fifty in a world to which sixty was ancient, and the young woman had no doubt been married to him against her will, in accordance with custom and her father's wishes, cementing an alliance between two knights, or perhaps even their lords.

Magnus bowed again and turned away, determined to have nothing to do with the lady, nor with her invitation.

"Be easy, knight." Her touch was featherlight on his arm, but sent the current coursing through him again, and he stopped in spite of his good intentions. "I do not seek to turn thee from a course of honor, but only to give rest and comfort to a valiant warrior who, I doubt not, hath ridden long and is both a-hungered and weary." She moved around to his side, far enough that he couldn't help but see her, her eyes wide and imploring. "Nay, wilt thou leave me lorn?"

He knew he should have—but the lady was very beautiful, and Magnus's pulse was pounding in his ears, and what harm was there in sharing a breakfast with her? "The Mass," he protested, in a last feeble defense—but he had the door open, and could hear the priest chanting the Lavabo.

"The Book has been moved," the lady said with a lazy smile, lips full and moist. "The mass is half-spent, and thou must needs come again to the church at another time. Thou hast done as well as thou might, to honor holiness on the day of rest—but travellers have ever great difficulty in finding a priest, and thou art surely to suffer no blame if thou hast not had a Mass."

"Half a Mass is better than none. . . ."

"Not to the Church, who would have thee come again if thou dost come too late."

Which was true; coming in after the Credo meant that his Sunday obligation was not fulfilled.

"Rest thee, then," she said softly, smiling almost proudly. "Come away to my castle, and find repose and refreshment."

The church door slipped from nerveless fingers; he turned

away from the chapel, following the sway of her hips, and telling himself there was no harm in light conversation.

Sir Spenser's castle was tall, but not large—scarcely more than a curtain wall surrounding a square keep, perhaps fifty feet on a side. This was no nobleman's wife, but a country knight's. Still, Magnus reminded himself, Dole was a good man, and deserved no slur on his honor.

The lady did not take them in over the drawbridge, however, but around to the narrow plank bridge that ended at the postern gate. Magnus knew, right there, that he should turn and go, but the lady's voluptuous figure swayed before him, and he told himself that he would stay just long enough for polite conversation, then leave. After all, she could scarcely invite him openly to her bed in front of her husband's servants.

But there were no gardeners in sight, nor grooms, as he passed through the postern. He told himself that they were only gone to church, and followed the lady through the door to the keep, resolving firmly to turn on his heel if he didn't see any servants inside.

But he didn't—see any servants, and didn't turn on his heel—because, as soon as they were through the door, the lady turned and pressed up against him even as he stepped forward, molding the curves of her body to his, parted lips seeking his mouth with an urgency that took him completely by surprise, and his body responded automatically. He yielded to temptation and the deepening of the kiss, putting his arms around her and pressing her hips against his own.

Then he realized what he was doing, remembered that this was another man's wife, and broke off in alarm.

She laughed with triumph, low in her throat. "So, then. Thou art not so godly as all that, art thou?"

Wrong choice of words; it reawakened Magnus's conscience. He stepped back, releasing her. "Nay, then, thou hast the right of it—I should be in church, even as thou sayest. I thank thee for thine hospitality. . . ." He was turning back toward the door, when she scoffed, "What, a Sunday man? Art thou then so afeard of Hell that thou wouldst turn from heavenly pleasures?"

She was, Magnus thought as he turned, highly overrating herself—but when he looked at her again, eyes bright, face flushed, bosom heaving, he wasn't so sure. Still, he tried his best to affect a frosty demeanor. "Thou hast a husband, lady, and I a duty to chivalry." This time, he did manage to turn around.

But her voice was all contrition, demure and shamed. "Nay, then, thou hast the right of it to scold me so. Have no fear—I'll be a seemly matron. Yet thou must needs permit that I make amends. Come to mine hall, and taste some wine to refresh thee."

Magnus hesitated, his hand near the latch.

"Wilt thou make me feel to be a thing of evil?" she pleaded. "Nay, turn, and have the grace to let me do my penance."

Magnus relented and turned back. "Why, I cry thy mercy, lady, and will gladly taste thy wine, for I am parched."

She gave him a tremulous smile of gratitude and turned away, leading him into the keep, and Magnus followed, relieved that the situation was no longer compromising, but wary still.

His wariness increased as she led him up the spiral staircase, but not so much—the great hall was, after all, for public occasions, and it wasn't terribly surprising that a single guest would be entertained in the solar.

They came out into a gallery, and the lady, no longer swaying, but still with a movement that Magnus found enchanting, led him to the door at the end. She opened it, and they came into a small chamber filled with sunlight from three tall windows in its outer wall. Magnus was surprised—he would have expected the solar to be larger, even in so small a castle as this—but it was well appointed, a carpet on the floor and tapestries on the walls, with an hourglass-shaped chair, a scroll-carved bench, and a small table.

The lady took a flask and glass from the silver tray on the table, gave the goblet to Magnus, and filled it with wine. "Recline thee, sir, and tell me—whence hast thou come, and whither goest?"

He found it unnerving that she did not ask his name, but perhaps it was wise, under the circumstances. He sat on the bench, the chair being behind the table. "I wander without purpose, lady, to see what may be found in Gramarye."

"Dost thou seek wrongs to right, and damsels in distress?"

"I have found the first, but not the last," Magnus admitted, "though, to tell truly, I know not what I seek."

"Wilt thou not taste of my wine?" she pleaded.

Magnus tipped the goblet against his lips, looked up, and nodded. " 'Tis sweet, milady, and full. I thank thee."

"I would thou couldst thank me for more," she said ruefully. "What hath set thee to thy travels, then?"

Magnus took a long swallow of wine to give him time to mull over the answer. He couldn't exactly tell tales outside the family, after all. "A yearning to see more than I have known in my youth, I would have to say—and a yearning to be away from the folk of my childhood for a space." Which was true enough—but Magnus had travelled throughout the Isle of Gramarye as he grew, and knew most of it fairly well; the broader vistas he longed for were not to be found on his home planet.

"I have yearnings, too," she sighed, "but a man may wander, and a woman must stay."

Magnus looked up sharply, feeling compassion for the

first time. "Nay, surely if thou dost long to see more of the world, as I do, it must needs go hard on thee to rest."

"I shall rest, as I must," she sighed, "for I know full well that a wanderer's life would pall, and I would long for house and husband. Yet I may dream."

Magnus smiled with sympathy. "Aye, at the least, we all may dream. That is not denied us, is it?"

"To dream, aye." She rose in a graceful turn, took up the flask, and refilled his glass. "But only to dream—never to be free."

"Even so," Magnus commiserated. "I have longed for such freedom, and do now seek it—yet I begin to suspect that I shall not find it." He sipped the wine.

"How so?" The lady frowned. "Thou dost wander; how canst thou not be free?"

"Why, for that I am still what I was reared to be," Magnus explained. "I look upon the peasants, and though they may scarce see more than a hundred square miles in their lives, they have a boisterousness, a looseness to their actions, that I have not, and never will. A nobleman, a gentleman, is born to restraint in action, lest he give cause for broils that may include hundreds—and he can never shake off the notion that the welfare of those about him is his care."

She leaned toward him, and lowered her voice. "That others' happiness is thy concern?"

"Aye." Magnus felt too warm, but he smiled. "Even though I've known them not, I know that all the folk of Gramarye must be as much my care as the King's and Queen's—and if they are sad, I feel the need to cheer them."

"But I am sad." She leaned closer, and her eyes seemed huge. With a surge of lightheadedness, Magnus noticed that her neckline was cut lower than he had realized, and her lips were trembling with sadness. . . .

He leaned to those lips as if drawn by a magnet.

For a minute, nothing existed in the world save her lips, and the sensations they aroused in him, the blood beginning to pound in his veins, the need for her so hot it would not be denied. . . .

He broke off, alarmed at himself. "Nay, lady," he gasped, "I am like to abuse thine hospitality." He set the goblet down and forced himself to his feet. "I cry thy pardon. I must away, ere I give offense. . . ."

"But if thou dost leave, though wilt most shrewdly offend!" she protested, her breath catching in a sob.

Alarmed, Magnus turned back and saw her eyes overflowing with tears that ran down her cheeks as she looked up at him, forlorn. His heart twisted, and he reached down to comfort her, but she rose into his arms; her lips enveloped his, her body pressing against him, curves melding to his angles, churning against him with her need, moaning low in her throat; and his hands began to move over her back, then down, caressing her hips, and up, to cup her breasts. . . .

He broke off, staring down at her, seeing half-closed eyes, her shoulders bare as her gown slipped down, and his gaze was riveted to the high, soft curve of her breast. . . .

She caught his hand, pressed it up against that curve, and sought his lips again. The kiss was longer, more urgent; she mewed in her throat, almost sobbing, and Magnus traced the contours of her body, entranced. . . .

A crash, and a bellow.

They sprang apart; then Magnus leaped between the lady and the door to shield her, but an iron gauntlet slammed into the side of his head and sent him reeling, a spear-point jabbed his ribs, and he looked up to see the guardsman who had confronted him at the church, leering with vindictive glee, while behind him, a terrible old man cuffed the woman as though she were a hound, bellowing, "Wanton! Traitress! A night gone, scarce three hours on the road, and thou hast found another fool to warm thy bed! Nay, thou hast stained mine honor once too oft, and never shall again!" He yanked his sword out of his scabbard, and the lady fell back, screaming.

Magnus gathered himself and shot upward, knocking the spear aside and slamming into the guardsman. The man reeled back and Magnus twisted the halberd out of his hands, whirling toward Sir Spenser . . .

Just in time to see the lady spinning away with a scream, to slam into the wall. Her husband advanced on her, face red with rage . . .

. . . and a blow struck Magnus from behind; he staggered, seeing stars, but anger flamed through him, and he turned as he hit the wall, to see the soldier swinging a club and two more guardsmen coming up behind him.

Magnus sidestepped automatically, caught the man's wrist as it went by, and hurled the soldier against the stones. He whirled to parry one spear with his captured halberd, brought the butt around to crack the pate of the other guardsman and, as he fell, turned back to the second, parrying his next thrust and swinging the halberd-butt at his head. But the guardsman managed to block in time—and Magnus lashed a kick at his kneecap. The guard howled and fell, and Magnus turned . . .

To find himself facing Sir Spenser, steel in his hand and blood in his eye, breathing in hoarse rasps and closing fast.

Magnus almost turned and ran right then; the old man was a sight to make even the most hardened soldier quail, with his glaring eyes and gleaming sword. But training came to the fore, and Magnus whipped out his own blade, blocked a cut, riposted, parried, counterthrust, and settled down to some fast and furious fencing.

The end was foretold—fifty years cannot last long against twenty, and the older man's experience and skill were countered by Magnus's training, which made him as adept as Sir

Spenser, while his reflexes were faster and his endurance much longer. And, though Sir Spenser had thirty years' experience in battle, Magnus had fifteen that had started in his childhood. Outraged honor warred against frustrated hormones—but as the rage cooled, Magnus began to be able to think again, and contented himself with parrying and occasionally thrusting, just a little, to keep the older man off balance. Sir Spenser's breath came harder and harder, his movements slowed, and in ten minutes' time, Magnus caught his sword in a bind, slapped it from his hand, and pinned him against the wall. "Now, Sir Spenser," he said sternly, "though I've shamed myself as well as thee, thou shalt answer to thy peers for this day's deed, and I shall bear witness against thee."

"And I will bear witness against *thee*," said a guardsman's voice behind, "that the lady was abed with thee when Sir Spenser came in this chamber. And thou, Nigel?"

"I too," the second guardsman answered, and the third grunted assent.

The lady cried out, and Magnus backed away to help her to her feet, never taking his eyes from the four men. One of the guardsmen made a tentative movement toward his fallen halberd, but Magnus's sword tip flicked toward him, and the man halted.

"Not a trial," the lady moaned, but Magnus didn't flinch. "What is a peasant's word, against a lord's? Nay, Sir Spenser, will you or nil you, you will stand before the assembled lords for this."

"Why, then, I will, and there's not a one of them will blame me when they know the cause," the old knight growled. "I had thought to spare the lady public shame, and so forebore to charge her to her father's face when first I caught her in her adulterous games—yet I see I was wrong in my patience. Nay, if thou must needs shame her and her father before his peers, have at it! The lords of this dukedom shall meet in Sterling Meadow two days hence; I rode to meet them, when this loyal soldier came to warn me that a whelp was sniffing after my bitch."

Magnus held his temper and made his own guess as to the guardsman's motives; loyalty was the least of them. The lady only sobbed and moaned, shaking her head.

"Ah," Magnus breathed. "So that is the way of it, eh? That it may not come to court."

"Do not humiliate me before them all!" the lady said through her tears.

"I would not, though I've strong cause," Sir Spenser said, his face stony. "Wouldst thou be so cruel, youngling?"

"Nay," Magnus said slowly. He straightened, sheathing his sword, but turning so he could keep an eye on the guardsmen. "Dost thou wish satisfaction of me, then?"

Sir Spenser's eye kindled, but he said with regret, "I've had what I may. Get thee gone."

"Why, so I will," Magnus said slowly, "yet I hesitate to leave this lady to thy revenge."

She moaned and clutched at his sleeve.

Sir Spenser gave them both a look of disgust, then said, "I will visit her with no punishment."

The lady went limp, sobbing.

"Yet I'll not keep her by to shame me more," he added, his voice grinding. "Back to thy father, lady! And do not think to tell him lies, for I and all my men will meet him in Sterling Meadow in two days' time, to tell him of thine infidelity."

"No-o-o-o," she moaned. "Not my father! And how should I face my mother? The shame . . ."

And the punishment, Magnus realized—but within the family. It was no concern of his.

"Thou hast forfeited thy place by me," the older knight growled. "I shall not divorce thee, for 'twould shame me as

much as thee, and thou shalt have thy dower lands again, to
dwell on in what comfort thou mayest—but we cannot live
as husband and wife more, for thou hast broke that bond."
He looked up at Magnus, and his voice was a whip crack.
"Take her hence! I wish thee joy of her!"

Magnus knew very well that he would have no joy of such
a woman—he wouldn't be able to trust her for a second. On
the other hand, he couldn't just leave her in the forest alone.
They came out of the castle, to find two grooms holding
their horses. The grooms helped the lady to mount her palfrey, and she and Magnus rode off into the forest, he silent,
she weeping.

But as soon as the leaves closed about them, she turned on
him. "And a fine knight-errant thou art! Couldst thou not defend me from his anger? Thou, who didst seek to seduce me,
and would have forced me had he not burst in upon us?"

The unfairness of the lie struck Magnus speechless. He
could only stare at her for the moment.

" 'Tis thine advances have left me bereft of house and
place!" she said hotly. "Nay, I am therefore thy charge now,
to house and feed! Thou must needs take me to the altar!"

The horror of the prospect jolted Magnus out of his stupe-
faction. "Why, what a lying shrew art thou! 'Twas *thou* didst
bend thy wiles to seduce *me*, and hast brought this coil upon
thyself!"

"Liar!" she screamed, and her hand swept around for a
ringing slap. "I am a lady bred! Never would I stoop to such
indignity!"

Cold rage cleared his head, and Magnus narrowed his
eyes, probing with his mind.

She must have been mildly telepathic herself, for she
screamed, clutching at her head, and he felt her horror at the
mind-probe. "Thou art a witch!"

"A warlock." He barely glimpsed her memory of the event, but knew that she was aware that he had seen it.

"Warlock or witch, thou art surely no gentlemen, thus to peer among a woman's secrets! Nay, thou art wholly undeserving of knighthood, for thou art most unchivalrous!" She bowed her head, weeping bitterly, a broken woman.

But Magnus knew better now than to trust appearances. "I am no knight, but a squire only; I have not sought higher rank. Thou hast the right in that, if in naught else. Surely there is no truth in thy claim that I am in any wise beholden to thee for thy welfare, for thou hast played this game with many men before me."

"Mine husband lied, in saying . . ." Her hot accusation trailed off as she looked into Magnus's eyes. "Nay, thou wilt seek within my mind to prove thy contention again, wilt thou not?" she whispered.

"Nay." Magnus's lip curled. "Yet there are witnesses, I doubt not—the servants and, though thou mayest not have thought, the Wee Folk. Hast thou kept thine hearths clean, and left them their bowls of milk?" He paused, long enough to see in her face that she had not. "They owe thee no debt of gratitude, and will not lie for thee. Shall I call them to testify?"

She hesitated just long enough to realize that a warlock probably could do just that, and be answered; then she took refuge in anger again. "Thou canst not know the shame and horror of forced marriage! Of maidenly dreams of love, torn asunder by a forced coupling with an aged partner who doth inspire in thee naught but disgust!"

Magnus did feel a stirring of sympathy; he had experience that enabled him to imagine.

"I, but a lass of sixteen!" she cried. "Nay, canst thou be amazed that I found no delight in him? Can it astound thee that I took my pleasure where I might?"

Magnus did feel sorry for her, but realized it was the

course of folly to admit it. "Yet thou didst take that pleasure with no thought for the hurt or shame thou didst heap upon thine husband, or even on thy lovers."

"What concern had they for me?" she demanded. "What concern hadst thou? Did any of thee care for aught but the pleasure of my body? Nay, if thou hast had shame, thou and they, thou hast had naught but thy just desserts!" She glared up at him. "Or wilt thou tell me thou hadst true concern for me?"

"Nay," Magnus admitted, "yet I do pity thee. Therefore will I conduct thee to thy father's house, and see thee safely there—yet no further."

"Oh, valiant man!" Her words dripped scorn. "O squire worthy of knighthood! Hast thou no thought for the shame that shall be mine? Aye, my father may yet grant me my dower house—yet there he will be sure that I shall live alone, apart from all folk of any degree, the jest of the other ladies, and never again to know human company—for a castoff wife is better dead!"

That, Magnus knew, was true. Medieval society was hardly generous to those who were divorced, especially females.

"It falls to thee," she snapped. "Thou wast the final cause of my humiliation. 'Tis for thee to give me place and station among my peers! 'Tis for thou to call for annulment, and to marry me! Come, carry me off! Steal me away! For there is no man but must have a woman in his charge!"

"Wherefore I, and not one of these other young men who have shared thy bed?" Magnus snapped.

"For that they have fled!"

"Why, then, so shall I. Lady, farewell!" Magnus turned his horse into the underbrush, but the crashing of scrub growth couldn't drown out her scream of rage.

He didn't go far, of course—just a dozen feet off the road, just out of sight but not out of hearing. He shadowed her as she rode on down the track, weeping as though she were heartbroken. Magnus felt pity stir within him, but told himself sternly that she was not his care. Nonetheless, he followed, wanting to be sure of her safety. He endured listening to her rail against all men, cataloguing their duplicities and wickedness; he heard her vicious cries of hatred, and rejoiced that he had turned away. Nonetheless, under the circumstances, he found that he could blame himself as much as her.

Then suddenly, five men burst out of the trees, surrounding the lady and catching her horse's bridle. The palfrey reared, neighing in alarm, but the men wrestled it back down. The lady screamed, but the biggest man clapped a filthy hand over her mouth and laughed. They were all slovenly and unkempt, crusted with dirt and reeking of grime. They brayed, chortling:

"Why, what a prize is here!"

"Thou dost hate men, dost thou, sweetling? Nay, we'll give thee greater cause!"

"Thou dost wish a husband, dost thou? We'll give thee five!"

The leader took his hand from her mouth, letting forth a tearing scream that was cut off as he clamped his own mouth over hers, pricking her throat with a dagger. She froze, wide-eyed in fear, not daring to close her teeth.

Magnus burst out of the roadside with a roar, laying about him with his sword. A man howled and fell with blood spreading over his nose; another bellowed and turned to fight, but flinched away with a yelp as Magnus's point scored his arm. The other three turned on Magnus with clubs and a rusty sword, but they were poorly trained indeed; he knocked their weapons aside with a dozen blows.

Then a club cracked on his shoulder, no doubt aimed for his head. He howled, and his right arm went limp. The other outlaws shouted victory and leaped for him, but Magnus reached out with his mind to twist the weapons from their hands, even as he caught an outlaw's club with his left hand and began to lay about him almost as efficiently as with his right.

"A witch!" one of the outlaws howled.

"Warlock!" Magnus bellowed, and cracked the man's pate. He laid about him, knocking down the others with three quick blows, then watched them roll about and moan, clutching at their heads, while he stood panting, only just beginning to be aware of the pain in his shoulder.

Then he turned to the lady. "They have not hurt thee, have they?"

"Nay, only filled me with loathing—thanks to thee. But thou art hurted!"

"The arm is only stunned, and will return to function presently." Magnus didn't say anything about the pain.

"I thought thou wert fled."

"I was, yet could not let thee travel at hazard. I heard thee cry, and came to ward thee. Go now to thy gate straightaway, madam, and do not tarry." He turned to the outlaws, who had regained their senses and were trying to creep away into the woods. He caught the biggest one by the front of his tunic and yanked his face up to within an inch of his own. "Get thee hence," he snarled, "and tell all thy fellows that this lady doth ride under the ward of a warrior who is a warlock as well. If any should seek to touch a hair of her head, I'll appear and cleave his pate. Dost ken what I've said, sirrah?"

The man nodded, face working in fear. "Ah—aye, milord."

"Then go!" Magnus flung him away; he staggered back, sprawling against a tree trunk. "Take thy mates," Magnus added, "and tell them what I've bade thee. Get thee hence!"

The outlaw fairly yanked his companions to their feet and turned them away, with frightened glances back over their shoulders. They carried the one with the wounded leg, and disappeared into the forest.

The lady started to speak, but Magnus ignored her and rode again into the woods, hearing her scream in impotence, "Wretch! Dog! Swine!" Then she broke off weeping, and turned her horse back down the road.

Magnus hardened his heart and followed at some distance, mind open, listening for any others. Twice that afternoon he detected outlaws lying in wait, heads filled with avarice and lust, but with an underlying fear of the warlock they'd heard of. He nurtured that fright, touching their minds with a hint of nameless dread, and felt them think better of their plan, then turn away to slink back into the wood.

At length she came to her father's gate. The sentries before the drawbridge straightened in surprise and cried out, "Lady Maisy!"

Magnus turned away; she was safe now—and he didn't want to hear the anguish of her explanation to her father. He felt consumed with guilt at her suffering, since it was in part his fault—but he reminded himself that she had initiated the incident, not he, and that he was only the latest in a series of lovers she had invited. Yes, he was guilty, but not to the point of having any responsibility for her actions. Her father would have to claim a larger part of that, having forced her to marry a man she did not love—but, when all was said and done, the greatest part of the blame was her own. She had not had to retaliate by promiscuity; that had been her own decision. That, no one had made her do; she had taken it upon herself. She would have to answer for her own deeds.

She would not see that as justice, of course. Magnus began to realize, for the first time, that the woman had expected a man to take responsibility for her, in every way—but had not been willing to accept responsibility in her turn.

6

Magnus rode ahead, feeling quite shaken, but determined not to show it—or to seek a confidant; the only ones he knew were members of the family. So, all in all, he was quite surprised when he rounded a curve and came upon his father, riding down the road only a few feet ahead. Magnus stared, then frowned as anger rushed. He kicked his horse up even with Rod's. "What dost thou here, Father?"

Rod looked up and did a double take. "My Lord! Magnus! What're *you* doing back here?"

"I might ask the same. Indeed, I did."

Rod shrugged impatiently. "I know it's odd, but I'm going back to Wealdbinde, that pious, nasty little village we left yesterday."

"Thou wilt not seek to overthrow their priests!"

"It's an idea," Rod admitted, "though I hadn't really decided on it yet. Why? You think that would be bad for them?"

Magnus was silent a moment, taken aback by the question. "Is that not for them to decide?"

"Yes, if they have the chance. But I think that alleged

bishop has such a tight choke-hold on them that they couldn't get rid of him if they wanted to."

"Nay." Magnus frowned. "He is a man of the Church; assuredly he would not use force."

"Uh . . ." Rod bent his head to rub his chin for a moment, then said, "You've heard of the Crusades? The wars of the Reformation? The Knights Templar?" Before Magnus could answer, he rushed on: "And about his being a man of the Church—I'm not too sure about that, really. Did you notice his vestments? The mitre was so exaggerated, it looked like a caricature—and he wasn't wearing a cassock or a chasuble."

"Aye; he wore a robe, such as a nobleman might wear about him. What matters that?"

"A real bishop would be pretty much of a stickler for tradition. And, as we've already noted, Gramarye has never had a bishop—just the monks from the monastery, who expanded to fill the spiritual gap."

Magnus frowned, mulling it over. "What dost thou say?"

"I'm saying that what we're looking at here is a great little example of do-it-yourself religion, a cult that was set up by some cynic to give him personal power. Sure, he based it on the Catholic Church, that being the only one he knew—but he made the changes that would guarantee his power, and improvised what he couldn't remember."

"Thou dost perceive this bishop as ruling this village?"

"Yes, which is in itself rather ironic—he calls himself a bishop, but his jurisdiction is scarcely the size of a parish. What we're looking at, son, is a very tight little theocracy." He looked up at Magnus. "Care to come with me and find out? Or are you afraid of disturbing your preconceptions?"

Magnus gave him a very cold look. "I shall come, if thou wilt give me thy word not to seek to unseat a government that the people have chosen."

"Agreed—provided they still do choose it. After all, you

may be right—this nasty little government could just be accurately representing a bunch of nasty little people."

They came out of the forest to hear a choir singing. They were very obviously amateurs. Rod looked up at the church on the hilltop.

"I mislike thine expression," Magnus said. "Thou hast a wicked idea."

"Oh, not wicked. I mean, I'm a good Catholic, aren't I?"

Magnus started to answer, but Rod cut him off quickly. "All right, forget about the adjective. But I've seen enough Masses to know what they're supposed to be like—especially since you grew old enough to go to church. I was just kind of wondering if it's the same liturgy."

"Is not the Mass the same everywhere?"

"Basically the same, with local variations—but you always recognize the basics."

"And thou dost wonder if thou wilt? Or dost thou wish to be sure the bishop doth notice thee?—as he will of a weekaday morn when so few come to hear."

"What, you suspect me of having an ulterior motive? I'm surprised at you, son—you should be sure of it. Shall we go?"

They rode up the hill, tied their horses to the graveyard fence, and went in to find Mass in progress. Rod halted, and stared in amazement—the church was packed. It wasn't all that small, either.

"They truly believe," Magnus murmured in his ear.

"Or don't dare stay away," Rod muttered back.

They stepped aside into the shadows at the rear. The bishop went on with the service, seeming not to have seen them, which he might not have—in fine old medieval style, the church had no pews, and everyone was standing.

Right away, they knew it wasn't a real Mass—or at least not the one they knew. For openers, the crucifix was at the side of the altar, not in the center, and there was something subtly wrong about it. Its customary place was taken up by a rather rough statue of a man wearing a costume identical to the one the bishop wore, like a poor memory of the real episcopal regalia. The Kyrie had turned into a communal chant of "Lord, forgive our disobedience"; the Gloria was mostly about man's unworthiness, not God's goodness; and the Confiteor went on interminably.

"Who will confess their sins?" the bishop cried, and when no one answered, he signaled to a couple of burly peasants. They strode into the crowd, seized a young man, and threw him down on his knees in front of the altar. "Confess!" the bishop thundered, pointing at the young man as though he were hurling a lightning bolt. "Confess thy lustful desires for Julia!"

A girl not far from the front turned beet-red with embarrassment.

"But I did not . . . I . . ." the lad protested.

"Thou didst treasure thy perverted desires in thine heart! Three elder folk saw thy face as she did pass by, and saw that thou didst look after her with thine eyes till she was out of sight! They saw the look in thine eyes! Confess!"

"I did naught . . . I . . ."

The bishop nodded to the burly men. One of them stepped forward, caught the boy's arm, and twisted it up behind him. The lad let out a yelp, and the bishop thundered, "Confess!"

Magnus started forward, but Rod put out a hand and caught his arm. "We're just observers, remember?"

The boy was babbling, an account of carnal thoughts that grew more lurid each time the bishop pressed for details and the usher twisted his arm. The poor girl who was supposedly the central figure in this episodic fantasy, nearly died of embarrassment as other parishioners glanced back and forth from her to the young man, crowding each other to be closer to the front, not wanting to miss a single syllable. When the boy was done, the bishop pronounced absolution (coming from himself, not God), and dismissed the young man back to the congregation. Then he singled out two more sinners, who seemed surprisingly willing to confess, one to the theft of an egg, the other to having missed Mass the day before, both berating themselves as useless and corrupted excuses for human beings. At last, satisfied, the bishop launched into the sermon, which was an elaboration of the decadence of Ranulf, the suicide, and the sins of his father, Roble.

Finally into the Mass of the Faithful. Rod was amazed that there was no collection, until he reflected that it would be pretty pointless, considering that the people gave the bishop everything they didn't absolutely need, anyway—but he was taken aback to see there was no offering of gifts or washing of hands, just taking out wafers and pouring some wine, pronouncing a quick blessing, and then the Communion, or what passed for it. The bishop and the priest gave Communion to each other, the three altar boys, and the two nuns, and that was it.

"No Communion for the congregation?" Magnus asked, flabbergasted, as they came out of the church—quickly, and ahead of the crowd.

"Apparently not," Rod said. "Presumably, they're not worthy." He untied Fess's reins. "How long were we in there, Fess?"

"An hour and a half, Rod."

"And the Communion itself couldn't have taken more than ten minutes, if that."

"Is not that supposed to be the core and heart of the Mass?" Magnus asked.

"Supposed to." Rod raised a forefinger. "That's the key phrase—'supposed to.' And, one might ask, who did the supposing? No, son, this isn't the Mass as I know it."

"Local variations . . ." Magnus muttered.

" 'They knew Him in the breaking of bread,' " Rod quoted. "They didn't crack a single Communion wafer, just blessed them as they were. He wasn't about to share the Eucharist with the parishioners—and he didn't mind in the least embarrassing and torturing sinners. Catholic confession is supposed to be private; Catholic Communion is supposed to be public, including everybody who wants it. 'By their fruits ye shall know them.' "

"Therefore is this bishop not truly Catholic." Magnus nodded as he swung aboard his horse. "That service was a virtual parody of the Mass I know. Nay, my father, I must agree with thee—whatever these people are, they are not of the true Roman Catholic Church."

"Not at all," Rod agreed. "Somebody remade the Mass to suit his own convenience."

"Naetheless," Magnus said firmly, "if they are pleased with this form of worship, who are we to say them nay?"

"*If,*" Rod said. "I can name you two who weren't pleased—the boy who had to confess, and the girl he was confessing about. She wasn't guilty of anything—but the bishop sure made it sound as though she was!"

Magnus shrugged. "Today they did not like it. Tomorrow they may. I learned in the schoolroom something of the psychology of religion, my father, and the mainstay of it is this: that people do need some form of Church, and of clergy, and of service."

"I can't really argue with that," Rod sighed. "Every time somebody tries to come up with a religion that doesn't require ministers or services, they always evolve again. Well, let's see if this town has anything to offer in the way of breakfast, son—if we still have any appetite, that is."

By the time they came to the first huts, Magnus had taken the initiative in the conversation, doing his own critique of the funeral service, and had worked his way up to the sermon, his mouth a thin, grim line. "What manner of bishop can this clergyman think himself to be, to so berate a widower in the hour of his son's burial?"

"I think," Rod said carefully, "that our good prelate knows exactly what kind of bishop he is."

Magnus frowned down at him. "What . . . ? Oh. Thou dost mean that he hath appointed himself to his episcopal chair."

"I certainly don't think the Abbot did," Rod returned, "and I don't think he would approve at all, of this man's version of Christianity. In fact, I think His Grace would tell this alleged clergyman to shut up—if he let him stay in Holy Orders at all."

"Thou dost assume this bishop would recognize the Abbot's authority," Magnus said, with the ghost of a smile.

Rod looked up at him sharply. "You know something I don't know?"

"Not *know*," Magnus hedged. "Not yet." '

Rod frowned, and almost demanded that Magnus explain; but a bunch of dried greenery swung at his face, and he had to duck. The distraction was enough to make him remember to give the young man room to find himself. He pulled Fess to a stop and, looking up, saw that the bundle of straw that had almost hit him was hanging by a yard of twine from a pole, which was sticking out of a very roomy hut. He dismounted, tying Fess's reins to a tree. "Well, this hut being a little larger than the others, and having a bush hanging out, I'd assume they're trying to pretend it's a tavern. Looks like we eat, son—something besides our own cooking."

"Alternatives to journey rations are ever welcome." Magnus swung down and tied his horse beside Fess. The stallion rolled its eyes toward the robot-horse, moving just a little away. Fess gave it a placid, almost disinterested look.

"We're not fooling anybody, are we?" Rod said under his breath.

"Only humans, Rod—but I think the equine will at least accept me as not being a threat." Fess lowered his head, pretending to graze. After a moment, Magnus's horse followed suit.

Rod nodded, satisfied. "Hope we have as good a case of luck with the locals. Shall we go in, son?"

"Wherefore not?" Magnus stood aside and gestured for Rod to precede him. Rod did, still disquieted by his son's refusal to give a direct answer—but he had been through this several times during the last few years, and wasn't about to make an issue of it. He led the way in.

The interior was dim; light filtered through a few horn windows. There were half a dozen tables with stools about them, and a long trestle table with benches. Rod looked around at the deserted room, shrugged, and knocked on a table. A moment later, a tall man came out of the doorway at the back, wiping his hands on an apron and looking surprised. "Gentlemen! What would you?"

"We would dine," Rod answered. "We've been on the road several days now, and have had little enough of proper food."

"Only dried crusts with which to break our fast this morn," Magnus put in.

The innkeeper glanced from the one to the other, seeming rather wary, but he forced a smile and said, "There is only some porridge, left from our own breakfast, and black bread—and ale, of course, though the brewing's a month old."

"That will do quite well." Rod smiled. "Don't get many customers in the morning, eh?"

"Only the widowers and orphan bachelors, gentlemen, and the bishop sees to it there are few enough of those," the man said, almost proudly. "Nay, we are here for the folk to meet and chat with one another o' nights, so we have little custom before sunset, in truth."

Rod frowned. "Odd arrangement. Your customers are just your fellow villagers, then?"

"Aye, though there be travellers, like to yourselves, one to a month or so. Yet we are mostly for a meeting place, though the good folk are as like to tarry outside in summer."

"Yet they'll tarry by the door," Magnus put in, "for this is the only place in the village from which they may have ale?"

The innkeeper bobbed his head, smiling. "Even so. 'Tis for me to do the brewing, and I manage it well, though I should not say it of myself. None others brew, of course. They bring me hops and barley, meat and grain, and I serve them ale and beer, and my wife serves them supper. They bring us flax and wool also, so that we need farm only half as much as they, that we may have time to brew and cook for them."

Rod had the feeling that he was hearing a public relations blurb, and braced himself for a recruiting speech.

But apparently it was too early for that; the innkeeper only said, "Wilt thou have ale with thy breakfast?"

Magnus maintained a stoic stone-face, and Rod managed a smile. "Why, yes, thank you." There wasn't much else to drink in a medieval village; no one trusted the water.

"Directly, then." The innkeeper forced another smile, bobbed his head, and withdrew.

"Well, this is as close to a view as we'll get." Rod sat down at a chair by one of the horn windows. "Light, at least. Seems like an odd way for a tavern to exist."

"Aye." Magnus sat down across from him. "From the look of the place, I'd have said that all farmed, and made all that they needed, from cloth to furniture and parchment—even soap."

"Except for the priests, of course."

Magnus flashed him a glance of irritation. "Must thou needs ever be suspicious of the clergy, Dad?"

"I don't have to, I suppose—it just comes naturally."

"Their time is fully taken seeing to the spiritual needs of their flock, I doubt not."

"Two priests, for a couple of hundred people? I don't think there could be more, here. Not to mention the nuns."

"Nuns?" Magnus frowned.

"Female clergy, who don't marry," Rod explained. "But they can't hold worship services, so they're not priestesses."

"Ah." Magnus smiled. "Like to the Order of Cassettes, who did save thee when thou wert left for dead."

"Very much like them, in that they decided to set themselves up as a convent, without anybody's sponsorship or approval—but unlike them, in that they're Catholic, and these people aren't."

"They are Christians, certainly."

"Oh, yes, certainly Christians—but they don't believe in the Trinity, from what I heard the priest say during that funeral sermon—if you can call it that. And Heaven only knows how many other differences there are."

"Heaven should know, indeed," Magnus murmured.

A young woman bustled out, bearing a tray, and set it down between them. "There, gentlemen! Thou wilt pardon my hurry, but I am like to be late for schooling if I haste not." She set a bowl in front of Rod, then another in front of Magnus—but her motions were more deliberate with him. Magnus followed the dainty hand as it drew back, and looked up along the arm to a round, pretty face with large blue eyes, framed in blonde curls that escaped from under the rim of a white bonnet. She wore a brown dress with a white apron, both cut very fully, almost as though she were trying to disguise her figure—which probably she was; Rod had noticed the same kind of dress on all the other women.

The sexual mores of the community apparently tended toward the puritanical. But the folds of the fabric were draped enough to hint at a voluptuous figure, and the apron cinched in about a very slender waist. Magnus gazed up at her face, and smiled slowly. Her eyes sparked with interest just before she modestly lowered them, blushing.

Calculation or innocence? Rod wondered. Too early to tell, either way. "You have a free school here?"

"Nay." The girl grimaced. " 'Tis not free; we must attend it, whether we would or no."

Rod smiled, amused. Didn't every young one say the same? "But you don't have to pay in order to go."

"Pay?" The girl smiled. "We've little use for money, gentlemen; the bishop keeps it for us all. Nay, we give him a tithe of all our crops, and timber, and cloth, even as our neighbors do in return for our ale. And we cook and serve the meat they bring, even as some wives sew the bishop's robes, and those of the curate and the nuns; others cook their meals, in turn. So there's little need for payment, at the least in coin."

"I expect you'll be glad of ours, anyway." Rod slid a few coppers across the table. The girl stared at them, wide-eyed, then picked one up for closer inspection. Her lips curved in a smile. "True money! So rarely have I seen it!"

"Then thou couldst mistake it," Magnus pointed out. "It could be lead, painted over. Bite, and if it shows not the mark of thy teeth, 'tis hard, and therefore like to be real."

The girl turned her smile upon him, her eyelids lowering. "And canst thou teach me what is real in the world, and what is not?"

Their gazes connected, and Magnus felt a thrill shoot through him, feeling her challenge and attraction both. Opportunity was calling—but opportunity for what? He smiled slowly, very much aware of the lush curves hidden by the rough, loose tunic, the full lips, the inviting eyes—but also marginally aware that his own defenses had risen, that he had become wary of demands in reserve, of the potential attempt to use him. He bore that in mind as he returned her smile, and found that he could think of things other than the girl herself. He tilted his head to the side, and answered, "I would think thou hast teachers enough. Didst thou not speak of school?"

"Aye," she said, "yet I have little wish to learn what the nuns teach. Thy matters, though, might entrance me."

Rod glanced from one to the other, very much aware of the girl's appeal for his son, and wondering already what her motive was. Somehow, he doubted that she was interested in the Gentle Giant for himself alone.

"I am hight Hester," the girl said. "And thou?"

"I am hight Magnus," the young man said with a slow smile, as though he was relishing the encounter.

And in truth, he was. Wary of the girl's motives though he might be, the sensations her interest aroused in him were quite enjoyable. The early stages of this game were very pleasurable, and he intended to appreciate every moment of it. Time enough to withdraw when the game became deeper, and the stakes needed to be put on the table. "Thou art not yet too fully grown for school?" Magnus asked.

The girl made a moue. "I have only some six months and a few days I must attend. Surely a dozen years of schooling more than suffice for any woman! Nay, to answer thy question, gentleman, I would say that I am grown enough, and more—but the bishop and his nuns would not agree."

"And their word holds sway?"

"Of course." The girl stared in unfeigned surprise. "Do they not ever?"

Magnus exchanged a glance with Rod, and said, "I have never met a bishop before—nor am I like to now, I warrant."

"Oh, he doth wish to speak with all newly come to our village!"

"I doubt me an we'll tarry long enough to be newly come," Magnus answered. He gave her a roguish smile, though, and added, "Still there might be benefit in dallying a while."

"Hester!" the innkeeper snapped, hurrying out of the kitchen. "Wherefore standest thou there in converse? Thou shalt be late for school!" He thrust a slate and a cloth bag at her.

"Oh, aye, Papa," the girl said, with a sigh. She took the bag and slate, and turned back to Magnus. "I must away, good gentleman." Again, the innocent's attempt at a sultry smile. "Shall I see thee when I am freed?"

"Hester!" the innkeeper barked, instantly angry; but she turned a saucy smile on him. "Ought I not seek to interest him in our congregation, Papa?"

That toned the innkeeper down to a glower. "In our congregation, aye . . ."

"And I am minded to see more of thy town and thy ways." Magnus stood, facing Hester. "May I accompany thee to the school, maiden?"

"Why, I should be delighted, sir," she chirped, and the two of them set off side by side.

The innkeeper stared after them, appalled, but at a loss—by the rules of their society, he couldn't object—at least not without stronger reason for suspicion.

Rod let him off the hook. "Don't worry, I'll be right behind them." He pushed his chair back from the table. "Thanks for the breakfast, innkeeper—it was quite filling." He gestured toward the pennies. "I hope that'll cover it."

The innkeeper stared at the money. "Oh, aye, sir! 'Tis too much!"

"Then I'll come back for lunch." Rod strode toward the door. "Sorry to be abrupt, but I'm going to have to hurry to keep up with them." And he set off after his son, as he'd been doing for most of the last ten years.

"Thy father *would* have to follow us," Hester said, nettled. "Can they not let us live as we would?"

"Why, he can, and hath done so aforetime," Magnus said, "yet I believe he, too, doth wish to see this school of thine. 'Tis rare, seest thou."

"Rare?" Hester looked up with a quick frown. "Why, how so?"

"Outside this forest, few of the commonfolk have schools of any sort," Magnus explained,

"Ah, fortunate are they!" Hester sighed. "Would I had grown in such a village.'" And, for no discernible reason, she gave Magnus a smile that would have melted ice.

"Why?" Magnus asked, with keen interest—not altogether intellectual. "Hath not knowledge made thy life richer?"

"Oh, I must say that it hath," Hester sighed, "for the nuns do tell us the Word doth enrich our souls, and increase our chances of Heaven."

"Oddly phrased." Magnus frowned. "Yet it doth, at least, tell me why thou hast a school. Thou dost wish Heaven, dost thou not?"

"Oh, aye," Hester said, with another sigh, "though only for its succor from the fires and torments of Hell, which the good sisters have told us of."

Magnus cocked his head to the side. "Thou dost not wish eternal bliss?"

"The bliss I wish is here and now—or could be." She stared directly into his eyes, hers seeming to become huge. "The Heaven in the sky is so dull a place, from all they say—only taking ease on clouds, and playing of harps and singing of hymns. The Heaven I wish is very much of this world."

Magnus forced himself not to flinch from her gaze, though he felt as much repelled as attracted. "The Heaven thou dost speak of on Earth is Heaven as I understand it to be hereafter—yet enduring forever, not for minutes only."

She started, shocked, and turned away. "Thou dost blaspheme!"

"Nay; for the bliss of the saints is even greater than that of the sinner in his fleshly preoccupation."

Hester eyed him warily. "The good sisters tell us 'tis a bliss of the soul only."

"I doubt it not," Magnus returned, "yet I tell thee of mine own knowledge, that the ecstasy of the flesh alone is a great anticipation and ascension into a moment's thrill that is far less than its expectation. 'Tis therefore that lechers forever pursue new conquests—they are ever in search of that which can only be gained by those in love. I cannot speak of the fullest ecstasy that is accorded true lovers, but from what I hear of it, it surpasseth mere lust as the ocean surpasseth the lake."

Hester stared up at him, shaken but fascinated. "Thou art a sinner!"

"That I am, to my sorrow—earthly sorrow of the here and now, not of the afterworld alone. There is great virtue in virtue, even that of chastity, though mayhap not as thy teachers tell thee."

"What thou hast said is not of their teaching."

"Gramercy for that. Yet in having any sort of school, thou art fortunate."

"I would trade such fortune gladly, for the chance to be free!" the girl said passionately.

Magnus was instantly on his guard—here was the ulterior motive. "Free? Why, what wouldst thou gain thereby?"

"Why, freedom!" She stared at him, open-mouthed. "Freedom to do as I pleased, without parents and teachers forever telling me what I must and must not do! Freedom to dance, to sing songs other than hymns, to taste of the delights of this world." She looked very directly into his eyes as she said it.

Magnus felt her gaze down into the pit of his stomach, but he tried to ignore it. "We all yearn for such freedom," he agreed. "It doth come with age."

"Nay—it doth come with marriage. And then art thou fettered to a husband's commands."

"Or a wife's." Magnus remembered the henpecked husbands. "In that, I am naive, Hester. I yet dream of a union in which husband and wife are so firmly delighted in one another that they act in concert, and take so much pleasure in one another's company that the bondage of never doing what one wishes, but ever tempering thine own desires by another's whims, seems of little moment."

"I, too, dream of that." Again, the eyes turned huge, the lips parted. "Hast thou seen such?"

"Aye, though it did not last," Magnus admitted. "As they aged, the one of them chafed the other."

"Age will make some difficult and contrary," Hester agreed. "I have seen such."

"And those of great anger grow to be of shorter and shorter temper," Magnus said with a sigh. "Yet still bide they, joined to one another, in hopes that the friction will cease."

"Before the love doth." Hester turned away, troubled. "Is there no freedom, then?"

"None that can be won once, and never striven for again—as I have heard, at the least. Freedom must ever be won over and over again."

"As must love?" Hester whispered.

Magnus nodded. "From all I have seen and heard, a wedding is not the magic charm we think it. A priest's blessing, and an exchange of rings, will not make a wild boy instantly into a prudent husband, nor transform a flirtatious lass at once into a demure and loyal wife. And, assuredly, a wedding will not make two folk who are unsuited to fall in love."

Hester winced, and Magnus wondered what she'd had in mind. "Yet still," he said, "I think there is freedom, though husband and wife must ever earn it by serving in bondage to one another." He frowned at his own words. "Do I make sense?"

"Nay."

"Praise Heaven; I feared I was too much like a pontiff. Nay, when all is said and done, I'll take the lesser, but more certain, freedoms."

Hester looked up, puzzled. "What are those?"

"Freedom of the mind is foremost among them. At the least, thou hast the world of books open to thee—if thou hast the good fortune to come by volumes."

"The world of books? How should we have such a world?"

"Why, by having learned to read and write."

"I have learned no such thing! What hath schooling to do with reading?"

It was Magnus's turn to stare, shaken. What kind of school was it that didn't teach people to read and write?

He was about to find out; they had come to the church. Hester murmured, "I thank thee for thy company," and hurried ahead, to arrive at the clustering of children and youths ahead of them. Magnus smiled; apparently he was already suspect in the community. Was that only by virtue of being a stranger?

The school was a small wooden building beside the church. Today, however, it was not going to be used, due to fair weather; two black-robed women came out of the cloister, took up stations before the group of youngsters, and

clapped their hands. Instantly, the children quieted and assembled into straight lines. The nuns nodded, then knelt with
ponderous ostentation. The children followed suit, and the
nuns began the Our Father. Magnus frowned; the words had
changed a bit from the ones he knew—due, no doubt, to having been passed down from generation to generation by
word of mouth. "Thy kingdom *has* come" did rather change
the emphasis—and that last sentence, "Make us obedient to
the priests whom Thou hast appointed to guide us," definitely wasn't in the Catholic version he knew—nor the Prot-
estant, for that matter; and from the grating tone in which the
nuns recited it, it didn't sound as though they were all that
happy about it, either. But recite it they did, and finished the
"Amen," and began the "Hail Mary." Again, it was not the
prayer as Magnus knew it. He certainly hadn't thought of
Christ as taking orders from Mary—at least not after He
grew up. He decided to look up the wedding in Cana in his
Bible at home.

"Thomas and Hester," said the eldest nun, "bring out the
slate."

Thomas looked up with a quick smile, but Hester kept her
face carefully neutral. Together they went into the school.
Thomas was instantly trying to chat with Hester, in a low
tone; she answered in monosyllables. The nuns couldn't
have helped but notice, but they turned a blind eye.

"Today we shall speak of the Holy Trinity," the younger
nun said, stepping to center, "of God our Father, and Jesus
His Son—and of the Spirit of God, which doth enkindle our
hearts with love. Therefore, if we live in God, we must love
one another, never speaking in anger, or striking one another,
or seeking another's shame or hurt." As she spoke, her face
became radiant, her eyes rising toward Heaven.

Then she whirled about, whipping a birch rod from her
voluminous robe and slamming it down across a young

man's knuckles. A single cry escaped his lips from sheer surprise, before he bit it back.

"And thou, Neil Aginson!" the nun shouted. "Dost think I have not seen that look of hate thou didst direct, but now, at Thomas's back? Nay, glower not at me, but smile, or I'll smite thee sorely."

The young man stared back up at her, eyes narrowing.

The elder nun came up behind the younger. "Think of thy father, Neil Aginson. Think of the tithe he doth owe the Church, that may be doubled. Come, let love fill thine heart, and smile."

The youth's face reddened, but he managed to draw up the corners of his mouth in a rictus.

"Think on love, and do better," said the younger nun, eyeing him with cold hostility. "But that will do."

She turned away, just as a sharp crack sounded from inside the school. Both nuns turned, eyeing the door narrowly. Then Thomas came stumbling out, bearing one end of a portable blackboard, a red mark flaming on his cheek. Hester came marching after, holding the other end of the blackboard, head high and shoulders back—but without the hint of a smile.

The nuns eyed the two of them, and the elder barked, "Hester! Be not so proud! Remember that humility is a virtue that doth become us all!"

Hester dropped her eyes. "As thou sayest, sister." She turned away to her seat on the grass.

The younger nun whirled to whack at Neil again. "Purge the hatred from thy soul, Neil Aginson! Aye, well I know what thou wouldst fain do—and I tell thee, unless thou canst school thine heart to love, and purge this hatred from it, thou shalt fry in Satan's skillet for eternity!"

Neil dropped his gaze and slumped his shoulders—but it looked to be only pretense.

"Beware of lust," said the older nun. "Beware the temptations of the flesh. I know thine heart; I have seen how thou dost regard Hester."

Now Hester's cheeks flamed. She sat at her desk, head bowed, every line of her body rigid with embarrassment.

"Purge thyself of impure thoughts!" the old nun orated, one hand held high in admonition—or threat. "Cleanse thine heart of every trace of concupiscence, lest the fires of desire condemn thee to the fire of the furnace in which God doth burn all impurities from mortal souls—burn, aye, for eternity!"

Magnus noticed that the term "eternity" was already beginning to have less meaning for him. He also wondered why neither nun had said anything to *Thomas* about lust—or did they think that Hester had slapped him for his conversation?

"Ten Hail Mary's!" The old nun's arm came down like a whip, finger pointing at Neil.

Every muscle stiff in protest, Neil bowed his head and began to move his lips. The nun eyed him coldly, but turned away.

She drew two large circles on the board, and turned back to the class. "What are these?"

A nervous giggle ran through the class.

"Be still!" The nun glared at them, face red and swollen on the instant, eyes staring in indignation. "What wouldst thou profane! Art thou all damned, even so young? Harold! What have I drawn?"

"Why . . . why, two circles, sister," an eight-year-old stammered.

"Thou liest, thou rogue!" WHACK! The ruler came down on the desk—but the boy yanked his fingers out of the way at the last second. The nun howled. "Thou wouldst, wouldst thou? Seek to avoid the punishment divinely meted out to thee? Nay, thou canst not turn away from God's chastisement, and if thou dost try, it shall be meted out to thee tenfold! Thomas, hold his hands!"

The youth leaped to obey with alacrity, a smile quivering at the corners of his lips, but contained, though his eyes betrayed his pleasure. The nun cracked the rod across the boy's hands ten times, impervious to his tears, then turned away. "Now, for one who did listen yesterday. Avila!"

"Wh-Why . . ." the girl stammered, "thou didst not speak of circles yesterday, sister."

WHACK! This time it was a slap across the cheek. "Did I not speak of God, Avila? Is not God a whole unit, sufficient unto himself? And is not a circle a whole, unto itself?" She whirled away, to point at the larger circle. "This is God!"

There was a smothered snort of laughter somewhere in the class, but the watching elder nun could see only blank, serious gazes. Several shoulders had shaken, though.

The younger nun tried again. "Why did God create us?"

"Wh-Why," the youngster stammered, "th-that he might have toys to play with."

"What! Dost thou think God to be a child? Nay, nay! Small time for play hath He—and would never think to profane the heavens with laughter or shouts of glee! The Devil is in thee, Rory! To confession with thee, and a long penance, too, whilst the others dine! Nay, God made us to love and to serve him, that he might have summat to love—for if thou dost not love Him, he will cast thee deep into the fiery furnace! Theobald!"

A ten-year-old snapped his gaze around to her. "Wh-what, sister?"

"Thou didst whisper to Harl!"

"Nay, sister! I-I but glanced at him!"

"And he glanced at thee, and thou didst set up a whole dialogue of grimaces and leers! 'Tis as bad as whispering, or worse, since thou dost seek to make others laugh and ignore the Word of God! Thou shalt stay when all others have gone, and scrub the boards of the schoolhouse floor!" She turned back to the blackboard, visibly striving to calm herself. "Now—let us discuss the ways of charity." She took the rod and pointed to the larger circle. "Let this stand for God the Father." She drew rays coming out of the larger circle, making it look like the sun. "And this is the Holy Ghost, which is the emanation of God's feelings toward us."

She whirled around. "Theobald! Why dost thou frown?"

The boy's look of puzzlement was instantly replaced by one of fright. "Why . . . Why, sister—is not the Holy Ghost a separate being from God?"

"Nay, silly fool! How could God's Spirit be separate from God? The Holy Ghost is to God as my love for thee is to me!"

The boy couldn't quite prevent the skeptical look that crossed his features, but you could tell he was trying, so the nun ignored it and turned back to the blackboard.

Magnus nodded; these people's beliefs were like their church service—whatever kind of Christians they thought they were, they weren't Catholic. Roman Catholics believed that the Holy Trinity consisted of one God in three separate persons, as separate from one another as the leaves of a shamrock, but even more unified than the plant as a whole. This nun, though, was saying that the Holy Spirit didn't really exist. And her next words made it even more clear.

"This Holy Ghost, as God's yearning for a son, did embrace the Virgin Mary, and enkindled in her the babe, born at Christmas, and named Jesus, the Christ. He was therefore the son of God—but do not commit the error of mistaking Jesus for God! He was a man, and only a man—a saint, and more than a saint; a perfect man, to be sure—but only a man withal."

The children sat attentively, as though they were listening

closely—but several eyes had glazed over. They had heard this before.

So had Magnus—it was called the Arian heresy.

"So God filled Mary with His Love, which we call the Holy Spirit," the nun summarized, "and Christ was born. . . . Hermann! Keep thine hands to thyself!" She descended on the luckless boy, whose hand had twitched toward the pigtails of the girl in front of him, and whacked him sharply over the knuckles with her ruler. As he squalled, she turned toward the elder nun with a sigh. "What ails these children this day? Have we been lax in our vigilance? Hath the Devil crept amongst them whiles we taught? Wherefore? And by what means?"

"Not the Devil." The older nun gazed across the heads of the class toward Magnus. "Yet there is a stranger present, who doth watch. 'Tis thy presence, young man, that doth encourage these children to disruption!"

Magnus turned very thoughtful. She might be right, he realized, though not for the reason she thought.

"I must ask thee to leave," the elder nun said, striding toward Magnus. "An thou dost wish to discuss the Faith with us, we will welcome thy questions—but after the school day is done." Her steps faltered as she came closer to Magnus, for he had turned a hard, brittle smile on her, and his eyes were glittering in a way that caused her to come to a halt ten feet from him. As soon as she had stopped, he bowed politely. "I would not be a burden on thee, Sister. Assuredly, I shall leave." He turned and stepped into the forest—with relief, if the truth must be known; even gladly.

After a dozen steps through the underbrush, Magnus turned to the side and broke through to the track. He looked back toward the schoolroom, expecting to see Rod standing there shadowing him. Instead, he saw only the class and the teachers. He frowned, puzzled, then glanced back into the forest—but no, his father wasn't following him there, either.

Well . . . Maybe he had trusted the young man not to get himself into trouble. Magnus smiled, and turned back toward the village.

He found his father in the village common, handing a skillet back to a housewife and chatting. Magnus remembered that Rod had disguised himself as a tinker before, and smiled at the old—well, older—man's slyness. He waited till the conversation was done and Rod had gathered up his tools and was turning away, then stepped up to him. "Ingratiating thyself with the housewives again, my father?"

"Huh?" Rod looked up, startled, then smiled. "Oh. Yes, son. How else am I going to learn anything? How about you?"

"I took a more direct path to the knowledge I sought. I went to school."

"Yeah, I followed you and watched for about five minutes. That was about all I could take."

Magnus nodded. "Thou hast ever had an aversion to child brutality."

"Yes, except when I lose my temper." A shadow darkened Rod's face, and the glance he gave Magnus was furtive. "I'm not too keen on psychological abuse, either."

"I ken the feeling, my father. For myself, though, I had a bit more trouble with the hypocrisy."

"Well, yes, there is that." Rod fell into step beside his son, noting that Magnus had changed direction to accompany him. "But I'm old and jaded, Magnus. I almost expect hypocrisy, these days."

Magnus frowned. "I would not say there is any great deal of it in yourself, or Mother—or the Elven King, Brom O'Berin, or Their Majesties."

Rod shrugged. "All that means is that you associate with

good people—who keep their hypocrisy down to a minimum. But some of it is unavoidable, son. Anyone who believes in two conflicting values is going to be a hypocrite, and there's nothing he can do about it. You caught me in it once—remember?"

Magnus lifted his head, gazing off into space, searching his memory. After a few minutes, he nodded. "I noted that thou didst denounce those who try to force their own system of government onto others, the whiles thou dost labor lifelong to woo the folk of Gramarye toward democracy."

Rod nodded. "And I could only reply that I'm wooing, but they're forcing. Of course, I'm not sure that distinction would hold up terribly well."

Magnus quirked a smile. "Less well than it might, when I consider that thou hast spoke of self-determination with religious fervor."

"Right. But I'm just helping them determine the form that I know they'll choose anyway—aren't I?"

"Yet it would seem that thine enemies, the future anarchists, know that the people, left to themselves, would choose to carve up Gramarye into separate, warring villages. Thine other enemies, the future totalitarians, know that they would choose a dictatorship."

"Not quite. They know those are the forms of government they could bludgeon the people into accepting."

"Whereas thou dost know the people of Gramarye truly choose democracy?"

Rod lifted an eyebrow. "Do I detect a note of skepticism there?"

Magnus broke into a grin. "Thou hast it; I have accused thee of hypocrisy."

"Rightly, too. But if I honestly believe in self-determination, but also honestly believe democracy is best for them, what choice do I have?"

"Why, only to manipulate them into growing a democracy of their own." Magnus nodded. "Yes, I see—the hypocrisy is unavoidable. For if thou wert to withold thine action for democracy in the name of self-determination, thou wouldst be equally a hypocrite, wouldst thou not? Yes, I see." He turned to Rod with a sudden frown. "What hypocrisy do I enact, then?"

Rod shook his head. "Too soon to say. Whatever your life's work is, I can't tell—you may not even have begun it yet. And you haven't exactly been outspoken about your personal beliefs."

"I would not kindle anger betwixt us," Magnus murmured.

Rod nodded, chagrined. "Probably right, too. Well, catch me in a good mood and tell me what you're thinking. Okay, son? I'd really like to know."

Magnus smiled with warm amusement. "Canst thou truly say thou wilt regard it as the confidence of a friend, and not seek to correct thy son in the error of his ways?"

Rod was silent for a few steps.

Then, finally, he nodded. "Yes. If that's what it will take to find out what my son really believes—yes. If you'll remember that my silence doesn't mean I approve or agree, I promise I'll just listen, and not try to talk you into seeing the truth."

"And show no sign of the hurt thou wilt feel?" Magnus shook his head. "Nay, my sire. I know not if I can find the willingness to wound thee."

Rod sighed. "Okay, let's try. Tell me your honest opinion of the governmental setup in this village."

"I cannot, for I have none yet—or rather, none that I trust. I have seen a raging priest, and cruel-hearted nuns, and a lass who chafes at the bonds of authority—but do not all, of her age?"

"Not . . ." Rod caught himself, and bit his tongue.

Magnus smiled. "Not all, thou wouldst say? Well, mayhap not. Yet, past that, I know not how the folk of the village feel about their spurious bishop."

"Well, I do—not a complete survey, you understand, just a brief sampling of public opinion, as heard by a tinker. But from what I can tell, most of them are quite happy with this arrangement. I'm sure there must be a few malcontents, such as that suicide who was buried yesterday morning and, probably, his father. . . ." A shadow crossed his face; he forced it past, and continued. "But most of them seem quite content to take orders from the priests and live their lives according to their version of the Bible. They don't even mind the priest yelling insults at them from the pulpit—they all want to know how unworthy they are, because that increases their chances of getting into Heaven."

Magnus shuddered. "Why, what a perverted catechism is this, that doth preach heresies as Holy Writ and perceiveth not its own hypocrisies!"

"Most people don't—that's why the real Church teaches that you have to be constantly examining your conscience."

" 'The unexamined life is not worth living'? " Magnus smiled. "The early Church fathers had been reading their Plato, had they not?"

"You disagree with the sentiments?"

Magnus shook his head. "At the least, the Church doth admire sound logic. This 'bishop' careth only for that which hath a good feel inside him."

"Glad you said 'inside'—that poor teenager who got lambasted for being jealous about his girlfriend this morning sure didn't think the outside felt too good." Magnus gave him a sharp look, but he plowed ahead. "*That* kind of hypocrisy, I can't stand—preaching charity and love, then turning around and humiliating someone in public."

Magnus hated it, too, but hearing it from his father somehow made him bridle and come to the nuns' defense, even though he thought very little of them. "There must be discipline in any social group, my father."

"Discipline, yes—but it can be administered without hatred, or pleasure in the victim's suffering. I don't have too much respect for someone who preaches love and understanding, and nurses a grudge at the same time. Needless to say, I'm sure that young man is one of the malcontents."

"I should think that he is," Magnus admitted. "Yet the bulk of them seem to see no conflict betwixt the preaching and the practice."

"None at all. It's as though they have two compartments in their minds—the one for 'religion' and the other for 'practical necessities'—and they never see any conflict in living by both precepts. The 'Church is fine, but business is business' mentality."

"Did not Christ speak to that? Summat about not letting the left hand know what the right hand doeth?"

"Which may come naturally to most people, but it's one hell of a way to play the piano. Yes, but you see—you're cheating. You've read the Book."

"Which these people have not," Magnus mused. "They have but heard as much of it as their priests do wish to tell them."

"There is that problem, yes. In addition to which, I'm not at all sure the local copy of the Bible is the same one the Church is using."

Magnus looked up, frowning. "Do not these people believe themselves to be Catholic?"

"Good question—and I asked it. The answer is, no, they think they're just generic Christians. Of course, that doesn't mean anything—anyone in Europe would have said the same thing, before the Reformation. But when I asked them if the Pope is infallible, they all said 'Yes, and the Bishop speaks for the Pope.' "

"I wonder an His Holiness doth know of it," Magnus murmured.

"I have my doubts. In fact, when we get out of this forest, I'm half a mind to hunt up the Abbot of the Order of St. Vidicon and rat on them."

"To tell the Abbot, so that he may send a score of monks to convince this audacious prelate of the error of his ways?" Magnus looked up, scandalized. "Surely thou wouldst not, my father!"

Now it was Rod's turn to be confounded. "Why not?"

"For that thou hast said thyself that the bulk of these people are content with this form of government, and the monks would surely unseat this bishop. Worse!" His eyes widened at a sudden, horrible thought. "When they sought to, the bishop would claim that he is the Abbot's peer, and would set his people to warring 'gainst the monks!"

"Then they would leave, and come back with soldiers." Rod nodded, face grim. "Yes, there is that little problem. But I can't let him go on tyrannizing these people, can I?"

"Dost thou not truly believe the self-determination thou dost preach?"

"Not as thoroughly as you do, apparently—but, yes, I still think I do. On the other hand, there's the little matter of his brutalizing the ones who don't agree with him."

"Like that poor wreck of a father we saw yestermorn?"

"Well, yes, I was kind of thinking of him. But there was that boy at the school, and that girl Hester from the tavern, whom he's obviously in love with."

Magnus's face hardened. "And where there are so many as that, there may well be more. Yet should not the majority rule?"

Rod opened his mouth to answer, but realized the implications, and left his mouth open while he did some quick re-thinking.

Magnus watched, managing to keep his face politely grave.

"Yes," Rod said finally, "but that doesn't mean the majority have the right to act as tyrants over the minorities."

"The tyranny of the majority." Magnus nodded. "Thou hast spoke of that before, and Fess hath taught me of it. Alexis de Tocqueville, was it not?"

"Still is—and I suspect Fess also taught you the counter to it." He certainly had taught Rod, repeatedly.

"Aye—that such tyranny is balanced by the individual's rights inborn. Yet those who dislike this bishop's rule are free to leave, are they not?"

"I certainly didn't get that impression, from that funeral sermon—if you can call that diatribe a sermon."

"I did not," Magnus murmured.

"I know—I did. But maybe we should talk to the object of that sermon, before we make any firm conclusions about the rightness of this nasty little theocracy they've got here."

" 'Tis most assuredly a theocracy, as the word hath come to be used—a rule by the priests," Magnus countered. "But it most assuredly is not what the word doth mean literally—a government by God."

"No—the proper term is *hierarchy*, rule by the sacred—but that has come to mean only a social status-order." Rod shook his head in amazement. "And people say semantics doesn't matter! Come on, son, let's find that bereaved parent!"

Magnus halted. "By your leave, my father, I find I've little stomach for that."

"Why?" Rod looked up. "Don't want to put your ideas to the test?"

"Mayhap," Magnus admitted, though it galled him. "Yet I find this whole village quite distasteful."

"Sickening, even?" Rod looked up at him keenly. "Then do something about it. Stand up for what you believe."

"And seek to impose mine own views upon them?" Magnus shook his head. "I have not that right."

Rod smiled, starting the quick gibe, then caught himself and frowned, thinking. He finally found a good alternative. "Would you, if you had been born as one of them?"

Magnus looked up, startled, then turned thoughtful, nodding. "Mayhap. If I were one of them, I would have the right of dissent, would I not?"

"Yes, if they acknowledge that right."

Magnus swept his hand wide in a dismissive gesture. "Acknowledge or not, the right is there. It is simply that if they do not honor it, there may be some fighting."

"Or some torture," Rod said grimly, "if there are more of them than of you."

"Such a consideration should not weigh . . ."

"How can you fight the system if you're dead?"

"A point," Magnus admitted, then stood frowning in thought.

Rod sighed and shook his head. "Whatever the right of it, you're not ready to act if you don't know what you believe. I'm not about to leave these people in the lurch, though."

Magnus looked up in alarm. "Thou didst give me thy word!"

"I know. That's the problem." Rod looked up, almost imploring the young man to understand. "If I were sure most of them liked this government, you see, I could just help the malcontents escape, and let it be—but I don't *know* that."

"And therefore thou must needs stay until thou dost?"

"Yes, or until I'm sure the majority really don't want the priests' rule, in which case I'll be free to do what I can to oust them."

Magnus stared, shocked and outraged. Then he reddened, and anger began to build.

"Oh, all right, all right!" Rod turned away in disgust. "I gave you my word. I'll tell you what—" He turned back to Magnus. "How about, before I actually do anything, I talk over the evidence with you, okay? Then, when you've made up your mind, we'll decide what to do together.'

"*If* I can make up my mind, dost thou mean?" Magnus was redirecting his anger.

"Now, I didn't say that." Rod held up a hand.

"Nay, but thou hast thought it. Belike thou wouldst like me to step aside and let thee do as thou wilt."

Rod frowned up at him. "That sounds like *my* line, doesn't it?"

Magnus stared at him, anger piling up over hurt. Then, without a word, he yanked his horse's head about and rode off into the forest.

Rod watched him go, then turned away with a sinking heart. "Blew that one, didn't I?" he said to Fess.

"I think you made your point, Rod," the robot-horse replied.

"Yeah. I won the argument and lost the boy's respect, right?"

"I do not truly think so," Fess said slowly. "In fact, I think you may have caused him to lose respect for himself."

"Oh, no." Rod squeezed his eyes shut. "That is definitely not what I wanted." He looked up and heaved a sigh. "But what could I do? *I* have to stand up for what I believe in, too, don't I?"

"Principles can be frustrating, Rod, can they not?" Fess murmured.

"They sure can—especially when they're my own, coming back at me. Come on, Fess, let's go."

7

Magnus rode among the trees, trying to stave off a feeling of guilt. What made it worse was not knowing whether he was feeling guilty about abandoning the people of Wealdbinde to their fate, or about betraying his father—or both.

And, of course, there was the girl, Hester. She certainly was no raving beauty, but was pretty enough, and there was something about her that wouldn't let go of his mind. Had he deserted her, too?

Then he remembered Neil Aginson, and decided that perhaps he had not.

"Women are ever a trial," someone sighed.

Magnus looked up, jolted out of his reverie, and saw the ragpicker ambling down the trail beside Magnus's horse.

"What, art thou come again?" Magnus demanded. "Get thee gone!"

"In good time. Twice now have I offered thee invulnerability for thine heart, and twice hast thou refused it—though in both cases, thou shortly thereafter hadst need of it."

"I will not take it," Magnus snapped.

"Be sure." The ragpicker grinned up at him, displaying

several missing teeth. " 'Twill cost thee naught to take it, yet may cost thee dearly to tell me nay."

"Then I shall pay the price of obstinacy!" Magnus grated. "Begone, fellow! I've no use for thee!"

"Yet thou hast, or thou wouldst not be so strenuous in thy denial."

"Can I never be rid of thee?" Magnus drew his dagger, and the ragpicker laughed. "Steel cannot harm me, youngling."

"Nay, but this can." Magnus unscrewed the top of the hilt and shook out the little yellow-handled screwdriver with the image of St. Vidicon carved into it. He brandished it toward the ragpicker. "Agent of Chaos, get thee hence!"

"Thou shalt rue this denial!" The ragpicker began to flicker, like an image poorly received on a video screen. "Thou hast the wrong Agency, also . . ."

"Begone!"

And the ragpicker vanished.

Magnus slid the screwdriver back into the handle of the dagger and sheathed it with trembling fingers. He drew a long, shaky breath, telling himself that he was a fool to be so upset by the apparition.

Then he began to believe himself. He could very well be just such a fool, and a coward to boot. He rode on through the woods, his self-doubt deepening and darkening.

Magnus rode out of the woods into a river meadow. A doe saw him coming, looked up in alarm, and whisked away toward the trees, her fawns behind her. Magnus watched them go, mouth twisting in self-disgust. He knew they were only fleeing at the approach of possible danger—but it made him feel as though even the wild animals didn't want to have anything to do with him.

He dismounted, tied his horse and took the bit out of its

mouth so that it might graze, and turned away to the river, following its course with his gaze, off toward the western glow where the sun had set. He thought of pitching a proper camp, then dismissed the notion as being too involved. He sat down on the bank beneath a huge old willow, to watch the water flow by, likening it to the stream of his life, wondering how so much of it could have gone by so quickly, and how his personal river had taken a wrong turning at some point. Instead of being his father's strong right hand, he had become an emcumbrance; instead of achieving rank and reputation of his own, he had become only an embarrassment to the Crown; and love seemed to elude him as thoroughly as though it had never known he existed. The only women he attracted were those who wanted to use him in one way or another, to debase him or feed off of him. He knew there were good women in the world, but they seemed to find him unappealing.

At least, he thought they were good. He hadn't come to know any of them well enough to be sure.

He threw himself back on the bank, heaving a sigh. Could he have done better? Or was this just the hand of genetic cards Fate had dealt him? All the titanic power inherited from his parents, all Fess's education and training—all of it came to nothing, less than useless, if he could not harness it to a good purpose.

There must have been a way he could have used those gifts in a more profitable fashion—more profitable for himself, and for all those about him. A huge longing welled up in him, to know, to see if he could have done better with what he had. . . .

And he remembered Albertus, his analogue in the world of Tir Chlis, far and remote in another universe. The two of them were almost exactly alike, so much so that Magnus had been able to borrow Albertus's power when he was himself

incapacitated; it was almost as though they were two different poles of the same globe.

Turn the globe. See what the other side was like.

He did. Trying to relax, he closed his eyes and concentrated on his memories of Tir Chlis, a land of silver woods
and magic, of monsters out of legend and a faerie race out of
folklore—not diminutive, gauzy-winged manikins, but tall,
impossibly slender people of amazing powers, whose moral-
ity was only barely recognizable, if it existed at all, and who
were as likely to be malevolent as beneficent.

Within that world of haunted nights strode Lord Kern, a
magician and aristocrat almost identical to Rod Gallowglass,
with a wife very much like Magnus's mother, Gwendolyn—
and two sons, Albertus and Vidor, who were virtual dupli-
cates of Magnus and his little brother Gregory. He visualized
Albertus's face as he had last seen him, then imagined how it
would change as he had grown—into a long, lantern-jawed
visage with a prominent nose and deep-set eyes, crowned by
a thatch of black hair—

The very image of Magnus himself.

The image began to gain substance; the world about it began to seem real. Magnus reached out in longing, a pulse of
pure thought winging to his analogue: *How fares it with
thee, my co-walker?*

There was a feeling of surprise, not unmixed with wariness, but both subsided into delight. There was a quick panorama of battles fought—evil wizards countered by Albertus
and his family, maidens alluring but demanding, other maidens devastating in their loveliness but only civil in their
greetings and shattering in their disinterest—of massive
frustration and feelings of failure.

Magnus felt commiseration surging up in answer—in
truth, the fellow was so much like him that they might be one
and the same! For a brief instant, their miseries mingled. . . .

Then a sudden, jarring jangle broke the trance, and Albertus was gone. Magnus sat bolt-upright, staring about him at a night suddenly gone silent, hearing the jangling diminish into a silver chiming. His pulse pounded in his ears; he looked about him wildly, and saw that one of the moons rode high over the clearing, its beams streaming down toward him. . . .

And down that beam of silvery light floated a gauzy shape, gaining substance as it touched the ground—a tall, impossibly slender lady on a milk-white steed, which, like herself, was so fine-boned as to be almost attenuated. Her face was as pale as the moonlight, with huge eyes and high cheekbones, and red, red lips. She wore a grass-green gown of silk, framed by a velvet mantle, and she chimed as she rode toward Magnus. It took him a moment to realize that the sound was coming from little golden bells that were tied to the horse's mane.

He realized he was staring. He shook his head, scrambled to his feet, and doffed his hat, bowing. "Greetings, fair lady! To what do I owe this pleasure?"

"To thine own efforts, Warlock's Child," she answered, smiling.

The term rankled. Magnus forced a smile. "Surely I am worthy of the title in mine own right, lady."

"Indeed." She tilted her head to the side, amused. "Thou must needs be so, if thou canst open a pathway betwixt this world and Tir Chlis."

"Open a pathway?" Magnus stared. "Lady, I but sought to commune with my . . . friend. . . ."

"Co-walker," she supplied. "Doppelganger. He who is like to thee in all respects, even to his miseries."

Magnus took a long, slow look at the lady, reassessing her—and feeling a chill at the thought of her powers. "Who art thou, lady, who knowest this of me?"

"I am a Queen among the Faerie Folk of Tir Chlis, young warlock," she said, "and I have come to visit thee."

She was easily the most beautiful woman Magnus had ever seen, with a face that would have made the greatest sculptors of the ages ache to carve her likeness; but no marble could be colder or more flawless than that moon-pale complexion, nor could any star glow brighter than her eyes. Her gown was low-cut, revealing an impossibly voluptuous figure with an incredibly small waist. In every way she was dainty, delicate—and hard, so hard. "Lady," Magnus murmured, "I am not worthy of thy regard."

"I believe thou mayest prove so." She reached down to touch his face, and his skin seemed to burn where her fingertips lingered. Suddenly, she was the only thing that mattered in all the universe; home, parents, siblings, king and queen, even God himself, seemed remote and unimportant. In a strange, detached way, he knew he was enchanted, but did not care. "All I wish," he breathed, "is to prove my virtues in thine eyes."

"Not too many virtues, I trust." She gave him a sidelong look through lowered lashes.

Magnus reddened. "All virtues that become a man—such shall I prove." "

"Thou must needs come with me, then." Her tone became peremptory. "Thou must now run beside mine horse, for thy poor nag of mortal flesh ne'er can go where we shall wander. Thou must needs come with me now, and serve me seven years."

"Only that?" Magnus protested. "Must I leave thee then?"

"That, we shall speak of anon," the lady said. "For now, follow." She turned her horse about and set off.

"As thou wilt," Magnus murmured. He followed, running lightly by her side, unable to take his eyes off her face—and amazed to find that he could keep pace with her horse.

Dimly, he realized that he was running up a moonbeam, that what he was doing was totally impossible—but the moonlight dimmed, and darkness closed all about him, unrelieved even by starlight; he ran only by the glow emanating from the Queen of Elfland herself, through a darkness that made the night seem bright—but he found that he did not mind, did not care at all, so long as he was by her side.

She glanced at him once, pleased and amused, then turned her face toward the direction in which they were travelling and sang a low, soft song of a cambric shirt.

Up into the sky they ran, with the moonbeam beneath them, till Gramarye was a small irregular shape on a huge globe behind them. They came into the light of the smaller moon, just as the larger seemed to swing behind them, blocking the planet from their sight. They were in the dark of the moon now; its face was black behind them, its rim etched by scattered light, but they ran on a beam from the smaller moon, ruby beneath them. Then that ruby deepened and thickened, until it seemed to Magnus that he ran through liquid; his legs began to ache, and his steps slowed. His breath came in huge, tearing gasps, and he saw, dimly, that the smaller moon had turned dark too, while the larger had disappeared completely, and with it, the planet wherein lay his home; but the sight bothered him not at all, strangely, and he slogged onward, through a liquid that became thicker and thicker, yet his speed seemed not to slacken.

"Thou wilt never come to Elfland thus," the lady said, and reached down her hand toward him. He caught it, feeling himself unbelievably privileged to be allowed to touch her fingers; but she lifted him up behind her as though he weighed no more than a lady's fan, and he swung about onto the horse's rump, gripping its sides with his knees. She pulled his fingers down to her waist, saying, "Hold fast." Magnus did, with both hands, astounded that something that looked so dainty could seem like spring steel beneath velvet, and by the wonder of the curve of her hip beneath the heel of his hand. They rode in total darkness now; the only light was the glow that emanated from the lady herself, and from the sluggish crimson tide below them—but from the darkness all about came a hissing surge that grew into a roar, then retreated to a hiss that grew again and again in a regular rhythm, like the surge and ebb of the tide, but was compounded of white noise.

"Where are we, lady?" Magnus shivered, though he felt no chill.

"We ride between the worlds, young warlock," the Queen returned. "We ride in the Void."

Magnus felt his scalp prickle; the eerie sensation spread down his back and into his thighs.

But light blossomed ahead, swelling into a vista of trees and grass and a turquoise sky. "Are we come to Tir Chlis, milady?"

"Nay, wizard-knight," she returned, "for so I shall call thee, thou hast yet to be knighted, for I perceive thou dost merit it."

Magnus stared. "Why, how canst thou know?"

"From the tang of Cold Iron about thee, which runs deeper than bone—for here between worlds, it is the essence of a man that shows, not the dross of his skin and visage only."

"Muscle and bone may yet matter, in Tir Chlis." Magnus spoke from vivid memory.

"Aye, yet we are not come there yet." The vista grew wider and wider about them, till the horse's hooves thudded on solid earth. It slowed, nodding its head and blowing through its nostrils, then stopped. Magnus looked up at transparent leaves that seemed to have been carved from slices of emerald, growing from boughs that wore a golden sheen. Fruit hung from that tree, swelling with ripeness, like pears with double tops that turned at angles to one another. Magnus gave a cry of joy and swung down from the horse, leaping to catch at one of the fruits.

"Oh, nay, sir wizard!" the lady cried. "Do not touch the fruit of this garden!"

Magnus yanked his hand back just short of the fruit, and turned as he dropped back to the earth. "Oh, lady, I implore thee, let me pull some of it down for thee to feed upon! For we have journeyed long, and journeyed far, and thou must needs be a-hungered. Only fruit of such beauty as this could be fit for so fine and fair a lady as thyself!"

"Right gallantly spoke." She smiled, her eyes glowing. "Yet know, Sir Wizard, that he who doth touch that fruit will feel horror touch his heart, and he who doth seek to eat of it will die in torment."

Magnus looked up at the fruit sharply, then closely. "Lady, how can this be? For never saw I fruit that looked more marvelous and wholesome than these!"

"They are fair," she returned, "but this little world is but an island in the Void, with many worlds about it—and some are places of torment for souls that seek viciousness, who believe that only by strife and hurting of one another can they thrive. Nay, further—they might swear that only by beating and slaying of one another can the worthiest be found."

" 'Tis hellish," Magnus breathed.

"Hellish indeed, and corrupt—and corruption doth breed disease. Nay, all the plagues that are in these hellish worlds do light here, and are gathered up by these fruits. 'Tis on this they batten—the energies of misery and agony that arise from millions of tormented souls."

Magnus drew back with a shudder.

"Therefore, seek not to satisfy thine hunger with such

fruits as these," she counselled, "and be not concerned for me, for we of the elfin blood know hunger only rarely; for the greater part, we dine for pleasure alone. Yet thou, I see, art sore a-hungered, now that thou hast paused to think of food. Thou mortal folk must ever be gathering substance into thyselves, for thy bodies do spend it most extravagantly." She cupped a hand in her lap; something twinkled there, and gained form. "Yet I have here a loaf of bread." She held up both hands; energy sparkled between them, taking the form of a bottle. "And here I have a claret wine. Nay, take them from me, that I may descend, and thou mayest dine and rest thyself a while."

He came to her gladly, took the loaf and bottle in his left hand, and held up his right. She clasped it and stepped gracefully down from her mount, who immediately lowered its head and began to graze. The lady drifted over to a tree, folded herself beneath it, and spread her skirts about her— but in such manner as to reveal the outline of hip and thigh. "Come." She reached up toward him. "Sit by me, and dine."

Magnus sat gladly, set the bottle down, and took up the loaf—but, on the verge of breaking it, he remembered what he had heard about faerie food, and hesitated.

The lady laughed like the tinkling of the bells in her horse's mane. "Thou dost fear that tasting of the food of Elf-land will bind thee to the elven kind, dost thou not? Yet thou art bound to me already by thine own desire and will, and I promise thee, this food will hold thee no longer than they."

Heartened by her promise, and not even thinking to question it, Magnus ate. A few bites were enough to satisfy him, and a single draft of the wine. The Queen folded them away, still amused, and patted her knee. "Come, lay down thine head and rest thee, and I will show thee fair visions that shall amaze thee."

Nothing loathe, Magnus lay down, breathing in the sweet

aroma of her perfume, amazed at his own delight in her presence. "Why, then, show me, fair queen—but they must be sights wondrous indeed, to rival my first view of thee."

"Silver-tongued knave!" She gave him a playful tap on the lips—and he parted them immediately, but too late. "Now behold." She laid one cool hand across his forehead and pointed with the other.

The turquoise sky seemed to thicken there, churning in a whorl of smoke that opened like an iris to show a picture of a hard-packed dirt road, little more than a trail, running arrow-straight through a thicket of thorn bushes and briars, clustering so thickly that the road was frequently lost to view.

"See thou yon straitened track?" she asked.

"I see." Magnus was even more impressed with the huge panorama of leaden sky that stretched above the briars, even to the horizon, for the land was as flat as a tabletop. "What gloomy road is that?"

She gave him a keen look, though he could not have said whether it was of amusement or wariness. "That is the path of righteousness, young wizard, and few indeed are they who inquire after it. Why, then—wouldst thou live a righteous life?"

Magnus chilled the automatic answer on his tongue and seriously considered the issue, searching his feelings. Then, slowly, he nodded. "Aye, lady. I find it within me to hope that I shall. I do wish it, verily."

"Thou art a most rare man indeed." Her manner seemed frosted suddenly, though Magnus couldn't have said how; he could detect no outward sign. "Rare, and more so, in that thou art a wizard, and might have what thou didst wish of this mortal world."

" 'Tis not the mortal world I hunger for," he said quickly, "but thine."

"Yet my folk are not concerned with righteousness, young

man, nor with aught but their own needs and amusements."
She waved a hand, and the picture shrank in on itself, becoming again a roiled knot of smoke. She gestured, and it
widened, opening again like the iris of some giant eye, to
show another view. Magnus looked, and saw a wide and glittering road that wound easily up across a gentle rise, then
dipped down out of sight, but rose again, twisting through a
gently rolling landscape that was filled with flaming flowers
under a cerulean sky adorned with clouds like bursts of incense. He even seemed to smell the perfume of the flowers,
thick and sweet, and immensely sensual. In spite of its enchanting prospect, he found it oddly repulsive. "What track
is this?"

"Yon broad, broad way is the path of wickedness, young
wizard, though many think it the road to Heaven. Yet the delights it doth seem to promise are fewer than those it doth
bring, and its destiny is the death of all joy." She looked
down at him with a smile of odd interest. "Dost thou not find
it appealing?"

"It doth tug at me," Magnus admitted, "yet it doth repel
me, too. I would be loathe to set foot upon it."

"I should be glad to hear thee say so." But the lady didn't
say she was; she only waved a hand, and the picture drew in
on itself until it was obscured by the knot of smoke again.
Another gesture, and it opened once more, but was filled
with haze this time. Magnus peered through the mist, but
could only vaguely discern the form of a lake. "What pond is
that?"

"Say rather, what form it hath." Her other hand dropped
suddenly so that both were now touching his brow, and Magnus found his mind strangely turning. He could not remember how he had come to be here, nor on whose lap his head
lay—but he was very glad to have it so. "Look keenly," the

lady said. "Look keenly at the lake, and let thy mind show us its form."

"Why so?" But even as Magnus looked, the haze dispersed, revealing a body of clear blue water, so lucid that he could see even the pebbles at its center, for sunlight filled all the world about it, even the waters themselves, and made the depths luminous. The verge about it was soft green grass, dappled with flowers in many hues.

"Ah," the lady breathed. "Thus did it seem to thine heart, so short a time agone." Her hand moved on his forehead, and suddenly, Magnus remembered following his father into the forest, arguing with him, and going alone to meet the hag in the tower, the lady at the church door, the girl in the cult village, and this Queen of Elfland, as she styled herself. As he remembered, the sky in the picture grew cloudy, the flowers curled up and hid their faces, and the waters took on a dark green hue, no longer clear, hiding something in their depths—and there was a feeling of danger, of something threatening that hid below the surface. "What change is this?" Magnus gasped.

"The change is in thee," the lady said, "for when first this pond thou didst see, I had cleared the memory of this past week from thy mind; yet now I have restored it—and thine image of the unknown pond hath changed."

Magnus frowned. "Why, how should this be? And what should it signify?"

But the lady only waved her hand, and the picture drew in on itself, whirling as a knot of smoke, then blossomed out again, into a bright, fair road strewn with golden sand, bordered by wands adorned with gaily colored pennons, about which twined flowers of every hue and tint. The road wound back and forth over a rolling landscape into a distance that glittered and promised . . . what?

There was a beauty to it that was alien somehow, yet immensely beguiling. "What track is that?" Magnus breathed.

"That," the lady said, "is the road to fair Elfland, whither thou and I shall ride."

Magnus shivered with a sudden thrill and rose to his feet in a single smooth motion. "Why, then, let us ride, milady! How quickly can we come thereto?"

She smiled up at him, amused. "Art thou so keen, then? Nay, if so, thou art bound most truly, and 'tis thyself hast forged the bonds."

"Right willingly," he assured her. "Nay, gladly would I pass all my days in that fair land."

"Come, then," the lady said, "mount up behind me—for my horse is rested, and ready to flee again. She hath need of only a few minutes' respite in a world's air, and will bear us now to Elfland."

Magnus came back and mounted behind her. "Is this world like to a stepping stone in the Void, then?"

The horse sprang into the picture, and Magnus cried out in alarm, then stared in wonder—for as they passed through the ring of smoke, the enchanted landscape spread out on both sides of him, and the bright pennons pointed the way. Looking behind, he saw the Void through the frame of smoke, closing in about the circle of grass and trees as the worldlet shrank behind. Then the smoke swirled in to hide the view, dissipated, and was gone, leaving only the clear blue sky of Tir Chlis above them. " 'Twas not a stepping stone," he breathed.

"Nay," she said. "Say rather, an island in the stream, a way station for a weary traveller—yet one that doth hold the gates to three worlds, for she who doth possess the key."

Magnus shuddered. "I'd liefer not meet the 'she' who doth hold the keys to the gate to Hell."

"Yet thou hast," the faerie queen said softly. "Thou hast

met her, in several guises—but hast not yet determined to walk through the portal."

"Not thyself!" Magnus cried, appalled.

"Even as thou sayest," she confirmed. " 'Tis not myself. Yet neither am I she who might speed thee on the road to Heaven."

Magnus thought that over for a few minutes, then said, "I'd as lief not meet her, as the other."

"Granted," the faerie queen purred. "Thou hast not."

They rode into the east, and the day dimmed about them with alarming suddenness—alarming, until Magnus realized that the faerie horse galloped so quickly that its velocity, added to the rotation of the planet, was bringing night on far more quickly than he had expected. He was seized by a sudden sense of *déjà vu*—the feeling that he had been through this event before. He realized its source, of course—for he had come to Tir Chlis once before indeed, though he had been only eight at the time, scurrying along beside his mother and father, guarding his sister and little brother. It was all as he had remembered, as he had seen it then and in his dreams a hundred times since—the velvet sky, the flickering stars, the jeweled grass. It lacked only the silver-leaved wood, for they were coming into rolling land, without a tree in sight. The sunset faded, and stars pricked the indigo dome above.

Their image was reflected on the plain below, as dozens of lights appeared.

"What lamps are these?" Magnus asked, awed.

"These are the torches of the elven people," the lady explained, "that do light them in their midnight revels. Wilt thou now join our promenade?"

"Aye, gladly!" Magnus sprang off the horse.

"And gladly shall we dance. But, my wizard, thou must needs hold thy tongue, no matter how strange or wondrous or—aye, dire—the sights that you may see. Thou must needs be mute, responding not to any question, nor to any challenge or gibe, no matter how small, or thou wilt no longer be within my protection, and may be parted from me—and shouldst thou chance to speak any word, thou wilt never come again to thine ain country."

"Small loss," Magnus breathed, his eyes upon her, "when so wondrous fair a being as thou art, is ever near to me."

The lady may have blushed; at the least, she turned away, and went on. "Now, when thou dost come to our court, young man, see that thou dost comport thyself as a gracious, well-bred, and learned young man ought."

"I have never claimed to be learned," Magnus murmured.

"Naetheless, by the common mortal standard, thou art so. And bow for answer, and smile fairly, for they will question thee, one and all. Yet speak no word, for thou must needs answer none but me."

"Shall I not be judged a rude and churlish fellow, then? And shall they not think the less of thee for having me in thy service?"

"Nay, for they know this game, and there be not a few of them do hope to gain a servitor thereby. Yet an thou dost hold thy tongue, they will by and by come to question me. Then will I give them answer, having proved thy fidelity, and tell them that I got thee at the Eildon tree."

Magnus remembered the large, branching tree with the huge leaves under which he had sat to brood, then to commiserate with Albertus. "I had thought it a common willow, though a great one. What doth that tree signify?"

"There are in every world a few like to it, that do respond to each of their fellows in all other worlds, and thereby serve as gateways and anchors for roads through the Void."

Analogues, Magnus realized—a few trees that had bred from the same ancestors, in the same locations in each universe. But surely there had to be more than a few in each world?

Perhaps not, considering the multiplicity of universes, and the factors of chance in environment and chromosomes, compounding one upon another geometrically with each generation. For a moment, he had a brief notion of the magnitude of the variables, and his brain reeled. It was almost impossible that any one individual would be duplicated in more than a few world-lines, let alone one so distant that its natural principles resembled magic.

But he was just such an individual himself—he, and Albertus.

For a moment, he shrank from the thought that there might be more of them—of him—in other universes, some of which he might not even have been able to imagine. The notion was startling, but intriguing—it tickled at his thoughts as a possible explanation for something he couldn't identify. . . .

But the Faerie Folk were coming out to meet them, dancing to the music of harps—tall, slender men of whipcord and sinew with long swords at their hips, turquoise eyes, wildly blowing hair; women dancing in gowns that glittered in every extravagant shape and form, women like the Queen, impossibly slender, impossibly voluptuous, with billows of fair, almost silver, hair, and huge eyes that glowed as cats' eyes do.

"Why, how is this?" cried one of the men. "What hath our proud lady caught this day?"

"Aye!" said another, hand on his sword hilt. "What art thou, mortal?"

"He is but a thing of no consequence," a third said with a languid wave.

Indignation surged, and Magnus opened his lips to answer. . . .

The whole crowd leaned forward, lips parted, eyes avid.

Magnus remembered the Queen's injunction, and bit off the words before they formed.

The Faerie Folk leaned back, mouths tightening with disappointment.

Magnus glanced up at the lady and found her looking down at him with a small smile of amused approval.

"Nay, handsome fellow!" A beautiful woman who looked almost new to life compared to the ageless youthfulness of the others, swayed toward Magnus, eyes half closed. "I do not wonder at thy taking, for thou art truly comely. Wilt thou withhold thy favors from all but one alone? Or wilt thou not bestow thy blessings on others who would welcome thee?" She leaned close, very close, and she was so tall that her lips were only a few inches below his. Almost without willing it, he found his eyes gazing deeply into hers, his head lowering, lips parting. . . .

"Come, thou must give answer," she breathed. "Thou must needs say if thou wouldst have me or no." And she drew back just a little.

Again, the words were on the tip of Magnus's tongue—a gallant reply that, fair though she was, he must needs be loyal to his mistress. But the thought of the Queen made him hesitate, remembering her injunctions; whatever she had bade him do or not do, he would devoutly heed. So he tried to show his apology and regret in his look, giving the lovely lass a sad smile and a shake of the head. She drew back with a hiss, though more of excitment than of anger. She looked up to the Queen. "Nay, Majesty, when thou dost tire of this one, thou must needs let me have him to toy with."

The term "toy" bothered Magnus in some vague way that he couldn't identify.

" 'Tis for him to give of himself, not me," the Queen retorted, and the whole throng burst into laughter. Magnus frowned about at them all, wondering at the nature of the jest.

Laughing, they dispersed, turning away to their pastimes, pausing for a drink while the faery harpers took up their instruments again. Then they began to play, and the dancing resumed.

"Take, my wizard."

Magnus turned away from the dancing and saw the Queen holding down garments for him.

"Take off thy gross and palpable garments," she said, "and don the robes of Faerie."

Magnus took the garments, glancing quickly from side to side, but could see nothing resembling an enclosed space, not even a grove.

"Thou hast no need of a tiring house," she admonished. "Come, take off thy mortal dross; no folk of Faerie fear to be seen in the glory of their naked skin."

His was scarcely glorious, Magnus thought—but he overcame his reluctance with remarkable ease, and stripped off his clothes, though he did feel immensely exposed. The faerie queen's eyes sparkled as she watched him, but she made no comment.

Magnus put on the hose rather quickly, but was somewhat disconcerted to discover they were little more than leggings. He pulled the tunic on, and found it to be more of a coat, of good, dark broadcloth—something less than his own brocade doublet, but cooler, too. He slipped his feet into the shoes—soft and supple soles, a very limber leather, with uppers that were green velvet.

"Thou art right handsome, when comely clad." The Queen reached down a hand to Magnus. "Come, aid me to alight, that I may tread the measure."

Magnus reached up, and she took his hand to steady herself as she dropped, feather-light, to the ground. Then, still holding his hand, she led him away to the ring. Turning about, she led him through the measure. He was about to protest that he did not know her dances, when he found that his shoes were guiding him through the steps, even taking the lead, with a stately deliberation that showed he knew them intimately.

But that stately deliberation became less and less, as the music began to beat faster and faster. Magnus was amazed to find that his feet kept pace with the increase of the tempo, swirling about and about, faster and faster, until only the Queen was clear in his vision, rotating in the center as he capered madly about her, all others only a blur of colors and faces behind her in the moonlight, churning through their own madcap dance, weaving about as he revolved around their queen. And the two of them swung about the musicians in the circle of the ring, faster and faster, Magnus giddy and delighted, feeling the sensations rising through his legs, up past his knees into his thighs, even as his delight in the dance seemed to coalesce, drawing together into an actual physical thrilling in the center of his abdomen, then pushing lower, as the Queen became not only the center of his vision but also the totality of it, her face seeming to be all that he could see, her lips growing more deeply red as they parted with excitement, her eyes seeming to swell, to absorb him. . . .

A shout and a clash, a jarring of discords, and the music fell apart. The Faerie Folk keened in high anger, and the men whirled toward something that had come into their center. Magnus turned with them, shouting in fury, instantly enraged at whatever had stopped the progress of ecstasy, to confront . . .

Himself.

Or it might just as well have been himself—tall and gaunt, lantern-jawed and muscular, cold steel glittering in his hand in the shape of a long and naked blade, and the faerie men shied away with oaths of anger.

Magnus, though, had no need to fear a steel sword any more than any other weapon, and strode forward to meet the interloper, hand slapping toward his own hilt . . .

And finding it gone.

Of course; it was with the clothes he had discarded in favor of the elven garments. For an instant, he felt terribly vulnerable; then anger surged, and he remembered the training in combat his father had drilled him in so long, and so often. He strode toward the sword with only a little fear, glaring at the interloper; yet his spirit quailed oddly at the feeling that he should know this man, this mirror image of himself, whose eyes sparked with his own anger, and whose lips parted to say:

"Thou hast stolen my place."

Magnus stopped, rooted to the spot, galvanized.

"Get thee hence!" the doppelganger snapped. "Is't not enough for thee that thou must needs wear my face and body? Must thou also needs steal my doom?"

Magnus found his voice. "I have stolen naught."

"That hast ta'en my fate! For she who should have ta'en me, took thee instead!"

"But dost thou not see!" cried a voice at his side. Magnus looked down, and was shocked to see Gregory standing by the doppelganger, calling up to him, imploring. "Didst thou not see what a fool she had made of him? Didst thou not see how he capered at her whim, how she dressed him in these foolish rags, how she stripped him of his sword?"

"What matter these?" the doppelganger grated. "She gave him pleasure, she gave him delight! Nay, even more, and greatly more—she gave him forgetfulness, that he might think no more of what he might have been but had not become, that he might go unmindful of the ruin of his life!"

"Thy life is no ruin, and thou hast in no way failed!"

"Failed to win glory, in mine own name? Failed to hew out a place of mine own? Failed to find love? Most surely I have failed in all of these!"

"Thou art Albertus," Magnus whispered. "And this lad is not my brother Gregory, but thy sib Vidor!"

"Even so," the doppelganger grated. "Get thee back to thine own world, find thine own place, and leave me to mine!"

Vidor looked up at Albertus, pleading. "I would not have him harmed—yet I would not see thee in bondage, neither. Canst thou not see what he doth not? Canst thou not see thou shalt be demeaned, a lord's heir debased to the role of a footman? Hast thou no pride?"

Magnus discovered, to his dismay, that he had not. Small wonder that Albertus had none, either.

"Thou shalt not take him from me." The Queen was there, slipping between himself and Albertus, hiding Vidor from his gaze, and her eyes were all that he could see again, her eyes with her face about them. "I have told thee aforetime, 'tis thine own yearning that doth hold thee in my service. Dost thou not still wish it?" She swayed closer, eyes half-closing. "Nay, if thou hast doubts, thou must needs kiss my mouth—yet if thou wilt partake of the embrace of my lips, thou must not miss my fair body, hips, breasts, and thighs— aye, all of me, all shall be given thee, that thou mayest say thou hast lain with a lady of Faerie." Close, so close, and her lips still parted from her words, parting more, closing with his. . . .

A cry of agony, almost despair—then something slammed into him, knocked him rolling. Magnus swung up to his feet with a roar of anger, and saw himself fastened deeply to the faerie queen mouth to mouth, arms coming up about one another, hip pressing to hip, bodies moving to a music that only they could hear . . .

. . . a music that began to sound where others could hear it, as the faerie musicians began their melody, taking their rhythm from the embracing couple before them, and all about, faerie men and women paired up to imitate their actions.

"She careth not," Magnus whispered, his anger turned to bitter despair. "She careth not whose lips she doth press, whose body she doth caress, whether it be his or mine!"

"Mayhap," said a voice at his elbow, and he looked down to discover Gregory—no, Vidor, he remembered. "Yet be mindful, she came a long and twining road to seek thee first."

"Yet doth not care if she doth find him instead," Magnus grated. Then realization swept him; his eyes widened. "Yet she could not, could she? He held aloof; he was beyond her power! Cold Iron protected him, and thy father's spells!"

"More my mother's," Vidor returned. "And he could hold aloof from the Faerie Folk, so long as he knew they would ever welcome him." He looked up at his brother sadly. "Yet when he realized thou wast here in his place, and the Faerie Queen no longer burned to possess him, then was he cast into despair, for the final road that he might take for solace in this world had closed to him."

"And therefore did he batter at the portal, and enter by force, where before he had resisted the temptation of the invitation," Magnus concluded.

Then he whirled toward the gyrating couple, howling, "Yet I wish it too! Where now shall I turn for nepenthe!"

Albertus broke off from the kiss, looking up at him with a cold and implacable glare; his voice started as a groan that rose to speech, and Magnus trembled with dread as he heard the words of the old incantation: "What dost thou here, what dost thou here? Seekest thou mine end? Thou art not to be taking my place, my place here in my world; for these, these are mine, and get thee gone, get thee gone to thine own place and time, get thee hence!"

The maelstrom seized Magnus, whipping him about and away with the cry of despair on his lips, the cry that there was no Faerie Queen in his own reality. But the Void swallowed up his words as the power of the young warlock's mind unleashed the tension of the warp in space-time that his mind had twisted, and in its unleashing spun Magnus about and about, stars blurred to streaks, a roaring of white noise in his ears, filling all of creation. . . .

Then it diminished, and the whirling slowed, stopped; the roaring faded away to a hiss of static, and was gone. Dizzy and nauseous, Magnus clung to the surface that had come up beneath him, found his fingers were clenched into grass, saw the streaks coalescing again into lights . . .

The lights of the stars of Gramarye.

Trembling, he lifted his hands carefully, most carefully, but found that he still remained on Earth—and relief at his escape welled up in him, but clashed against sorrow at losing the magical kingdom. He lowered his eyes . . .

And saw his clothes.

They lay in a heap near him, sword and dagger glinting in the moonlight. Of course; if Albertus had banished him as not belonging to Tir Chlis, his clothes would have been banished, also.

Which meant . . .

Looking down, Magnus discovered he was quite naked. Of course; the coat of the even cloth, and the velvet shoes, had remained in their own proper place. Albertus wore them now, without a doubt, and wore them in Magnus's place by the Faerie Queen. . . .

In the balance, he wasn't sure he was glad of it.

But he shivered in the night's chill, and reached out to take up the clothing of this mundane world.

He had pulled on his breeches when he finally realized he was not alone.

Turning about, he saw his little brother sitting there beneath the Eildon tree, eyes closed, legs folded, back ramrod straight.

Suddenly, Magnus understood a great deal. He pulled on his doublet and said softly, "Wake now, Gregory. Ope thine eyes, little brother. I am well; I am come home again."

Eyelids fluttered; the teenager looked up, staring, a little wild-eyed. Then he reached out, touching his brother's arm. "Thou art loosed!"

"Aye." Magnus patted the hand gently. "Thou hast given me rescue, my brother. I am free." In a few years, he might be happy about it. "Thou hast quite ably held ope one end of the road that could bring me back. Yet how didst thou know where I'd gone?"

"I sought with my mind, as I do every night," Gregory answered. Magnus nodded; he had long known that his little brother could not sleep unless he knew where every member of his family was—the legacy, no doubt, of his babyhood abandonment by his parents and siblings, when they had all been kidnapped to Tir Chlis.

"I sought," Gregory explained, "and could not find thee."

"Surely thou hast not kept vigil ever since!"

"It hath not been so long as that," Gregory assured him, gaze drifting. "Nay, and this trance hath restored me even as sleep doth."

"And how didst thou track me?"

"Why, I knew where thou wert yestere'en, so I went to the marge of the stream and touched soil and rock, till I found traces of thee."

Magnus's eyes widened; he had not known Gregory

shared his own mixed blessing of psychometry, the ability to "read" the residue of emotions left in inanimate objects. "So thou didst track me by the echoes of my feelings? Eh! Little brother! I would not have had thee share mine agonies so!"

"I could bear it." But the paleness of the youth's face made clear how deeply the experience had shaken him. "Yet I was grieved to find thee so sorely wounded in thine heart, and shocked to find . . ." He broke off, looking away.

"Shocked to learn that even I, the eldest, might feel I had failed?" Magnus asked softly. "Shocked that even I might feel my life had been to no purpose?" He cast about for something reassuring to say, but could only manage, "All men feel so at some time or another, little brother. Being eldest, and accustomed to command and achievement, doth not make me immune." And, with a shock, he realized that was true.

"I had not known," Gregory muttered.

Magnus nodded. "Big brothers, too, are human, my lad." And some, he reflected, were more human than others.

"But how thou couldst perceive thyself as failing, when thou dost succeed in aught thou dost attempt—!"

"I have not suceeded in the finding of love," Magnus reminded him.

"Thou art young yet," Gregory returned, which was quite something, coming from a thirteen-year-old.

"Gramercy; I had feared I was ancient. And I have not succeeded in the world of Faerie, as I doubt not thou hast perceived. Nay, I have made a fool of myself."

"Yet thou didst succeed!" Gregory looked up, surprised. "Didst thou not know? Thou and thy co-walker succeeded, where one alone would not have!"

"Succeeded?" Magnus frowned. "Why, how is this? Succeeded, in bringing him into the Faerie Queen's clutches, when by himself, he would have been able to resist her blandishments?"

"Not forever," Gregory said firmly. "If his despair was a match for thine own, his resolve would have crumbled, and he would have gone to the Queen—aye, and that ere long, too."

Magnus had to admit that Gregory was probably right—but, then, he usually was.

"Yet by himself," Gregory went on, "he would ne'er ha' been more than a servant. Nay, she would have dandled him after her endlessly, he ever hoping for some sign of favor, ever yearning for the ecstasies she promised—yet would never have attained to them, for the game to her was to see how deeply she could bind him by his own desires, with the least satisfaction."

"Must the Faerie Folk ever be playing games?"

"Aye. What else shall they do with their interminable lives? They have no need to labor, they have no duties to occupy them. What else shall save them from dying of boredom, save games of one sort or another?"

Magnus was amazed all over again, not at how much his brother knew—he was getting used to that—but at the depth of his understanding.

"Yet thou, by thine appearance and imminent departure, won through to her," Gregory explained. "She could see that the force of Albertus's resentment, of his will to banish thee, was stronger than thy desire to stay—so she took the only means she knew, to increase thy desire."

"And his." Magnus stiffened in a moment of insight. "She could not lose thereby, could she? For the action that inflamed my passion, inflamed his also, till it burst the bonds of his reserve and made him abandon all else in his need for her."

"Even so," Gregory agreed. He started to say something else, then caught himself.

"I am a cat's-paw, eh?" Magnus's mouth twisted in a sardonic smile. "Thou dost think that she but made use of me, as a tool to win the other whom she truly wished."

"Nay, not so," Gregory quickly assured him. "She would have been as glad to have thee as him."

"Why, what tolerance!" Magnus said, with a hard laugh. "How gracious, to accept either one! How open-minded of her! Yet I think she would rather have had him, brother, for he was of her world."

"Mayhap." Gregory frowned.

"And so." Magnus pulled on his boots and stood, buckling on his sword belt. "So he hath gone to the elven kind, and is lost. Doubly lost, tenfold lost, for winning the favors of the Queen's body; the ecstasy she brings him will have him ever panting after her for another favor."

"Aye; and she must give them," Gregory said, "or his desire will curdle into hatred, and he'll storm away from her."

"I doubt it not. So she will bed him now and again, ever in time to keep him from turning away, and will hold him all his days—or till she tires of him." He turned a bleak gaze upon his little brother. "How then? How then, when he is cast out of Elfland? Will he not despair, and seek death?"

"She dare not enrage him too greatly," Gegory pointed out, "for he is a mortal who can wield Cold Iron, and a wizard, who doth know the ways in which to wield it most shrewdly 'gainst the elven kind. Nay, if 'tis as much his desire that holds him, as her own, then she must needs quench his yearning when her own doth lapse."

Magnus frowned down at him. "Dost thou know this of thyself?"

"Nay; I had it of Vidor. Such liasons are naught new, in Tir Chlis. They endure seven years—or at the least, 'tis seven years till the one enthralled returns again to mortal kind."

"Time may run at different rates within the Faerie's spells." Magnus nodded. "So he is gone from his enemies for that long. How will the land fare without him?"

"His father, his mother, and Vidor endure," Gregory reminded him. "They may mourn his loss, but will preserve his inheritance."

"If he doth wish to take it up."

"He will," Gregory said, with some certainty. "The Faerie-taken return to waste away, or with greater zest for life—and I think that Albertus is not the kind to pine."

Looking within himself, Magnus had to agree. He would survive out of sheer stubbornness, if nothing else—but he was equally likely to stay alive just out of anger. He nodded. "He will live, and thrive. Thou sayest he will have greater appetite for life?"

"Aye; Faerie will drain him or fill him to bursting, the one or the other. And he will return with knowledge of elven magics, added to his own."

Magnus shuddered at the thought. "He will be a most puissant wizard."

"Aye, in the future—and for now, he is happy. Or if not happy, at least living in delight."

Magnus wondered at his brother's distinction, but decided he didn't want to hear it explained.

8

Rod looked up, then looked up again, wide-eyed. Sure enough, that was Magnus, riding into the village square. But why the look of cold determination? What had happened to his son in the forest?

Somehow, he didn't think he should ask. The lad would tell him, if and when he was ready.

But there were some things he could say. He stepped toward the young man, waving. "Good to see you back, son! Changed your mind?"

"Resolved it, rather." Magnus dismounted and stood beside him. "We must have some purpose in living, must we not? And if we have none, we must make it." He glanced around to be sure no one was near, and lowered his voice. "Folk have the right to leave this place, if they wish it. Let us see if there are any we should aid."

Rod grinned and slapped Magnus on the shoulder while he wondered at the boy's words. But there would be time enough to puzzle them out later. For now, mending fences was more important. "I don't know about you, but it's been a while since I've eaten. Let's go find a tankard of ale and something to munch."

Magnus glanced up at the sun. "Aye; 'tis noon. I find I could surround a flagon."

"Just take the ale out of it first, okay?"

They found the tavern, got a tankard each and some sausage, that being all the tavernkeeper had on hand. He served them himself, since Hester was still in school. Rod watched Magnus keenly for signs of regret, but didn't spot more than a sardonic twist of the lips.

They had no sooner begun to eat than a shadow darkened the doorway, and the grizzled peasant Roble came in, walking heavily, face pale and grim. He leaned on the counter and said, "Corin! A stoup of ale, an it please thee!"

Corin did a double take, then shied away as though he were looking at an unclean spirit. "It pleaseth me not, Roble! For I cannot o'erlook the sins thou hast committed in leading thy son to take his own life."

" 'Twas not I who pushed him thither, but His Grace the bishop!"

"Blasphemy!" Corin gasped. "I cannot serve thee, Roble, when thou wilt not confess to thy sins! Look no more upon me!"

"Since when was it blasphemy to criticize a priest?" Magnus murmured to Rod.

"Since that priest decided it was," Rod murmured back. "Hush, son, and listen."

Roble narrowed his eyes. "I will look most shrewdly upon thee, till thou dost give me mine stoup of ale."

Corin's face set itself into grim lines. He turned away to dust and polish.

Roble stood and glowered at him.

Corin's shoulders squared, and he went on bustling about, then turned away and went out to the kitchen.

Roble sagged and lowered his eyes.

Magnus glanced at Rod, then stood and stepped over to

the bar. He leaned across and hooked a tankard off its peg. He beckoned to Roble, who looked up in surprise, then followed him back to the table, where Rod and Magnus were each pouring half their tankards into the empty one.

"Drink." Magnus set the stoup in front of him. "We are not of the village."

Roble looked them slowly up and down, with suspicion but also with relief, then growled, "I will—and bless thee, strangers." His lips quirked with a mirthless smile. "If the blessing of a sinner and an outcast will do aught for thee."

"I certainly can't cite anyone else for being a sinner," Rod rejoined, "and the blessing of a father should certainly . . ."

But Roble was sinking again. "I am parent no longer. Call me not 'father,' goodman."

The innkeeper came bustling back out and jarred to a halt, staring at them, shocked. Then he remembered that he wasn't supposed to even see Roble, and turned away.

Magnus decided to press his luck. He stepped over to the counter, calling, "Ho, goodman! Fill the bowl again, if thou wilt!"

Corin turned to stare at him, then let a slow smile show. "Aye, stranger." He refilled Magnus's tankard, took down a new one and filled it, too. "For thy father." Then he turned away quickly, back to the kitchen.

"So," Magnus murmured, sitting, "he hath some fellow-feeling after all."

"Corin was ever a good-heart," Roble allowed. "Dost say thou art this man's son?"

"I have that honor."

Rod looked up in pleased surprise.

" 'Tis a holy bond," Roble growled. He turned to Rod. "Rejoice in him."

"Good advice," Rod said slowly. "I do."

"I'll give thee better: leave this village, and quickly. The bishop will be angered with thee for thy mercy to me, as will his curate, his acolytes, and his nuns—and what they hate, all the folk will hate. An thou dost gain the enmity of the clergy, thou dost gain the hatred of all the town—which thou wilt, by naught but thy converse with me, for such hath been declared to be a sin."

"Whatever the priests tell them is Gospel, huh? Well, I think we'll take our chances. Being from out of town can be a big help."

"Such conduct is odd," Magnus pointed out, "for they who preach Charity."

Roble shrugged. "There are virtues, and other virtues. For all their preaching, they will tell thee quickly that obedience is of greater import than charity."

"Obedience?" Rod frowned up at Magnus. "I don't remember that as being one of the cardinal virtues."

" 'Tis an aspect of Faith, goodman—for if one hath Faith, one doth obey God's Word."

"And God's Word is whatever the priest tells you it is?"

"Aye, and he doth say Faith is the greatest virtue of all."

Magnus shook his head and quoted softly, " 'For there abide these three: Faith, Hope, and Charity—but the greatest of these is Charity.' "

Roble looked up, startled. "Whose words are these?"

"Saint Paul's, from the first of his Epistles to the Corinthians."

"The priest hath not read us that from the pulpit."

"And you're not taught to read for yourself?"

"Nay. Only they who are learned can correctly interpret God's Word. None others should read."

Rod jerked his head toward the outside. "I take it those boys we saw this morning are being taught their letters?"

"The acolytes? Aye. They have been chosen for their intelligence and faith."

Which probably translated as their fanaticism and willingness to do whatever the priest said, Rod imagined. "They're giving up a lot. Your neigh . . . fellow villagers tell me the priests and nuns really live very chaste lives."

"Aye," Roble admitted, "that they do. I ha' ne'er seen so much as a gleam in a priest's eye; they are consumed with devotion. Each hath a small house by the church, though the bishop's is larger than the others, and none ever enter those houses save the one who doth dwell there. Nay, they are pure in their zeal."

"If zeal is enough to make a man good. Yes. Of course, sparing someone else's feelings might be a factor in spiritual quality, too."

"Charity, aye—but it doth take second place, or third, when there is the matter of protecting all other souls from heresy—or thine own, from thine own error."

Magnus frowned. "Dost thou believe this of thyself?"

Roble's mouth hardened. "Nay. 'Twas that which drove my boy Ranulf mad with grief—for he had a mind that sought sense, mind you, and would protest to the nuns, even when he was a child, that the Holy Ghost would not be separately named if He did not truly exist, or that Christ could not be any more a son of God than any others of us if He was not in some sense God Himself."

Rod whistled. "That must have gone over like a whirling skillet."

"A most bright lad," Magnus murmured.

"Aye, much good did it to him. They took offense," Roble confirmed, "and screamed at the boy that he was a heretic and a damned and impious one, then beat him. His schoolmates beat him worse, on the way home, and he wept bitterly when he was come to his mother. She sought with gentle words to explain to him that he must never question the nuns' teachings—and the bishop came to accuse me of poisoning the lad's mind with my incessant questioning of Holy Doctrine, and to read me the passage in which Christ says of the one who leads younglings astray, that it were better for him to have a millstone bound around his neck and be cast into the depths of the sea. Yet I had been careful not to speak of my own questions in the lad's presence—aye, or even in his mother's, when first I found that she was frighted by my wonderings." He lapsed into a brooding silence.

"So thou, too, didst note the contradictions in the bishop's teachings?"

"Aye, when I was young myself. The old bishop, who came before this one, told me I had a twisted and rebellious mind, and was over-fond of listening to the Devil. I will own that I chafed at the authority of the priests, for I could not see that they were that much better in soul than any other men, save in the matter of mastering their fleshly lusts. I wished to leave the village, and even crept away one dark night—but the old bishop sent men after me, with dogs to trace my scent, and they beat me and brought me back."

Magnus's eyes widened; he exchanged a quick glance with his father. "So, then. Thou art *not* allowed to leave."

"Aye, for, saith the bishop, I fled toward the Devil, entranced by his wiles and snares. The whole forest is the domain of the Adversary, seest thou, and the great wider world beyond it is there only to corrupt the innocent." His mouth twisted in bitterness. "I think they may have truly believed such. Surely they did lock me in a darkened cottage, to meditate upon my sins, and mine only company was a curate who came to preach to me an hour at a time, three times daily. At last I was so desperate for release that I came to believe I had been misled by the Tempter, and confessed my sins. They loosed me then, but watched me closely. They need not have, for I was cowed, and truly believed myself to be evil. I lived in penitence, and at last the bishop judged that

I should marry. I balked at this, but he lectured me sternly, to show me that 'twas my obligation either to serve God as a priest—and I lacked the strength of Faith for that—or to wed and rear up babes to witness the glory of God—for there were, after all, only those two vocations."

"Nay," Magnus said sharply. "There are three—the chaste and single life is another, even without the call to the priest-hood."

Rod nodded. "Of course, it has its own burdens and responsibilities—and it's a very lonely life."

Roble gave him a brittle smile. "The bishops have told us, throughout the ages, that no soul should endure such loneli-ness and the temptations with it, if he cannot—and therefore all should marry, if they are not priests or nuns. So they matched me to a lass whom no one else wanted, and wed us—and she never forgave me for marrying her out of force, not love. She shrilled at me, she scolded me, she nagged, and I thought again about fleeing to the forest—but she bore a son, and proved as gentle and sweet a mother as she was a hard and bitter wife. Yet she would not tolerate the slightest sign of impiety in Ranulf, and as he grew older, began to beat him sorely for daring to speak of it. As he grew, and questioned more, she grew harsher and harder, even as the nuns, and then the priests lectured and upbraided him, and told him he was corrupt in his very nature, and bound for Hell, because he was my son. My wife would have turned me out from the house then, were divorce not sinful—and 'twas not long thereafter that she died. The bishop pro-claimed her saintly, for having striven so hard to raise Ranulf in the fear of God, and for enduring the presence of the re-bellious soul who was her husband." He said this all without expression, his tone level.

Rod felt his heart wrench within him, and felt a huge upwelling of gratitude that he had found Gwen—and his old abiding sense of guilt in that he had been so poor a husband.

Magnus murmured, "And thy son questioned God's wisdom, in taking his mother when she was not yet aged?"

"Aye, and in his grief, he spoke of it aloud—nay, he ranted and demanded that the priests should explain how a good God could take a woman who was in the summer of life. The bishop thundered at him that he was a blasphemer and a lost soul, and that I had driven his mother to her death. God bless the lad, he would not believe it—and God pity him, for he said it aloud, and the bishop commanded his priests to beat the Devil out of him. He was pilloried and whipped, and I with him, then cut down to limp home as best we might, and do what we could to bind each other's wounds. 'Twas then he spoke of fleeing, and I, in fear of their dogs and whips, cautioned him against it; nay, pled with him. And at my asking, he bided, and tried to be good by the bishop's rules—but he had lost all faith in the priests by then, and saw them as villains."

"And therefore saw himself as evil," Rod murmured.

Magnus looked up at him, startled, but Roble nodded. "Aye, for he had lost all faith in aught but God Himself, or so he told me. And so it befell that he sought to flee one night, without telling me. I knew naught of it till the small hours of the morning, when the hunters brought him back with a huge clamor, and waked the whole village to witness the shame of the apostate. They scourged him as they had me, and locked him in the hut, and preached at him mightily—but he was made of sterner stuff than I; he never wavered, and would not give in. At last, two nights agone, he hanged himself by the thongs of his shoon." His whole face squeezed shut; his shoulders trembled. Magnus put out a hand toward him, but Rod waved him back, and the younger man slowly withdrew his hand.

Finally, Roble opened his eyes with a gasp. "Thy pardon, strangers. I should not burden thee with a father's guilt."

"I wouldn't say the guilt was yours," Rod said, keeping his voice low. "This variety of religion you're taught here, goodman Roble, is not the Church as it exists in the outside world."

Roble turned to him, staring. "In truth? Is the Church outside this forest, then, possessed by demons, as our legends say?"

"Not a bit, though it has its share of weak and fallible mortals in it. It preaches Charity as the most important virtue, and its punishments are much gentler—so much so that if a really vile crime is committed, it hands the victim over to the King's men for punishment."

"We are of that Church," Magnus murmured. "We believe that the Father, Son, and Holy Spirit are each separate persons, but at the same time, each completely and fully God."

Roble stared. "But how can that be?"

"How can a single triangle have three sides? Naetheless, that is too simple an example; true understanding is beyond our mortal minds." Magnus wondered if that was because human beings could only perceive three dimensions, but suspected it was only one among humanity's many limitations. He didn't cloud the issue, though.

"There are other differences," Rod said, "but the sum and substance is that, no matter what your priests and bishop tell you, the Church that rules you here is not the same as the real Roman Catholic Church. In fact, my son and I have been wondering how this cult could ever gotten started."

Roble lifted his head, gazing off into the distance. "There is a history, that we are each of us taught."

Rod glanced at Magnus. "I think we'd like to hear it."

Magnus nodded; if nothing else, it would take the older man's mind off his grief.

"An thou dost wish it, then," Roble said slowly.

Magnus reached over and refilled his tankard.

"I thank thee." Roble smiled, then began the tale that, in their village, passed for history.

"This village, strangers, was begun by a group who found summat in the Bible that made them believe the Church of the outer world was sinful."

Rod nodded. "I take it there was some kind of leader who pointed that out to everyone else?"

"Aye; he was the Eleazar whom these folk name a saint. He called upon all who believed in the pure Faith to follow him to the wildwood, and went off to the forest."

Probably with the sheriff one step behind him, Rod thought to Magnus. The young man's lips quirked, then smoothed; he kept his look of close attention to Roble's words.

"The folk struck off by themselves into the forest," the peasant told them. "Our legends say they had to slip away by twos and threes, for fear of the soldiers. They met Eleazar at his hermitage, a great rock in the forest, and all went together in search of a place where they might worship as they pleased."

"Or as Eleazar did," Rod murmured.

Roble gave him a bitter smile. "Aye. After some weeks' wandering, they did find this clearing in the forest—where the church and school now stand. They cleared the trees to make them fields, and proceeded to dwell in harmony."

Rod nodded. "I can believe that. After all, Eleazar had selected only those who agreed with him. They all believed the same things, so nobody was discontent."

"Not at first, mayhap," Roble said, "but they sought to live without priests, look you . . ."

"Aye." Magnus smiled. "Few clergymen would wish to company a troop that thought the Church was wrong."

"Even so. Yet after some ten years or so, the wives found the burden of rearing children without a priest to teach them right from wrong too heavy to bear. They felt the need so strongly that they besought Eleazar to go and find them a clergyman; some of them even began to mutter that their life in the forest was too hard, and their need of a church too great, so that they began to implore their husbands to take them back to the villages outside the forest."

"But the husbands were escaped serfs, and knew they'd be punished sorely," Rod interjected.

"Aye, or slain. To quiet them, Eleazar went back out from the forest, to find a priest who shared their views."

"Nice trick . . ." Rod said slowly. "Who'd he find?"

"Himself. He was gone several months, then came back wearing a cassock, and shared the glad tidings—that the Abbot of the Monastery had found him worthy to become a priest, and had sent him back to minister to them."

"Oh, did he truly?" Magnus said softly.

I doubt it. Suddenly, it all made sense to Rod. *Of course, he truly said so—otherwise, he would have lost his power over these people.*

Aye. That is all Eleazar truly wanted, is it not so? Power over his own small mud puddle.

"So the villagers dwelt content, and in harmony," Roble said, with a certain amount of irony, "for they had a priest to guide them toward Heaven."

"And to tell them what to do on Earth."

"Indeed. Yet as he became old, the blessed Eleazar became afraid for his flock; he did not wish them to be without a priest after his death."

"So he made another little trip to the outside world?"

"Aye, and came back still alone—but with a mitre, and bearing a crozier."

Rod stared. "Bishop's regalia?"

"Aye, for only an abbot or a bishop can ordain a priest. So the Abbot of the Monastery had appointed him to be Bishop of the Forest, that he might ordain new priests without the risk of the long and arduous journey to the outer world."

"How considerate of the Abbot," Magnus murmured.

"He ordained a new priest, a curate. He chose him from the most zealous of the altar boys, taught him to read, and taught him the holy things a priest must know . . ."

Translation, Rod noted: the people didn't know just what a priest needed to know.

". . . and founded a seminary," Roble went on, "a school for priests. He chose, as candidates, the boys who had the greatest zeal, who felt the pull to the priestly vocation. . . ."

"They wouldn't have happened to be the sons of the people who were especially friendly with the bishop, would they?"

"I cannot speak of the first bishop, but whiles I have lived, aye, it hath been ever as thou dost say. Is't not as thou wouldst expect, that the most devout are the sons of the most pious? They are the pillars of the Church, look you, those who give most unstintingly of their time. . . ."

In brief, as Rod well knew, they were the ones who were best at currying favor with the clergy. It was depressing to realize all over again that even in a little village like this, parish politics held sway, and that an elite was assiduous in establishing itself. "I take it the curate inherited the bishop's see?"

"Aye; on his deathbed, Eleazar elevated the curate to the crozier and mitre. The second bishop realized that some of the young women were as devout as he himself, and founded a convent. All were most pure, and zealous in their devotion, and truly celibate. Could they have been less than holy?"

"Yes," Rod said. "Their prayers and celibacy are all very laudable, goodman Roble, but it's the spirit of the law that counts, not just living it to the letter. Do these people live as though other people's welfare is their greatest concern? Are they understanding? Are they patient?"

Roble sighed. "Christ said the most important commandment is that we should love the Lord our God with our whole hearts, our whole souls, and our whole minds, and that the second is like it—that we should love our neighbors as ourselves. Surely, then, Faith is more important than Charity, and the priests are right in berating those of us whose faith is weak. Their anger must be righteous anger, since it doth come from holy men, and their punishments of the ungodly are only just, not uncharitable."

"There is such a thing as mercy," Magnus pointed out.

"Aye, but protection of the flock is of greater import. They must quash such heresy as mine, say they, to protect their lambs from the wolves. For all of this, there must be obedience, exact adherence to each commandment of the priests."

"So they rule, and everybody has to do what they say."

Roble shrugged. "There is some sense to it. They must punish those who break the Law, the Ten Commandments, and that punishment must be strenuous and public, to teach others to resist temptations to sin. Disobedience must likewise be punished, that all will live by God's Law, and those who seek to flee from God's jurisdiction must be prevented—for their own good, lest they mire themselves in sin."

"And nobody notices that all of this just incidentally gives the priests total power over the people in this village?"

"Hush!" Roble glanced over his shoulder. "Say no such word, stranger, on thy life! To say that worldly power is of greater import to the clergy than God and His flock, is blasphemy."

"And you believe all this?"

"Nay!" Roble's face suddenly contorted with a swift and intense rage. "I have tried—the dear Lord doth know I have tried! And for fifteen years I had nearly believed that I believed—but my son's pain hath torn aside the veil of my pretense! I can credit their teachings no longer!"

"Good to hear." Rod hunched down low, speaking softly to Roble. "From what I know of the monastery, goodman, the Abbot would never appoint a bishop—in fact, the issue has come up before, and the upshot was that there has never been a real, official bishop in Gramarye, anywhere. On top of that, it takes four years to learn what you need to become a priest, and I don't think the Abbot would have been willing to ordain Eleazar in only a few months."

Roble stared. "Dost say Eleazar was a false priest?"

"A false priest, and a falser bishop. In fact, I'm saying he was a charlatan, who played upon the people's faith and confidence to make himself undisputed ruler over his own petty kingdom. All he really wanted was to be top dog, and he didn't care how small his pack was."

"So." Roble sat up straighter, life coming back into his eyes—life, and a gleam of fire. "I thank thee, stranger. Thou hast freed me."

"Don't go jumping to conclusions, now," Rod cautioned. "Just because you know the truth doesn't mean they'll let you leave. And it certainly doesn't mean they'll let you tell it."

"I shall take my chances with the dogs and the hunters," Roble said, smiling, "and if I die, at the least I'll see my son again."

"Assuredly they would not slay thee!" Magnus said, aghast.

"Aye. They would take my life, to save my soul from the temptations of Satan."

The words gave Rod a chill, but he shrugged it off and

said, "Good enough. I think you'll live to see the outside world—that is, if my son doesn't feel that helping you get loose will interfere with your neighbors' right to choose their own form of government?"

Roble frowned, at a loss, but Magnus said, "No fear, my father. His right to leave is equal to their right to stay."

"Yes," Rod said softly. "It all comes down to the freedom to choose, doesn't it? About something a little more important than which kind of beverage you'll be drinking." He turned back to Roble. "Meet us at the edge of the forest after dark, goodman, at the deer track near . . ." He broke off.

"Near my son's grave?" Roble nodded, hard with determination. "A fitting place for my farewell to this village. Yet I would not have thee share my punishment, strangers."

"We will not," Magnus assured him.

Rod looked at his son's face, and felt a thrill of delight and apprehension. He knew Magnus was quite capable of murder, but he hoped the boy wasn't looking forward to it. "Believe me," he said to Roble, "your chances will be a lot better with us."

"Then I should not be seen talking any longer with thee." Roble rose, drank down the last of his ale, and said a loud "Farewell!" then a softer, quicker, "Bless thee, strangers." He turned, and strode out of the tavern.

Rod glanced up, but the innkeeper was still in the kitchen.

"Well," his son said, "thou hast given him comfort, of a fashion."

Rod turned to smile at him, but saw the look on his face and froze with the smile half-cracked.

"Let us have air, and space for free talk," Magnus muttered, and stood up so quickly that he almost toppled both table and bench—and father, too. Rod scrambled to his feet, but Magnus had turned away and stormed out of the inn. Rod stared after him, surprised, then hurried to catch up. He didn't speak, just went alongside his giant son, matching him stride for stride, which took some stretching.

"Thus may we see," Magnus said at last, "how religion may twist and torture the soul of a man."

Rod stared straight ahead, astounded.

His son turned a dark and brooding gaze upon him. "Do I shock thee, then, my father?"

"No," Rod said slowly, "but you did kind of take me by surprise there."

"Wherefore?"

"Because," Rod said carefully, "I would have said that what you're looking at is a twisted version of a good religion, not a good religion twisting a man."

Magnus slowed to brooding. "Aye. This is not the same Faith that you and my mother taught me."

"Not at all—in several major particulars. Oh, the forms are the same, but Eleazar made several major changes in doctrine to increase his own power, and the spirit of this religion is diametrically opposed to the Faith of the good Friars of St. Vidicon. The Faith I learned says that Charity is the most important virtue, not obedience."

"Is't so?" Magnus demanded. "Hath not the Church ever insisted that none diverge from its dogma? Hast thou forgot the persecutions of heretics, the wars 'twixt different sects, the Inquisition?"

"That was long ago," Rod said, brooding. "I'd like to think the Church of Rome is above such hypocrisy now."

"Indeed! And how wouldst thou say this current bishop hath twisted that Faith?"

"By using it," Rod said simply. "Oh, I don't doubt that he believes what he was taught—but I do doubt the sincerity of that first bishop, Eleazar. We'll check the records at the monastery, and I'll bet we'll find absolutely no mention of this place, nor of him. He just left to put on a show, not to see the

Abbot. Probably never got more than ten miles from the forest."

"Aye. His sole purpose was to gain power for himself, was it not?"

"Yes—and he used the Catholic religion for that purpose. In the process, he made a few significant changes, such as claiming he was only a man, not God. Anyone who's after power has to start with that—so that he can claim almost as much authority as Christ. Then, too, there's this business of requiring unquestioning obedience of every member of the parish, and giving himself the power to declare any behavior that he didn't happen to like, to be sinful, such as doing any thinking for yourself."

"Oh, aye." Magnus smiled. "The Church hath ever encouraged free thought, hath it not? So long as that thought hath freely agreed with all that the Church did teach."

"Touché," Rod said. "But at least the Church did encourage thinking of some sort—and the bishops were willing to explain errors and discuss ideas; they didn't automatically say every new thought was a sin."

"There is some truth to that," Magnus mused. "And the form of this community, my father, doth seem more that of a cult, than of a religion."

"I wouldn't disagree with that for a second—especially since it started out as an attempt to have religion without priests. Several cults, and even sects, have started out that way, but they always developed clergy of one sort or another. People try to live without priests, but always wind up reinventing them—they need them too much. And the priests are sometimes corrupted, either by power or by other lusts. But just because some people use religion to exploit other people doesn't mean that religion in itself is bad—just the person who misuses it. There will always be people who will find a way to twist something good and use it for their own purposes."

"That may be so, my father, but it does not mean that religion in itself is right, either."

Rod looked up at him sharply. "You're seeing something I'm not—or that I wasn't saying, at least. What is it?"

"That 'tis not the priest alone who doth use the Faith," Magnus answered, "nor even his curate and his nuns. Nay, every single person in this village doth use this religion, to prop him up and to ease him of the burden of forming his or her own conscience, and of thinking matters through for himself or herself. They take Revealed Truth, dost thou see, and thereby have no need to seek Truth for themselves, nor to labor to understand the purpose of life, or what God may be—and thereby do not come closer to Him, as they should."

Rod frowned. "You're not infallible either, Son. Should you be delivering judgements like that on your fellow man?"

"I do not judge the people, but the structure they have built, that they call a church. I do not judge the people, but the beliefs that I may or may not espouse."

Rod eyed him askance, then turned away with a sigh. "Well, at least we can agree on one thing—theocracy is a very demeaning form of government."

"Not so," Magnus countered. "These folk are happy in it; it doth give them what they need—the means to cooperate with one another, to resolve disputes, and to comfort them in their strife." He shook his head. "I cannot say this form of government is evil, my father—not for them. For others, mayhap, and for Gramarye as a whole, it would be injurious—but not for these folk."

"So you still think this government-by-pulpit has a right to exist?"

Magnus turned to stare at him, taken aback. "Aye! For they to whom it gives what they need."

"Okay for those who like it, huh?"

"More than that—if they wish to live thus, it is their right!"

"How about those who don't wish to?"

" 'Tis their right to leave!"

"Well, then." Rod gave him a brittle smile. "Let's set about enforcing a few rights, shall we?" He noticed movement beyond Magnus's shoulder. "Here comes another case."

Magnus turned about, and saw Hester hurrying up to him, cheeks rosy with exertion, eyes bright, bosom heaving. Magnus stood rigid, and Rod couldn't blame him—she was very pretty, to a callow youth.

"Praise Heaven!" she gasped, catching Magnus's arm. "I feared thou hadst left the village!"

Magnus held his face immobile, than let a small smile show. "Would that have distressed thee?"

"Aye, greatly!" she panted. "I most earnestly wish to know thee further!"

"I am pleased to hear my company is so pleasant," Magnus said gravely. "Or is't that thou dost wish to have me take thee away from the village?"

She stared at him, her expression fading, her face growing pale, and Rod just barely managed to keep his jaw from sagging. The boy didn't mind using the direct approach, did he?

"How canst thou say such a thing?" she whispered.

"Because I have seen how unhappy thou art, here in thy village. Yet wherefore dost thou think I could loose thee from this bondage, when the village is so closely guarded?"

"Why, they would not dare to meddle with a stranger!"

"I think they would, if they could be sure he would not leave ever, to tell what he hath seen."

The blood drained out of her face. "Thou dost not speak of murder!"

"Nay—only a legal execution. I am certain thy priest will discover a way in which my soul can be saved only by killing my body."

Hester stepped back, one hand going to her bosom as she stared at him, appalled. Then she dropped her gaze. "I—I could not ask thee to so risk thyself."

"Nay, thou couldst, and I will—for I think it wrong that folk not be able to leave if they wish. Yet there's another that I think would gladly go—thy schoolfellow Neil."

She glanced up, startled and astounded, then looked away, blushing furiously.

"Aye." Magnus's smile was sardonic. "Thou hadst meant to ask me to bring him also, hadst thou not?"

She turned on him, embarrassment transmuting to anger. "Thou dost think thou dost know me fully, dost thou not?"

"Not a whit," Magnus assured her. "I know only what thou dost wish of me. Nay, I will bring Neil too, and gladly—for thou dost love him, dost thou not?"

She seemed to loosen up a bit, growing thoughtful. "Aye," she admitted. After all, for Magnus to want to bring Neil along as a favor to Hester, that was all right.

Rod could understand—she'd feel much safer if she thought Magnus were doing it because he loved her. She didn't trust charity, having heard it preached too often and seen it practiced too rarely. Of course, that didn't mean Rod couldn't blame her for trying to use his son.

Magnus nodded. "So I had thought. Meet me as soon after sunset as thou mayest, at the base of the hillock on which doth stand the church, at the side nearest the forest."

"Why . . . 'tis where lovers do meet," she said, astonished.

"I had thought as much; it is as far removed from sight of the village as any place may be in this clearing. Surely, there, none will suspect us of aught but the worst."

"But they watch like hawks, the old biddies! Neil and I

would never come within a furlong of't without a nun bustling out to shoo us home!"

"Then come alone, and bid Neil await us elsewhere."

"Yet an they see us come to meet him, assuredly they shall stop us!"

"Then we shall rendezvous at a place they are not apt to watch. Do thou seek him out first, and tell him to meet me within the fringe of the forest, out past the threshing floor, at sunset."

Hester frowned. "Wherefore two meeting places?"

"Why, if any see all three of us foregather, they shall drive thee and Neil home, as thou hast said. Nay, we'll all three meet within the wood."

Hester shivered, but plucked up her spirits. "I shall tell Neil." She looked up at Magnus. "I . . . thank thee, stranger. I . . . cannot thank thee enough."

"Time enough for thanks, when we are all away clear. Already we tarry too long; any seeing thee in converse with us will grow suspicious. I shall see thee in the gloaming."

"Aye. I thank thee. Till then." Hester turned away. She went a few steps down the path, glanced back with misgiving, saw Magnus's gaze still upon her, flushed, and hurried away.

"Not the way she had planned to have it happen, I'm sure," Rod murmured.

"Oh?" His son turned a bland smile on him. "What did she intend, then?"

"Why, to have you fall madly in love with her, so that you couldn't bear to be without her. That way, she would have been sure you would have taken her away. Then, at the last moment, she would have asked if her childhood friend Neil could come along, and you would have been jealous as hell, but you would have done anything she'd asked."

Magnus smiled, amused. "'Tis like to a scene from a play upon a stage, is't not?"

"You think that wasn't what she had in mind?"

"It most definitely was."

Rod smiled. "Glad we can still agree occasionally. But just to err on the side of caution, how about I be the one to meet her?"

"Nay." Magnus frowned. "Dost thou think me unable to ward mine own heart?"

"Let's just say it's going to be less suspect for us to meet them separately than for you to be seen chatting with each one, just before they take off for the tall timber."

"A good thought, but I think they'll be more suspicious of thee than of me—for with myself, they will suspect only dalliance, where with thee, they'll suspect escape. And 'tis no answer to my question. Thou dost still think me defenseless before a pretty face, dost thou not?"

"Well, not just the face."

Magnus laughed, true and unfeigned mirth, to Rod's great relief. "No fear, my father. She never had so strong a hold upon my fancy as all that. In truth, she scarcely had even a pinch. I assure thee, I have been harrowed by experts, 'gainst whom she is the veriest amateur."

"Well . . . I'm glad to hear that," Rod said slowly; but there was an undertone to the boy's words that chilled him. "Just so you're able to recognize your one true love when she comes along."

"*If* she doth come," Magnus said, his voice flat. "I misdoubt me an such a woman doth live. Yet if she doth, I hope I'll not have so calloused a heart that it will not respond to her touch. For all others, though, I warrant I'm proof against them."

Rod hoped he was right—but the words did have an overtone of arrogance to them.

• • •

They hiked back to the tavern and had dinner; then Rod inquired about lodgings for the night, just to establish a cover. The innkeeper looked worried, but told them that he had no beds for strangers, since they came so seldom. He did, however, say they might ask the bishop for the privilege of sleeping in the village hayloft.

"Thanks, but I wouldn't want to trouble him," Rod said. "We'll camp out in the fields—we've done that before. Besides, that way we'll be all set to strike out again tomorrow morning."

"I can offer porridge, to break thy fast," Corin assured them, perhaps a little too quickly.

"Thanks." Rod gave him a bright smile. "We'll take you up on that. G'night, now."

He waved a hand as he went out the door. Magnus did the same, and they strolled away from the inn. "Well done, my father. Thou mayest be certain the bishop will know of our 'plans' within the half-hour."

"That long?" Rod feigned surprise. "Well, let's find us a chunk of pasture with a nice view, and put on a good show."

They found pasture land not too far from the church on the hill, and not too close to the livestock, and spread out their blanket rolls. There they sat and chatted as they watched the sunset, passing a wineskin back and forth. No one needed to know that they took only sips from it, not gulps. When the rosy glory had faded into dusk, Magnus lay down while Rod went off, none too steadily, toward the nearest thicket—but as soon as the leaves screened him, his step firmed remarkably.

He stepped into the forest, found a likely looking sapling, then called Fess. He took a special dagger from the saddlebag, pressed the right rivet, and a scarlet beam shot out of the ruby on the pommel. Rod moved it slowly across the base of the sapling. Smoke rose as the laser cut, and the sapling came free. Rod let up on the rivet, put the dagger away, and stripped the twigs off his new quarterstaff.

Then he slipped around the village to come out near the threshing floor. Neil was waiting, ostentatiously sweeping the boards. Rod strolled past him, whistling. Neil thoughtfully put away the broom, picked up a small pack, and followed.

Meanwhile, Magnus tossed and turned, then got up and went down to the nearby stream to have a drink. He went on over the rivulet, though, slipped into the brush along its border, and followed it around behind the hill with the church.

As he stepped out of the leaves, he saw Hester waiting, nervously swinging a parcel. His mouth tightened in chagrin—the pack was as good as an advertisement that she intended to run away. But as he came closer, Magnus revised the notion—she had kept it down to something that could believably be a gift of food to a travelling friend. He mentally gave the girl points for brains. "Good eve, Hester."

She jumped. "I-I had not seen thee come up, Magnus. Good e'en." She glanced upward and behind her; looking that way, Magnus saw a figure in a black robe watching them—one of the nuns, keeping an eye on the chastity risks. "Let us stroll," he said. "So long as we are on our feet, and away from cover, surely they will not cavil."

Hester smiled a little. "Nay, surely. Whither shall we wander?"

"Everywhere and nowhere, so they shall see—but we shall tend south and west." Magnus proffered his arm. "Wilt thou walk?"

Startled by the courtesy, she took his arm, and they ambled off into the gloaming. "My conscience doth trouble me," Magnus said, "at thought of thy parents' distress when they find thee fled."

"They have given me their blessing," she said, with the afterechoes of shock. "They each have told me they longed to go, even as I have, when they were mine age."

"I rejoice to hear it." But Magnus's tone was hard.

"Have no fear, they'll speak not a word! Neither of them would wish to see me shamed in the pillory—and they are such firm friends of the bishop that I misdoubt me an he'll blame them for my wayward flight."

Magnus nodded, relaxing. They strolled on into the evening, managing some very strained small talk. Magnus started trying to work in every old joke he knew, and sure enough, to her they were new—so she was laughing quite merrily, when she looked up to see the heap of bare dirt, and the three men standing near it. Her good humor vanished on the spot, and she stared, eyes huge, suddenly trembling.

"There is naught to fear," Magnus said gently, "and here is thy young man. Go to him, now."

She glanced up at him once, flashed a grateful smile, and hurried over to Neil, to be swallowed up in his embrace. Roble watched them, his face bleak, then looked away—but Rod covertly eyed Magnus, and saw the tiny tightening of the face that betrayed emotion held in check. His son hadn't been quite so carefree about Hester as he had pretended. If nothing else, it was a blow to his pride.

The lovers broke apart, and Hester turned to Rod. "How shall we . . ."

"Hist!" Neil raised a hand, looking off into the darkness. "I hear the watch!"

They were all still, and heard a distant murmur of voices—but Rod and Magnus, listening to minds, heard several men talking about the bishop's orders for extra vigilance this night, because certain corrupted souls might try to flee to the forest, the domain of Satan. "Thou hast keen ears," Magnus said.

"Take them and get lost!" Rod caught his son by the shoulder and pushed him toward the track that led into the forest, then shooed the others after him. "Go on! Move as fast as you can, and cover your tracks as well as you can! Wade a stream! Swing from the branches!" He knew Magnus would take that hint. "Just get gone!"

Roble hung back. "But thou . . ."

"I'll stay here and feed the bishop's men a tall tale! Don't worry about me—I can escape very quickly, if I have to." Roble should only have known just how quickly. "Just go!" He gave the man another push, watched him step into the shadows and disappear, amazingly deft and graceful, then turned and strolled toward the oncoming watch.

He met them just as the first rays of moonlight touched the meadow grass about him. They looked up, startled, as though he had appeared out of the night—which he must have seemed to do. "Halt!" They were three burly men, with cudgels at their belts and a dog on a leash. He saw Rod and started barking. One of the men cuffed him into silence as another demanded, "Who moves?"

"I do—and I breathe, too." Rod raised a hand. "I'm the stranger who's travelling through, remember?"

"Aye, and hath left discontent and troubled hearts in thy wake! What dost thou here?"

"Couldn't get to sleep, so I went for a walk." Rod waved behind him and toward the village. "We're camped out a mile or so away."

"We took note of it. Is not a mile a longish stroll?"

"Not for me. This is a very peaceful setting you have here."

"And we wish it to remain so," said the biggest fellow. "What of thy son?"

"Back at the campsite, presumably." Rod frowned. "What's the matter?" ·

"Naught yet, and we shall be sure it doth so endure. What of Roble?"

"Roble?" Rod frowned. "Oh, you mean the father whose son was buried two days ago. I give up—what about him?"

The watchman bit down on anger and snapped, "Hast thou seen him?"

"Yes, several times during the day. We even had a chat with him over a tankard of ale."

"So we had heard," the left-hand bully boy growled.

"Kind of thought you would. Why? Is he missing?"

"He hath not been seen since sunset."

"Did you check his house?"

"Aye."

Rod shrugged. "Probably out walking, like me." They should only know how far. "I'd expect that he wouldn't be able to sleep tonight, at all."

"The guilty conscience doth ever make for the wakeful night," the third guard pontificated.

"Grief has that effect, too." Rod gave an elaborate yawn. "Well, I think maybe I'll be able to sleep by the time I get back to the campsite. Was there anything else?"

The biggest watchman glowered at him, but growled, "Nay."

"Then I'll be toddling along, if you don't mind. Good night."

They snarled surly replies as he stepped past them. Twenty paces further on, he was just congratulating himself on having allayed their suspicions when a shout sounded from back toward the village. Rod looked up and saw half a dozen peasants running toward the watch with a black-robed priest close behind them, like an embodiment of the night. Every alarm bell in his head started ringing, and he decided to stroll back toward the watch.

He came up in time to hear one of the peasants panting, "Aye, gone! Both of them, and their beds not slept in!"

"Pray Heaven they do not seek to share one!"

"Raoul!" barked the priest—no, the bishop himself, Rod saw. "Shame on thee, to think such!"

"Thy pardon, bishop," Raoul muttered.

"What's the matter?" Rod asked.

They jumped and whirled about, not having heard him come up. "What dost thou from thy bed?" the bishop demanded sharply.

"Just taking a walk, to get sleepy—but all this commotion makes me feel wakeful again. Something wrong?"

The bishop eyed him narrowly. "Hester and Neil are missing, as though thou didst not know."

"If they're missing, it doesn't make any difference whether I know it or not, does it?"

"Speak more respectfully to the bishop!" a watchman barked.

Rod turned to give him a level stare. "I speak to each man with the respect he deserves."

The watchman reached for his cudgel, but the bishop laid a hand on his arm. "Hold fast, Raoul. Let him not provoke thee." To Rod, he said, "What dost thou know of their disappearance, stranger?"

Rod shrugged. "What would I know? I gather, since you're talking about a boy and a girl, that the two think they're in love."

"Lamentably, aye," the bishop growled, "for so sweet a lass is far too good for an heretic like him."

"A heretic?" Rod looked up sharply. "I thought you didn't allow them."

"We will beat the Devil out of him ere long, I assure thee. What dost thou know?"

"Well, if they're in love, wouldn't they have found a hiding place where they can be alone for a while?"

The peasants' eyes kindled, but the bishop shuddered. "Perish the thought! And 'tis mistaken, in any case—our good sisters have searched every such nook and cranny."

Rod didn't doubt that the nuns knew every single trysting place, and had posted "NO POACHING" signs on every one. "Even for Rob . . . What did you say the name of the other missing person is?"

"Roble," the biggest watchman snarled.

"Yeah, him. Wouldn't he have found a hiding place, too?"

"We have spoken of it," the watchman reminded him.

"Yeah, but!" Rod said brightly. "Maybe he found the two kids!"

"Heaven forfend!" the bishop snapped. "He would mislead them as surely as he did his own son!"

"Okay, so maybe he's hiding out alone. After all, since you've told everybody not to talk to him, wouldn't that make sense?"

"Wherefore would he not lie in his own house?"

"Memories," Rod said promptly. "It'd make his loneliness worse."

The bishop peered closely at Rod. "I think thou dost know more of this matter than thou dost tell."

"How can I? I've answered every question you've asked."

"I say that thou dost lie!"

The watchmen tensed, hands on their cudgels; the dog began growling.

"I can't have been lying," Rod said reasonably, "because I've scarcely made a single statement. I've only asked questions."

"Then I ask thee straight," the bishop barked. "Hast thou sent this benighted Roble, and these two straying lambs— nay, this lad and lass!—into hiding?"

"Not hiding, no."

"Thou hast aided them to escape!" the bishop howled.

"Don't you mean 'to flee the village'?"

"Call it what thou wilt." The bishop's eyes narrowed. "Hast thou done it?"

"Well, now that you ask—yes."

The watchmen leaped for him, and the dog, excited by their movement, set up a furious barking.

Rod twisted, ducked, and wasn't there. The watchmen looked about, astonished, and saw Rod right beside the bishop, chatting. "Of course, it really would be a bad idea to set your bully boys on me. I'm tougher than I look."

"Have at him," the bishop snapped.

The three toughs fell on him.

Rod twisted aside, staff whirling, and clipped one on the crown. The man fell to his knees, grasping his head—and dropping the dog's leash. The beast pounced, snarling. Rod dodged, just enough for the biggest watchman's lunge to carry him between Rod and the hound. Then Rod whirled to block a swing from the third man's cudgel. The fellow was stronger than he looked; the blow jolted Rod's whole arm, and the pain reminded him that he wasn't as young as he thought any more. But he managed to riposte and jam the butt of his staff into the watchman's stomach, and the man fell to his knees, the wind knocked out of him.

The dog leaped over him and went for Rod's throat, eyes blazing.

Rod dodged aside; the dog convulsed in midair, trying to follow him. It landed off balance, and while it was scrambling to get its hind legs under it for another pounce, Rod swung the staff and cracked the mutt's head. Then he had to whirl to slap the cudgel out of another watchman's hand. The man howled, and nursed bruised knuckles—as something cracked on Rod's shoulder from behind. Pain shot through his left arm, and he whirled about, dancing back, twirling his staff like a drum major's baton. The watchman hesitated at the sight of the windmilling wood, and the bishop shouted, "Pierre! Hugo! Montmorency! Do not stand and gawk! Have at him!"

But the peasants hesitated, seeing the biggest and toughest of them fallen.

"Don't try it," Rod snapped. "I'm a knight!"

"Thou hast the dress of a peasant!"

"I'm the modest type. I'm also in disguise."

The third watchman gathered himself with a snarl and charged.

Rod pushed the staff with a bit of telekinesis to help his single good arm; one end cracked down on the man's cudgel hand. He dropped the club with a howl, and Rod swung backhand at his head. The staff connected, and the watchman slumped to the ground, out cold.

Two of the braver peasants were gathering themselves for a try, but Rod whirled toward them, staff braced, and they froze.

"Art craven?" the bishop shouted.

"Your bully boys dropped their cudgels," Rod said softly. "Why don't you pick one up and try it yourself?"

The bishop recoiled at the thought, then realized how he looked in the eyes of his peasants, and blustered, "'Tis not right for a man of God to bear arms!"

"Then it's not right for that man of God to command others to bear them for him. Hypocrisy, bishop. If you think force is right, use it yourself!"

"Thou speakest with the voice of Satan," the bishop howled, "to tempt those of weakened faith!" He turned to the peasants. "Do not heed him! Raise the hue and cry! Bring more dogs, more men! We must hale them back to the village, for that path into the forest is the road to Hell!"

"Oh, stuff and nonsense!" Rod snapped.

The bishop rounded on him, red-faced, and bellowed in rage, "I shall have them scourged for their disobedience, and thou, too, if thou dost persist in their suborning!"

"I don't remember the commandment that says 'Thou shalt not disobey thy priest,' " Rod said.

" 'Tis the First Commandment, thou blasphemer!"

" 'I am the Lord thy God, and thou shalt have no other gods before Me'?" Rod raised a skeptical eyebrow. "You think you're God?"

"You have heard the blasphemy!" the bishop cried to the scandalized peasants. He turned on Rod. "If He is God, thou must needs obey Him—and, therefore, His priests!"

Rod shook his head. "No. The one doesn't require the other. A priest can advise, can teach—but he has no business trying to give orders. Look at the prophets in the Bible, bishop! They didn't give orders of their own—they just transmitted the Word of God! And they always prefaced His orders by saying, 'Thus saith the Lord.' "

The bishop stared. "Thou canst not know what is said in the Bible!"

"Oh, yes I can. I can read."

The peasants muttered in awe and fear.

The priest's eyes narrowed. "Who taught thee that?"

"My teachers, of course! In a world in which everybody learns to read and write, and reads the Bible for themselves!"

"They do not know Latin!"

"It's been translated."

"Thou art a heretic!" the bishop levelled a trembling forefinger. "Be silent, limb of Satan!" He turned to the peasants. "You have heard the heresy! Catch him, beat him, bind him fast! He must be burned at the stake, for in no wise else can his heresy die with him!"

"The Church teaches that all men should read the Bible

themselves." Rod fought to keep anger out of his voice. "The real Catholic Church, that is—not this twisted, distorted thing you false bishops have made for yourselves!"

The peasants gasped and shrank back, clearly expecting a lightning bolt to strike Rod down.

But the bishop knew better. "Seize him! Smite him! Silence him!" he bellowed. "He is possessed by a demon! He must be, to speak so against the priest of the Lord!"

From the direction of the village, faint but approaching, came the baying of hounds.

The game was just about over. Rod knew he couldn't hold his own against a mob. The diversion had lasted long enough; it was time for a fast fade. "I'm no demon, bishop, and I'll prove it! Give me a crucifix; I'll touch it without shrinking."

"I shall give thee the sight of it alone!" The bishop pulled out his rosary and held it up, the crucifix dangling before Rod's eyes. "Begone, thou limb of Satan! I banish thee from this village and its environs!"

With a swift grab, Rod caught the crucifix. The bishop yelped as his arm came with it; the beads were wrapped around his fingers. Rod held the crucifix up at eye level, turning to the peasants. "See? It doesn't burn me; I don't shrink from it. I'm not a devil."

"He hath profaned it!" the bishop cried. "That is why it hurts him not!"

The man was good at argument, Rod had to give him that. Of course, it helped that he didn't have to worry about mangling the truth, since it was already in pretty bad shape.

Mangling . . . Something about the beads caught Rod's eye. He stretched them out, and stared. "You've even changed the rosary! Twelve beads to a set!"

"Certes," one peasant quavered. "How many else should there be to a decade?"

"Ten, of course! That's what 'decade' means! And the crucifix—that, too! You've got Him with His feet side by side! He's supposed to have one foot over the other, held in place by one single nail!"

"What—what happened to the other nail?" a peasant stammered.

"A gypsy stole it." Rod let the bishop yank back the crucifix. "At least, that's the legend; the Gospel doesn't say. Does it, bishop?"

"Only a priest can know what the Gospel doth say!"

"But I'm not a priest, and I've read the Book."

"Thou art a demon or hast one!"

"How could a demon read the Bible? Wouldn't it annihilate him?" Rod sighed and rolled his eyes up to Heaven. "If you say it often enough, they'll believe you eventually, is that it? No luck—I've already proved I'm not a demon. But I am a Christian who's trying to be good, and who believes that it's wrong to use God as an excuse for abusing other people."

"I banish thee!" the bishop stormed. "Begone from this village! Never come near us again!"

Rod bowed. "I'll be glad to oblige—to the first part, anyway. As to coming back, I just may—with a tribunal from the Order of St. Vidicon behind me. I'd advise you to re-examine your theology, bishop, and be awfully sure you're right."

The bishop stared, eyes bulging. Then he whirled to his people. "Slay him! We shall burn his dead body—but do not wait! Slay him outright!"

The peasants started to move toward Rod, and behind them, much closer now, came the baying of the hounds.

Time to leave. Rod shrugged. "I'm not one to stay where I'm not wanted. Good night, folks." He stepped back, out of the circle of torchlight.

They stared, amazed that he had gone without a fight.

The bishop shook off his surprise and roared, "After him! He must not run free to spread his heresies and blasphemies!"

The peasants jumped and headed for the forest—somewhat reluctantly, if the truth be known. Then the hounds and the mob caught up with them, and they shouted with renewed bravery and plunged into the brush.

By that time, of course, Rod was coming out onto the trail and moving fast. *Magnus*, he thought. *Where are you?*

An image appeared in his mind, a picture of a hilltop with only a few small trees on it, and the forest spread out just below his feet. Rod concentrated on the image, thought of being there, and the trail about him grew dim as the hilltop grew more and more clear, taking on bulk and substance. . . .

Then it was real and all about him, and his ears rang with a double boom—the implosion of air rushing into the space his body had just vacated on the trail, and the explosion as he appeared on the hilltop, forcing air suddenly back. He looked about, feeling his knees trying to go weak, and leaned on his staff. He found himself gazing at Roble, who stared at him, crossing himself.

"It's all right," Rod said softly. "I'm only human, though I am what you call a warlock."

"I have explained it, my father, and told them how our powers have naught to do with Satan, nor with miracles, but are only the talents we were born with," Magnus said right behind him.

Rod turned and looked up. "Did they believe you?"

Magnus shrugged. "With their minds, yes."

Rod smiled and turned to the young lovers. "He brought you up here one by one, the way I just came?"

Hester nodded, huge-eyed and huddled in the arms of Neil, who wasn't looking any too sanguine himself. "Good thing he did," Rod said. "They've called out the posse, and the dogs."

The young couple listened to the baying borne on the night breeze, and shuddered.

"There is no cause for fear," Magnus said softly. "They could not possibly track us here, for there is no trail for them to find."

"That is one of the advantages of travel by thought," Rod agreed, "though it has its disadvantages, too."

"I have talked with them at length," Magnus said, "explaining that we are neither angels nor demons, but I am not sure they wholly believe me."

"I do," Roble croaked, "for even in our benighted village, we have heard tales of such folk as thee. Yet we thought that such a one had made a pact with the Devil."

Rod shook his head. "No, only with the King and Queen. You've heard of them, I take it?"

"Aye," said Neil, and Hester added, "though we know not their names."

"Catharine and Tuan, as it happens, and I'm their liegeman, Rod Gallowglass, Lord High Warlock."

They shuddered at the sound of the title, and made the Sign of the Cross.

Rod's mouth tightened with chagrin. "The only part of that which means anything to them is the word 'warlock,' isn't it? I assure you, though, the term is being used wrongly—they call us witches and warlocks, but we're really only espers, people who were born with strange gifts of the mind. I'm just as much a Christian as you are, though probably more of a sinner."

Hester looked up—almost in indignation, Rod thought. "Nay," she said. "We know of lords and kings, though our priests have told us they are all evil."

"Oh, as far as your bishop is concerned, I'm very evil, because I've stolen away three of his parishioners. What's worse, I just may take those people to the Abbot of the Monastery of St. Vidicon, and ask them to tell him all about their village and their priests."

Magnus looked up in alarm, and Neil frowned. "Why is that worse?"

But Roble smiled. "Why lad, if the true churchmen hear of our bishop and what he hath done, they'll unfrock him and tell him he is a bishop no longer."

"Nor even a priest," Rod agreed, "since he hasn't been trained in the real Church's doctrine. They might admit him to the seminary, though—and in the meantime, they'll send some real priests to teach your fellow villagers."

" 'Twould serve them as they should be served!" Hester cried, eyes alight with vindictive glee, and Roble nodded, eyes glowing. " 'Twould be just."

"Mayhap to the bishop, but not to the people." Magnus frowned down at Rod. "How is this, my father? What right hast thou to meddle in their ways?"

Rod shrugged. "It was just a thought—and we'll have to discuss it more fully, son. At least, we do agree that anyone who wants to get out of that village, should be allowed to." He turned back to the peasants. "Are there any other malcontents in your village—any other people who don't like the way the priests run things, and want to get out?"

Roble shook his head, and Hester said, "Nay. There were others, but they have been scourged into seeing the error of their ways, or—" She caught herself just in time.

"Or have taken their own lives," Roble said, his face bleak. "Do not stint the truth, lass. There were two others, milords."

Magnus frowned. "But the others, who wished to escape . . ."

"They have pious spouses now, and children. They will

not wish to leave them; they are bound to the grinding of their souls for twenty years and more."

Magnus winced. Rod knew the cause, and turned to change the subject quickly. "And that," he said to Magnus, "is why everybody who's left in the village likes that form of government."

Magnus looked startled—that wasn't what he'd been thinking about. Then he frowned in thought.

Rod turned to the fugitives. "We're probably safe for the night here, so you might as well bed down. My son and I will keep watch."

"I thank thee, milord," Roble said slowly. "I cannot thank thee enough."

"Just have a happier life than you have already—and don't think it's going to be easy. You'll still have to work for a living, and you'll probably find the lord of your manor to be just as overbearing as the bishop."

"But from a lord one might expect it!" Neil burst out. "They are no holier than we; they are not *supposed* to be more perfect!"

"I suppose that makes it easier to bear," Rod admitted, "though I think my wife might give you an argument about what's expected of a nobleman. Anyway, good night, folks."

It took a little more talking and soothing to get them settled, and Hester pointedly slept on the other side of Roble, rather than right next to Neil—but she gave the lad a few looks that made it clear it was more by duty than by desire. The whole pantomime even evoked a tired smile from the bereaved father, who made a few reassuring noises of his own, and finally got them settled down and breathing evenly. Privately, Rod thought that the byplay between the young folk must have given Roble a pang of grief, reminding him of his own Ranulf and the joy the lad had never had—but if his tears flowed in the moonlight, surely there was no one to see but himself.

Magnus drew Rod aside over a very small, well-shielded watch fire. "And now, assuredly, thou wilt lecture me over the sinfulness of a theocracy."

"No, really—I had in mind discussing the perils of do-it-yourself religion."

Magnus frowned, not understanding.

"That's one way of looking at a cult," Rod explained. "Somebody dreams up a new religion, or a new version of an old one, which exactly meets his own taste and whim—and, even if he's sincere, Truth is apt to get lost in the process."

Magnus nodded. "More to the point, given time he will remold his religion to assure his own power and wealth."

"Yes—and if he's mentally unstable, he'll lead all his people into lunacy."

"Say rather, delusion," Magnus offered, "yet those delusions he will present them will be most attractive ones, so that many will wish to join him—and be subject to him." He frowned. "Dost thou truly think the first of these spurious bishops, Eleazar, was so cynical as to pretend to a lie, in telling his folk the Abbot had elevated him to an episcopal see?"

"No, now that you mention it." Rod frowned. "He probably managed to justify it to himself—other people found it easy to believe his lies, but that made him feel guilty, so he start believing them, himself."

"And thus is delusion born." Magnus nodded. "Still, for those who are content, and even happy, to live in such a community, who are we to tell them nay?"

"The ones who are supposed to be their leaders," Rod countered. "We're supposed to protect the ones who aren't happy under that system."

"And assure them the right to leave? Aye, that we should—but if that right is given, and those who dislike the theocracy are filtered out without hurt, we would be wrong to attempt to change it."

Rod heaved a sigh. "I'm afraid that's something we'll never agree on, son. I suppose I'm a bit of a fanatic, myself—I can't rest easy knowing there's a government in power that I can see only as being false, exploitative, and morally wrong."

Magnus started to contradict his father, then caught himself and forced a smile. " 'Tis even as thou hast said—we will never agree."

"That's what I thought," Rod said, with a sardonic smile. "Well, if we're going to be able to protect the rights of these people tomorrow, son, we'd better get some sleep tonight. You want to take first watch, or shall I?"

9

They saw the peasants to the edge of the forest. When they could see the cleared land through the trees, Rod stopped. "You're safe now. You'll be out of the forest in another ten minutes." He reached into his purse and came out with a handful of silver coins. Distributing them, he said, "Use these wisely, and they'll get you a fresh start. Good luck."

"Good fortune to you all," Magnus said, and without waiting for an answer, turned and strode away, back into the forest.

Rod looked up after him, taken aback, then turned to finish the goodbyes before he hurried after his son. Fess paced along behind him, ever faithful—but ever tactful, too. Father and son needed to talk in private, if at all.

Rod caught up with Magnus and panted, "A little abrupt, wasn't that?"

"They had had all they needed of us, my father," Magnus said, his face grim, "and more than they may have deserved."

Rod guessed that Hester had taken a stronger hold on the young man's fancy than he had let show.

"If thou art so concerned for them," Magnus went on, "wherefore dost thou not accompany them to the nearest village, and see them set up in their new lives?"

Rod glanced back over his shoulder. "I should, I suppose—and I should take them to the Abbot, for that matter. But I find I'm not ready to come out of the trees yet."

"Nor am I," Magnus said shortly. "In truth, I am not ready for human converse, either. If thou wilt excuse me, my father, I must needs walk alone awhile." And he increased his pace, swinging off through the trees.

Rod slowed to a halt, watching after his son. "Touchy, touchy," he murmured, but wondering if it should perhaps have been "Touché, touché." He *was* being a bit of a nosy parent, he supposed—and the kid was a grown man now, and able to take care of himself.

All but his heart . . .

"Shall we follow him, Rod?"

Rod almost jumped out of his skin, then looked up to see the great black horse coming up beside him. "Follow? Of course not! It's just that, coincidentally, I happen to be going in the same direction. Think we can find a path, Fess?"

Disgusted with himself and the rest of the human race, Magnus paced through the trees, hoping to tire himself enough to be rid of the restless energy that seemed to push him onward. He did not notice that the leaves had begun to fall, or that occasional glimpses of sky showed leaden. He paced forward, not particularly caring where he was going, reviewing his most recent disasters. The witch of the tower, who had sought to entrap him by lust pure and simple; the Queen of Elfland, who had sought to bind him to her service by promises never stated nor meant to be kept (he wondered about the reality of that episode); Hester, a shallow and blatant flirt who sought to attract him just long enough to use him as her means of escape. . . .

"A rag, a bone!"

Magnus looked up, startled, apprehension coiling through him.

He came weaving his way between the trees, crying out, "A rag, a bone! Aught thou dost not wish, I'll have! A rag, a bone!" He stopped next to Magnus, grinning up at him, showing a broken tooth. "Good day, young master! Hast aught for which thou hast no use?"

It was the ragpicker, of course.

"Not a whit," Magnus said, through stiff lips.

"Eh, now! Come! Thou hast a weakness for the ladies, hast thou not? Thou hast no use for it—it hath brought thee naught but misery! Give it over, young master, give it over to me! Lose thine Achilles' heel—though 'tis scarcely thy heel, is't now? Lose it to me, and gain invulnerability for thine heart!"

Magnus was shocked to realize that he was sorely tempted. The notion of emotional invulnerability had become very appealing.

"Thrice before have I exhorted thee," the ragpicker reminded. "Thrice hast thou refused me—and gained sore pain as the price of thy stubborness."

"Thou wilt exact a greater price yet," Magnus ground out, though he no longer believed it.

Indeed, the ragpicker was shaking his head. "There is no price but the armor itself, young wizard. Come! Wilt thou not accept another's magic? Or must thou be hurted yet again, and again once more?"

For a moment, Magnus almost gave in, for something within him clamored for that imperviousness with an intensity that left him shaken. Perhaps for that reason he steeled himself against the pull and forced out the words. "Away with thee! Avaunt! And trouble me never again!"

The ragpicker sighed. "Ah, the suspicious nature of this younger generation. Well enough, lad, even as thou wilt— yet I'll come again, when thou shalt need what I offer. Farewell!" He turned away, sauntering back into the forest and calling out, "A rag, a bone!"

Magnus watched after him, hearing his cries grow fainter, then cease, wondering all the while if he had been wise or foolish to turn down the fellow's offer. He would be well served indeed never again to be susceptible to a woman's charms, never to fall into the traps of love, never again to be used as a woman's plaything. . . .

But, no, he reminded himself as he started walking again. No, he wanted to fall in love, wanted the true, deep intimacy that could exist only between a man and a woman, to have the peace and security of heart that he saw in his parents, in King Tuan and Queen Catharine, and with a few other couples he had watched as he grew. . . .

Peace?

Well, his parents had had their episodes, that was true. Marriage was not an end to a struggle, but a beginning to a long process of working together, against vanities and false pride and arrogance. And that intimacy was a prize to be won, again and again, every day. It was not the fruit of a magic spell worked by a priest at the altar. He knew that well, and was braced for it, even eager. . . .

No. He had to admit that, looking within himself, he was no longer eager for it. He had come to realize that the chances of being hurt, badly hurt—maimed even—in a place not even he himself could see, were too great. To take a risk like that would require a rare woman indeed, a gentle, tender but strong, loving, giving woman who would pay greater heed to him than to herself—and one with whom, moreover, he would be well and truly in love, even as she would be with him—and he had begun to wonder whether such a woman could exist. In fact, he wondered if he would ever meet a woman who could love him for himself alone, not for the social position or wealth he could give her—a woman who could love without seeking to use him.

He stopped stock-still, struck by a sudden realization. He could never find such a woman as long as he lingered in Gramarye, where everyone knew him as the son of the High Warlock, destined for power and wealth. No. No woman could meet him here without thinking how he could bring her to the most influential post in the land. Of course they could not love him for himself alone—they couldn't even come that far in their consideration!

Which meant he would have to leave Gramarye.

He shied from the notion—it was unthinkable! Though as soon as he had thought of it, a yearning welled up in him, to be someplace where no one would know him as anything but Magnus, just Magnus, by himself, alone, and able to establish his own reputation . . .

And discover his own abilities?

He shrugged the matter off and paced away through the forest all the harder, grim and angry.

Then, suddenly, the trees opened out into a meadow, gay with autumn flowers and the colors of the changing leaves. It struck him with a shock that, this year, he hadn't even noticed when the trees had begun to turn.

Then a woman stepped out from the glory of those leaves, and they faded into insignificance. Magnus stared, suddenly aware of her, and only of her. Her gown clung to her, showing how her thighs threshed as she walked; her whole body moved with each step, evoking the thought of sensuous music. Her hair was long and jet-black, her figure perfect (and the gown clung in just the places to make that clear). She was delicate, small-boned, and with a face finely featured, stepping so lightly that she scarcely seemed to touch the meadow grass. She reminded Magnus of the Faerie Folk of Tir Chlis, though she was nowhere near as tall, nor so elongated in form—almost as though she were a child of their kind.

Then she came close enough so that he could see her eyes clearly, and she seemed even more like those eldritch creatures—for those huge orbs were at once gay and sad, and wild, wild. They held his gaze, those eyes, and he lost all awareness of himself, knowing only that she was the most entrancing woman he had ever seen, and that all he wanted was to be with her.

"I greet thee, Sir Knight," she said in a rich, husky voice as she neared him. "Wilt thou dally with me awhile?"

"Gladly!" Magnus reached out, but hesitated, not daring to touch so divine a creature.

She saw, and smiled with a strange delight, and stepped in to sway closer, her lips almost touching his, but not quite. "Wilt thou not, then, carry me away?"

"Aye, far away, where there will be no world but our own!" Magnus turned and gave a high whistle. She laughed, and took up the pitch, making it high and eerie, avoiding the order of notes.

Magnus's horse stepped forth from the forest. Little wonder its nostrils were flared, its eyes wild, for Magnus had just teleported it from the place where he had left it grazing, near the forest village of Wealdbinde, to the verge of this meadow. The poor beast was alarmed and confused, though it hadn't really noticed much change—just a very strange sensation.

Magnus wasn't thinking of that, though. He wasn't thinking of anything, except the faerie child.

He caught her by the waist and swung her high, up to the saddle, then sprang up behind her. The horse danced sideways, disconcerted by the woman, but settled as Magnus kicked his heels against its sides, then began to trot.

"Faster!" the girl cried. "Faster! Faster!"

Magnus kicked the horse into a canter, and the girl

clapped her hands. Magnus made a frantic grab at her waist to keep her from falling. She laughed, a high, manic cry. "Faster! Faster!"

Magnus spurred the horse into a gallop, and they rocketed around the meadow three times—widdershins, he was to realize later—and the wood seemed to change around them in some subtle fashion.

"Away!" the girl cried, and Magnus felt the overwhelming urge to please her. He swerved the horse into the forest path. It whinnied in fear and protest, but Magnus had thought only for the girl's wishes, and for the thrill that went through him as he heard her wild, shrill laughter. They went careering through the wood, somehow missing overhanging branches and narrowly avoiding slamming into tree trunks. The girl leaned from side to side, and just as Magnus, in a panic for her safety, would reach to hold her, she would lean far to the other side, all the while singing in a high, lilting, eerie tone, a song in a language Magnus did not recognize, clear and wild and thrilling every fiber of his being.

At last the trees opened out to show them a lake, with steep hillsides sloping down toward the water. "Enough!" the lady cried, and Magnus reined in. He leaped down to help her alight, not noticing that the poor horse was lathered and white-eyed. He only turned aside from it, leaving it to stray where it would as he accompanied her along the hillside.

"Yon!" She halted suddenly, pointing down.

"What, lady?" Magnus looked, but saw nothing save fading grass.

"Beneath the ground! A tuber sweet! Pray dig it for me, for I crave it!"

Without the slightest thought of denial, he was on his knees and digging with his knife. Sure enough, the roots were there, and he ran down to the lake to wash them, then came running back with his offering.

"I thank thee." She took the tuber, bit of it, then held it out to him with a merry glint in her eye. "Partake!"

He did, at her word, and found the taste sweet, but strange and exotic. When he looked up, the world about them seemed to have become dim and dun; only she had color and life.

"Come!" She moved past him, almost dancing, and he followed.

She paused by a hollow tree. "Honey! Surely the bees may spare some! Fetch it for me!"

He didn't even consider arguing, just thought sleepy thoughts at the bees as he reached in and took out a honeycomb. Her eyes went wide at the sight of the unconscious bees that fell from it, but she took the comb, stuck out her dainty tongue and dribbled sweetness onto it, then proffered the comb to him. He dribbled honey into his own mouth and found it far sweeter than any he had ever tasted, with a strange wild tang—and looking at her, found that her form seemed almost to glow.

She danced away from him, laughing, and he followed, frantic at the thought that she might slip away from him.

She seemed to know where she was going—and, sure enough, they came to a little grotto carpeted with green moss and bordered by crocuses and tulips, its rocky sides bedecked with stones, roses and anemones and poppies growing out of its myriad crannies. Magnus was delighted to see spring flowers in the autumn, but she was the fairest blossom of all.

"I thirst," she said. "Fetch me water."

"Where is there a spring?" Magnus looked about.

"There is none, but there is dew on the rocks."

At her word, he turned to sweep the moisture from the stones, and was amazed to see it gather in large drops on his palm. She caught up his hand to sip the water from it, and the touch of her lips waked echoes in his chest and loins. But she pushed his hand up and said, "Drink," and he did, licking the last of the droplets—and looked at her, and could have sworn that the glow of her eyes was all there was in the world. She swayed close to him, murmuring something in the strange language—and, though he knew not the words, a thrill charged through him, for he understood her well, that she had said, in her most intimate form, "I love thee true." He reached out to take her in his arms, but she turned and twisted, and he held only empty air, her tinkling laugh resounding through his head.

Suddenly, though, a sadness seemed to sweep over her. She folded herself to the ground, drooping and dispirited.

"What doth ail thee, lady!" Magnus cried, dropping to his knees before her. "Tell me what will cheer thee, and thou shalt have it, though I must needs scour the world for it!"

She looked up, with a shy, sly smile. "A crown of flowers would cheer me, knight." She pointed. "Those flowers, yon."

Magnus turned on the instant, and was busy plaiting roses and moss roses and violets into a fragrant circlet. He set it on her head, and was rewarded by a single laugh before she drooped again. "I have no bracelets!"

"Thou shalt have them!" He turned to pluck flowers for her and returned, plaiting them into ringlets and slipping them over her slender, dainty hands. She looked up with a mischievous smile, then wilted again, sinking back against a pillow of ferns. Her body moved, restless and bewitching, with a twist of hips and an arch of back. Magnus stared, no thought in him but that slender body and the delights it promised—but her eyes streamed tears, and the movements of her breasts were sobs.

"Oh, what saddens thee!" Magnus dropped to his knees beside her. "Tell me, tell me what I may do to gladden thee!" But she only shook her head and twisted her whole body, lips parted for a soft and racking moan. Magnus couldn't bear it; his passion drove him, and he leaned to kiss her lips, ever so gently. . . .

Her body stilled, but the moan came again, desperate, demanding.

Magnus kissed her once more, his lips moving over hers, then lifted his head to see the tears had stopped, but the eyes drew him more deeply than ever. He lowered his lips to hers, and kissed, and her lips parted beneath his, her tongue touched his lips lightly, briefly, and he knelt, almost paralyzed by the sensation. She pushed his head up a little, gazing deeply into his eyes, then drew his head down again, and this time her tongue found his, and the kiss deepened and lasted. Little by little, Magnus stretched his form beside her on the moss, eyes closed, her mouth his whole world, drawing him down, down, into darkness.

For a timeless interval, he drifted, aware no longer of her kiss, but somehow of her presence. Then, in the night, a glimmer appeared, a diffuse glowing cloud that fluxed and thickened into whorls that took on human shape and form. He was shocked to see a dozen men or more, and behind them others in a band that seemed to stretch out forever. They were knights, though beyond them he seemed to see fur-clad barbarian warriors with stone-edged spears. Those in the front rank, though, wore crowns and coronets around their helmets, and their shields were emblazoned with elaborate coats of arms. All were gaunt, hollow-eyed and hollow-cheeked, and pale, very pale, but their orbs burned as they marched toward him, and he seemed to hear a whole whispering chorus saying:

Poor mortal, thou art ensnared and lost! Thy soul too will be mired and ginned, even as ours have been—for this elf-child is truly an ancient witch, who hath beguiled stronger and wiser men than thee, and will beguile many more. She doth drink heart's blood, as even now she doth drink thine; she will sap thy will to live, thy joy in life, and batten off it. And there is no hope of escape, no, none, for this beauteous lady doth know no pity, and is completely without mercy.

I shall escape! Magnus cried, inside his own mind, but their chorus bore down his voice:

Thou art lost already, for she hath cast her spell o'er thee, and thou has been glad of it. Thou hast gone willingly into bondage to her, and she hath thee in thrall, in company with us. Nay, soon, soon, thou shalt join us, for thou shalt wake to find thou hast no interest in life, no wish to feed, no lust, no love left within thee. Thou shalt waste away, as we have, pining for one more glimpse of this beauteous lady—but she will not vouchsafe even so much as that for thee; nay, she hath left thee already, for thou hast no more to give her. Thou art an empty husk, as are we all.

Their mouths opened, revealing an emptiness that rushed from a score of throats to shroud Magnus in darkness. He screamed and thrashed about, trying desperately to waken . . .

And did. He sat bolt upright, chilled and alone, lying on gravel within a grotto of bare rock, wetted by spray borne on the wind. He looked about in desperation, but of the faerie lady there was no sign.

And the despair welled up and engulfed him. He fought against it, struggling to rise to his feet, that he might stagger away from the slate-gray lake with its border of withered sedge. But the despondency overwhelmed him, and he sank back, meaning to rise again, but realizing that he would not, for it was too great an effort. He hung his head to weep, but found he did not even care enough for that. It was as the phantom warriors had said—the faerie child had taken all his energy for life, and left him too empty to care whether he lived or died, too apathetic even to think of suicide. He did not doubt that they had spoken truth—within a week, he would join them.

The prospect failed to move him.

And so he sat, alone and uncaring, listening for some sound other than the wind and the rippling of the water—but no animal barked or bayed, and no bird sang.

10

Rod was worried. It wasn't that he had lost Magnus's trail; he knew exactly where his son was. But he had seen him meet the wild-looking beauty, seen him swing her up onto his horse, and had discreetly turned away. Being accessible in case of emergency was one thing; spying was another. No, Rod had gone off and pitched camp and whiled away the time making amusing little carvings and writing in his journal. Not that there was anything to fear, of course, but some nagging concern kept him from just packing up and going home. Of course, if it hadn't been there, he never would have gone traipsing off after Magnus in the first place—but the young man was in very unstable condition right now, very vulnerable. Of course, he had only one real weakness under ordinary circumstances, but that weakness bore a thousand pretty faces and knew a million seductive movements, and was heightened by his current dissatisfaction with himself and his life.

So Rod camped nearby, and waited—and waited. When the gloaming gathered in to become night, he tried to sleep, but vague and dire dreams kept waking him. He rose in the false dawn, blew the coals to flame, heated water, brewed some herbal tea, and waited. And waited.

Finally, unable to take it any longer, he reached out, tentatively, very delicately and with total passivity, to try to eavesdrop on his son's mind—not closely enough for thoughts, mind you, just a general mood. . . .

It slammed through him and nearly dragged him into the earth with the weight of its sadness and despair.

Not even waiting to think it through, not even stopping to look, he sent out a plea for help with an urgency that verged on panic—but a plea to a very specific person. Some things, only a mother can handle. More to the point, there are some crises for which a parent would much rather have reinforcements, if they're available.

Instantly, he felt her response, colored with alarm: *What ails thee, husband?*

Our son, he thought back. *I don't know what it is, but something has him hip-deep in despair. No, amend that—I do know what it is, just not how or why.*

Another woman who doth seek to twist my son? The thoughts were tinged with hints of mayhem now, and incipient murder.

Something like that. Come quickly, won't you, dear?

Faster than the eagle flies, she assured him.

Rod relaxed a little. When Gwen said "fast," she meant it. He turned away to put out the fire and start a little skulking. It was time to spy.

Gwen landed on the bald spot atop the ridge, where lightning had blasted a pine and new growth had not yet sprung up. She hopped off her broomstick and ran to Rod—but she didn't get more than two steps before he swept her up in a crushing embrace. She yielded, letting herself melt into him for a minute or two, their thoughts mingling in mutual anxiety and reassurance; then she pushed him away and said, "What hath the shrew-witch done to my son?"

"I can't say for sure—I didn't spy on the deed, just its aftermath. All I know is that he met a wild maehad-type, and she went riding off with him, Apparently, she ran him through the wringer."

Gwen frowned, not quite understanding the simile, but certainly grasping its gist. "It may be that solitude is all he doth need, my lord. Thou hast hinted, more than once, that thou hadst been hurted by vengeful women of a time."

"Well, yes, but I was lucky enough to meet you, and you healed all those hurts."

Not completely, Gwen knew—in fact, she had later opened old wounds, quite unintentionally. She now realized just how deeply some of her careless remarks must have hurt him. "Gramercy, my lord," she breathed, and reached up for a long kiss. When at last they drew apart, she smiled and looked down, then looked up again. "And thou dost fear that Magnus will not meet a woman who will banish his memories of the others?"

"Or at least make them seem unimportant?" Rod shrugged. "Maybe. But he has to survive long enough to meet her, and right now, that's very much in doubt."

Gwen's eyes widened. "So bad as that?" Then her gaze lost focus as she turned her attention to the impressions coming directly into her mind rather than those of her other senses. Suddenly, she stared, shaken, and her gaze snapped back into focus.

Instantly, Rod was open to her mind and caught the impression of their son's emotions.

"Great Heaven!" Gwen cried. "He is sunk in a melancholy so deep that he is like to seek his death!"

"But how?" Rod groaned. "He just finished dealing with a

couple of females so predatory that they made wolverines look sweet!"

Gwen nodded, her face grim. "He is more easily swayed for having but just now been set aside, my lord."

"On the rebound," Rod translated, "and not in very good condition to discriminate between good women and bad."

"And she has snared and hurted him already." Gwen's face hardened with anger. "Hurted him, and cast him aside. How long hath she had for the doing of this deed, my lord?"

"A night and a day. I didn't want to seem to be following him too closely."

Gwen shook her head in wonder. "That such as she must feed their dwindled hearts off goodly men, and take the tenderness from them and cast them aside so quickly! Come, my lord—let us seek him and free him from her bonds."

Rod followed, reaching out to touch her hand. "I thought we were supposed to be able to relax and stop worrying about them, once they grew up."

"Never, my lord. Let us seek."

11

They found him sitting on the bank of a gunmetal-colored lake, shoulders slumped, sunk in melancholy. Rod and Gwen both halted, dumbfounded—this apathy was so unlike their son!

Then Gwen knelt beside him and touched his forehead. "What ails thee, my son?"

"Love." His voice was almost a monotone. "I am mired in it."

Gwen stared off into space a minute, probing his mind, then stood up, shaking her head. " 'Tis more than that, mine husband. 'Tis the work of a thought-caster, and one most expert, too."

"A projective?" Rod frowned. "To do *this* to him, she must have damn near hypnotized him!"

"She hath, and quite thoroughly. The posthypnotic suggestion binds him as no coercion could."

Rod's heart sank; for suggestion to work, it had to have struck some chord of despondency in Magnus. What had gone wrong in his son? The boy had always been so dynamic, full of such positive feelings. "Up and away, son! Don't let an enemy get the better of you!"

The vacant gaze turned in his direction. "How can she be mine enemy, when I am sick with love for her?"

"Because she tried to hurt you—and succeeded horribly well! I know it's tough, but you have to ignore the molasses your heart is mired in!"

"I cannot."

"But you know the feeling isn't real! You know it's just an illusion she's bound you into!"

"Nay, Father—'tis not a compulsion alone, but a reordering of my hormonal balance, and of the functioning of my brain. The witch-moss hath been crafted in suchwise as to alter my genes, however slightly."

Gwen drew her breath in with a sharp hiss, and Rod's eyes opened wide. "Witch-moss? What did she do, feed you a love philtre?"

"Aye, yet she held me spellbound from first sight. The philtre only assures that I cannot throw off mine infatuation."

"Come off it! No medieval femme fatale could know that much about physiology!"

"She had no need to; she had but to ponder on the effects she wished, and the witch-moss shaped itself to the pattern that would yield them. For look you, 'tis a substance that doth react to thought, and can therefore alter thought—and in this exacting mass of interactions that doth constitute our bodies and our minds, any alteration in the one doth transform the other. Nay, I know quite well what she hath done, but that doth not change the fact of it. I love her to misery, and will do all that I can to please her."

"But you know it's not a natural, spontaneous feeling— it's a synthetic emotion, not true love!"

"Aye, I know that—yet what use is knowledge? The feeling is still there, and cannot be altered." Magnus heaved a mile-long sigh. "Oh, my father! I feel as though the blood of life doth drain itself out from mine heart in a never-ending stream—and I can do naught to stanch it."

Rod looked up at Gwen in appeal. "Isn't there something you can do?"

Gwen shook her head. "There is much I could try, but I think 'twould be to no avail—and even if it were, the cure would be as vicious as the illness; for look you, ailments of the heart are such that a mother *must not* cure them, not in the way his need to be healed."

"But there has to be *some* hope!"

Gwen sighed. "There is a witch I've heard of, one whose gift is of healing, and her powers are of life."

Rod frowned in doubt. "More skilled than you? I didn't think there was any such."

Gwen was still a moment, then flashed Rod a smile. "I thank thee for thy kind thought, mine husband; yet though I've skill and force of many kinds, there do be some magics that others wield better than I."

"But none so many, so well?"

"Save my children; thou hast it. This witch doth dwell in the West, and is skilled beyond any in the ways of life."

"Funny I haven't heard of her."

"Few have; she doth not seek reknown, or those who are ill would give her no peace. Indeed, she doth hold her secret close, not even telling any her name, and will give aid to none who can be healed by others—unless they are near to dying."

Rod glanced at his son's pale face, at the haggard looks and slumped shoulders. "He might qualify on both counts. But how does he find her?"

"He must seek her out. The Wee Folk say that she hath posted sentries, creatures who watch for those so sorely hurt that only she can aid them, who guide the wounded to her."

"But the Wee Folk themselves don't know?" Rod frowned. "Just how powerful *is* this witch, anyway?"

"As I've said, she doth know the ways of all manners of life, without but even more within—and the elves have life. Nay, she doth know how to mislead even them; they can say only in what region she doth dwell, and tell only what those who have seen her, and been cured by her, do tell."

"Pretty good, since she probably swears them to secrecy—but the elves have some pretty good mind readers. So where is she?"

"In the West, as I've said—and she doth dwell by a curving lake that doth run between hills."

"A river oxbow, silted up till it's cut off from the river." Rod nodded. "But those are usually pretty close to its new course—so we can follow a stream?"

"Even so. The region is known—one of many lakes and ponds."

"The Lake Country?" Rod looked up. "I've heard of it."

"Aye. 'Tis therein she doth dwell."

"But that's a hundred square miles, at least! Isn't there any better hint than?"

"It must suffice." Gwen sighed.

Rod turned away, irritated. He clamped his jaw, then nodded. "Right." He bent down to clasp Magnus's arm. "Up, son. Time to go."

He hauled on dead weight. Magnus looked up, blinking. "I cannot, my father."

"Of course you can!" Rod spoke loudly, to hide the sneaking dread. "All you have to do is stand up and climb on a horse! Come on, son!" He pulled again.

Now Magnus actively resisted. "Nay, my father. The love of my life hath bid me stay; I will honor her wish."

"You'll atrophy! You'll die of stagnation!" Rod took a closer look at the grayish hue of his son's face, and wished he hadn't said that. "There's no real reason to remain—you know that. She just wanted you out of her way."

Magnus turned and bowed his head to his knees.

Gwen touched Rod's arm, feather-light. " 'Tis melancholia. You cannot jar him from it."

Rod felt his stomach sink. Whatever the murderess had done, she'd altered Magnus's biochemistry to force depression on him. He could save himself, but he had lost the will. "Can't you pull him out of it? Give him some sort of wall within his mind, that'll contain it?"

Gwen looked up, startled. Then her eyes took on a distant look as she considered; slowly, she nodded. "A wall within his mind, aye—and one to ward his heart. But there must needs be an outward symbol, husband, summat to show and keep him mindful that her spell is contained."

"What kind of symbol?"

"A shield, that doth ward him from fell magics. 'Tis therefore suited that it be of rowan wood, which will not turn a lance but will catch and hold Cupid's arrows."

"I suppose we do have to blame this on Eros, don't we?" Rod turned away to begin looking.

Gwen turned to her son, knelt by him, lifted his head, and pressed a hand to his forehead.

Rod left her to her emotional first aid and looked for fallen trees.

There were quite a few, not too far from the lakeside—the whole region was on the decline. He found a rowan, thumped it to make sure rot hadn't set in, and took out the dagger with the ruby in the pommel. Rod set it for a three-centimeter depth and starting carving. Ruby light lanced out—but only for the preset three centimeters. Rod pressed it slowly against the log, then drew it carefully across, then down, back, and up to meet the first line. He stepped away, eyeing the curved rectangle, nodded, and set the laser for two feet. He took his time burning through the log at each end, then cutting horizontally, following the lines he'd first made. He turned off the laser, lifted out a section of cylinder, and laid it face-down. Then he turned on the laser and began carving away the inside.

He came back to Gwen, holding up a shield that looked like a curved rectangle, a section out of the wall of a tube. She was still intent on her work within Magnus's mind, so Rod sat down with shield and laser and passed the time by cutting straps from his emergency leather supply and attaching them to the shield, then carving symbols into the face of the wood. It had been the easiest and quickest kind of shield to make, but it had come out resembling those the Roman legionaries had carried—so he outlined a pair of Roman eagles, then burned away wood to leave the eagles in bas-relief. He eyed it critically, added the letters SPQR, and put the dagger back in its sheath. He looked up just as Gwen was rising—slowly and stiffly; she'd been kneeling quite a while. Rod jumped to offer his arm; she took it, flashed him a grateful smile, then saw the shield. "Ah!" she breathed. "Well crafted, husband! Hale him up, now."

Easier said than done; Magnus was still well over two hundred pounds of bone and muscle. But if he didn't help, neither did he resist, and Rod managed to get him to his knees. Then, with his muscle and Gwen's telekinesis, they wrestled the young man to his feet. "Give him the shield." Gwen's face was taut with strain.

Rod lifted his son's arm and slipped it through the straps inside the shield.

"The rowan shield doth ward thy body," Gwen intoned, looking deeply into Magnus's eyes. "The spell that is linked to it doth ward thine heart. Walk, my son—the witch's compulsion can no longer hold thee."

Magnus stood stone-still. Then, finally, his brow creased

in a frown, and he took a single step. "I can move," he said, as though it were a puzzle, then took another step, turning his back on the water. "Away from the lake, I can step!"

"Thou canst," Gwen assured him.

The young man's shoulders sagged. "It boots little, Mother. My heart doth pulse out its blood within me; I bleed, and am sick in my soul."

"Even so," Gwen said softly, "and therefore must thou go to seek aid from one more skilled than I. There is a witch of green, a witch in the West who doth dwell by a curving lake, who can give thee healing that I cannot."

But Magnus shook his head. "Not even the waters of Life can lift me out from this slough of despond."

Gwen nodded. "This is a wound within, and even clear water cannot cleanse it. I ken not the way to make the dying grow again. None but this Western Witch can make thee whole again."

"Come on, son." Rod took his arm and turned him toward the horses. "Let's mount and be away."

But Gwen stopped him with a touch. "Nay. Thou art not wounded; the Green Witch will not let him approach if thou art with him, nor none of her sentries will guide him."

"You don't mean he has to go alone! In *this* condition?"

"Even so," Gwen said, her voice iron. " 'Tis the pity of my life that I must watch his pain and leave him to wander in solitude—but he must seek this healing by himself, husband. We may not company him in this quest."

Rod's face hardened; he felt the inner rebellion hot and stabbing; but he knew his wife was right. He caught his son's arm and turned away. "Well, at least we can see that you have the best guide possible. Down, Fess—I don't think he can get his foot in the stirrup, just now."

"It would seem unlikely." The great black horse knelt. In a daze, Magnus let his father guide one foot up and over the horse's back; then Fess rose slowly, and the young giant set-tled into the saddle.

Now Gwen went over to her son, reaching up to clasp his hands and looking up at him with eyes that, for the first time, betrayed the depth of her concern. "Godspeed, my son. Seek thou the Maid of the West."

"I feel as though I do yet bleed within, Mother," the young giant said faintly.

"There's none but the Western Witch can save thine heart's blood. Go well, my son—and quickly."

"Gramercy, Mother." For a moment, his gloved hand rested on hers, then reached down to catch his father's. "I thank thee, Father. Wish me well."

"I do," Rod said fervently. "I always will."

12

The sun had set, and the sky was filled with a pearly light
that darkened to gloaming all about him as Magnus rode out
of the little valley. Actually, Fess carried him; he was so
sunk in despondency that he let the horse bear him where it
would, totally passive, with scarcely enough will left to hold
on and bear up his shield. Five hundred years of experience
with humans had taught Fess when there was some point in
trying to get them talking, and when it was less than useless,
so he let the young man drift, only speaking to ask his choice
whenever they came to a crossroads or a fork in the way. Every time, Magnus roused himself, frowned about, and said
only, "I care naught. Go as thou dost think best," which was
exactly what Fess had expected, of course—but it did pro-
vide an excuse to bring the young man out of his stupor for a
few minutes every now and then. Fess was concerned that
Magnus not be left undisturbed long enough to retreat so far
within that he might never come out.

After a while, he came to a small dirt road, wide enough to
justify trotting. The jouncing roused Magnus to grab at the
pommel, then clasp with his knees and straighten a bit.

"Fess! Canst thou not go more smoothly? I had near to fallen!"

"I shall canter, Magnus." He speeded up, and the ride smoothed out. Magnus grumbled, but held on; though he drifted back into apathy, his stupor was not so deep.

Fess could have gone as smoothly as a rocking chair, at any gait, of course; but the diversion had worked.

Then they came to a greater diversion, which demanded real thought of the young man; for as they rode up to the crest of a ridge, they saw a gaunt old tree, stunted and twisted, devoid of leaves—and in its branches slept a huge black bird, its head tucked under its wing. But as they rode under the limb on which it perched, that head came out, fixing Magnus with a baleful yellow eye that seemed to glow in the deepening gloom, and the bird cried, "Carrion!"

That jolted Magnus out of his trance. "What manner of bird art thou!"

"One that doth live by corrupted meats—and there is the scent of putrefaction about thee! What part of thee doth moulder?"

"None." Magnus frowned, thinking to tell the bird it would be carrion itself—but it was too much effort.

"Thou speakest false, for thine heart's begun to turn. 'Ware, warlock's son!"

Magnus frowned up at the bird. His mind worked sluggishly, but thoughts did form. He fought to enunciate them. "Thou art of a witch's making, and no true bird."

"Art thou a true man?" the raven returned, "For I see thou art of the making of a warlock and a witch."

"Even so—yet how dost thou know?"

"For that my mistress hath told me. *Krawwwwk!*" The raven lapsed into cawing for a few seconds, while it dipped its head and raised a claw to scratch. Then it looked up at

Magnus again and said, "Wherefore dost thou ride by night?"

"For that I ride in haste, and must needs find the Maid of the West."

"Then art thou doomed to despair, for there's no such maid. *Krawk!* A wanton is she, and never pledged a troth to any man!"

"Why, how is this?" Magnus frowned. "I have been told that she doth ward herself closely, and is shy of mortal converse."

"The more fool she, young knight, and the more fool thou to seek her! *Awrrawwk!* Yet an thou must needs pursue thy folly, take thee ever the high road, and never the low! Yet far wiser wert thou to take instead the road thou hast come by! Begone!"

For a moment, Magnus was tempted to do just that—turn away, and go back to the tarn his love had commanded him to watch. But before he could decide to do so, Fess lurched ahead, and Magnus had to catch at the saddlebow. After that, it was far too much effort to tell him to change direction— but Magnus did turn back to glare at the impertinent bird. Its head was under its wing again, though, totally oblivious to his displeasure.

Night closed down fully as Fess turned northward, following the ridge line. The change of direction brought Magnus briefly to his senses. "Though hast turned from the roadway."

"The road tended downward, Magnus, into the valley. That witch-moss construct of a raven told us to ever seek higher ground—and there are mountains ahead."

Magnus peered into the darkness. "I cannot see them."

"Nor can I, Magnus—with visual senses. But radar shows a large mass looming ahead."

"Well." Magnus thought it over. "But how shall we come to her other sentries, then, if there is no road?"

"I suspect that the route to the curving lake is selected from a diminishing number of choices, and is known to all her constructs."

"And that the sentries are stationed at the places of those choices?" Magnus nodded. "Well, so." And he lapsed back into brooding—Fess obviously didn't need his notions.

They came out on a moor, the miles eaten away by Fess's tireless canter. Magnus rode through it, swaying in the saddle, so quiet that he might have been asleep—or dead. Fess rode on across the wasteland, sonar constantly probing the ground ahead, alert for bogs.

At last he came to one he could not avoid—it stretched out to either side for at least a hundred yards. In fact, the path seemed to run right into it—but as they came up to the end of the track, Fess saw that it joined another path that ran to left and right. He slowed and stopped, considering alternatives.

Roused by the cessation of motion, Magnus looked up—and it was he, not Fess, who first saw the two flecks of brightness beside the clump of heather. "I am Magnus Gallowglass, and I go in need of the aid of the Green Witch of the West!" he called.

"To whom do you speak, Magnus?" Fess asked—but the young man had somehow come alive, more or less, and was dismounting. Alarmed, Fess followed closely.

Magnus knelt by the bushes and parted them. A fox lay panting on the ground. As Magnus pulled the leaves aside, it scrambled to its feet and tried to run—but its rear leg stretched out taut with a chink of metal, and the fox yipped in pain.

" 'Tis caught in a trap." Magnus frowned, thinking it over—the elimination of local vermin was hardly his concern, and if he let the fox go, some nearby farmer might lose a few chickens.

But the sight of a fellow creature in pain, entrapped as he was himself, stirred pity in Magnus, and he laid aside the shield to reach out, murmuring in soothing tones as he coaxed the fox back toward the trap just a little, then pressed the jaws open. The beast surged forward, running a few steps away, limping—but the limp grew less and less pronounced with every step till, after a run of perhaps twenty feet, it was moving normally. There it turned, receding, until it was only two bright sparks of eyes in a pool of shadow.

Magnus frowned; it was odd behavior for a fox. "Surely, little friend, I will not hurt thee. Nay, go thy way, as I go mine." He turned to take up his shield and swing astride Fess again.

But the bright sparks came closer, and the form became clear behind it, muted fire and flowing fur, and the fox came up to sit beside the warlock's horse, gazing up at him with unblinking eyes. "Wherefore wouldst thou seek the Green Witch, mortal? Thou dost show no wound!"

Magnus stared, taken aback. Then he realized that he was seeing another of the Green Witch's sentries. "I am not wounded, but ensorcelled, Sly One."

"And thou dost think the witch can unbind the spell that doth hold thee?"

"I pray she may," Magnus returned, "for an she doth not, I am doomed to pine away."

"We would not wish to see so fine a man as thou languishing," the fox returned. "Nay, go thou northward yet, for the right-hand track doth lead up higher."

"And what shall I discover thither?"

"Mayhap a wood, whose trees never shed their cover." The fox grinned, tongue licking its chops. "Mayhap fat hens. An thou dost find such, save some for me."

Magnus knew a hint when he heard one. With the ghost of a smile, he reached down into his saddlebags, found some of the dried meat his father always carried, and tossed it to the furry one. The fox leaped and caught it in midair.

" 'Ware," Magnus advised him. " 'Tis salt."

"Meat is meat," the fox muttered around the morsel. "I shall dine. Fare well, young mortal." And it turned, to tail back into the forest.

Smiling, Magnus rode on, then lapsed into a trance again.

Around the bog Fess cantered, up the rising ground that left the moor behind, and into the foothills. Magnus jolted alert, every fiber thrumming danger. "What! Where!"

"There is nothing, Magnus. Have you dreamed, perhaps?"

"Nay, Fess! 'Twas a rider who came upon us, all black as midnight, and his horse the deepest of shadows! His cloak spread out like wings, and his eyes were coals!"

"None have passed us, Magnus. None have come near. The only life that stirs is that of the small creatures of the night, such as badgers and hedgehogs."

"Yet I could swear 'twas he!" Magnus looked up at the moon and gasped. "He is there! Upon the face of the moon, 'tis his form!"

Fess looked up, registered that the markings of craters that had always been on the larger of Gramarye's two moons were as they had always been—but could see how a young man in a semi-trance might interpret those markings as the shape of a horse and rider. "Let us assume, then, that he was another of the witch's sentries. From which direction did he come?"

"From the left, ahead of us."

"Then let us investigate that direction." Fess bore to the left, off the track.

"Might he not be warning us of danger?"

"Perhaps." Fess slowed to a trot, scanning everything ahead. "But I sense none."

"Is there sign of a pathway?"

The robot was silent for a few minutes, then said, "There are cairns of stones every few hundred yards, all piled in the same manner. Yes, I think there is some indication of direction."

Then, suddenly, the ground rose up before them, and they broke out into a broad, dusty roadway, bone-white under the moon. Beyond the track, a valley lay in shadow, and in that shadow was an evergreen forest. Around its fringe grew a few young oaks, leafless now in the chill of autumn, but glinting here and there with vines of white berries.

As they paused, regarding the forest and the mountain behind it, a shadow swooped across them from behind. For a moment, the form of a winged bird was clear against the white dust; then a small falcon swooped upward and away. Hard behind it came an eagle, which flapped its great wings and rode an updraft, rising higher and faster than the falcon, but following unerringly.

Magnus could see the game; the eagle would maneuver until it was just above the falcon, then pounce upon it. It was none of his affair, of course, but he couldn't help seeing himself in the smaller bird, and turned to glare at the eagle.

The predator faltered, then began to glide in a huge curve. Magnus spared a glance at the falcon, thinking a summoning thought at it too, and both birds, quite unwillingly, found themselves winging back toward the young man, impelled by the imperatives of his thoughts. They stretched their claws to light on branches of nearby but separate trees, one to each side of Magnus. He looked at them both sternly, and began a silent dialogue, mind to mind to mind, which, if it had been voiced, might have sounded somewhat like this:

"Eagle, wherefore dost thou pursue this falcon? Knowest thou not that he is not thine ordained prey?"

"He hath stole from me! An he doth take my food, he shall become it!"

"Why, how is this?" Magnus turned to frown at the falcon. "What hast thou ta'en?" Looking more closely, he saw a mouse in the falcon's claws.

"Only the small warm one."

"So small a morsel?" Magnus turned back to the eagle. "It should be beneath thy notice!"

"Should or not, 'tis mine! I stooped upon it, and this upstart did swoop betwixt me and it!"

"Game doth belong to him who doth seize it first!"

"Then thou art my prey!" The eagle stretched its wings.

"Give over thy claim!" Magnus thought sternly, and brought more of the dried meat out of his saddlebag. "Give over thy claim against the falcon, and thou shalt have this!"

The eagle eyed the meat with interest. "What beast is that?"

" 'Tis the flesh of a deer, which are too great to be game for thee."

"Give me!"

Magnus tossed a scrap of pemmican toward the eagle. The wicked beak snatched the morsel out of the air; it disappeared. The eagle nodded. " 'Tis good. More of that, and I'll give over pursuit."

Magnus brought out a larger piece of meat as he nodded at the falcon. "Begone!"

"I shall!" The smaller bird winged away. "I shall repay thee at need!"

Magnus tossed the large scrap to the eagle, who caught it and rose into the air on thundering wings, then soared away.

Magnus shook his head. "Let us go, Fess."

But the eagle banked and circled about, winging back toward them, but stalling, swooping lazily in the breeze, turning to stay near. "Name thyself, rider! For thine actions are well done, and not of the common sort. Wherefore comest thou here?"

"I am Magnus Gallowglass," the young man answered, trying to follow the bird's sliding movements, "and I seek the Green Witch of the West."

"Then gather such of the mistletoe as ye may find," the eagle called, its voice eerie in the moonlight. "Bear the berries with ye, that they may give ye guidance!" It wheeled away from him, crying, "Then up, even to the clouds! And find the channel of the stream that died!"

"Why, how shall I know such a channel?" Magnus called, but the eagle only gave a long and tearing cry as it turned back to him. Remembering his manners, Magnus came alive long enough to snatch another bit of dried meat from his saddlebags, and tossed it up. The eagle dipped in flight to catch it, then circled away, crying, "Fare thee well, mortal man! Persevere! And if thou shouldst have need of me, why, call!"

The night swallowed it up.

"At the least, it seems, she hath deemed me worthy of her care," Magnus muttered, "or her guardians have. Come, Fess—I must ride by an oak, to gather berries."

Fess went ahead, secretly delighted that Magnus was showing so much sign of life.

He even summoned the energy to clamber up standing on Fess's saddle, holding onto the tree's limbs for balance—he, who should have been as surefooted as a mountain goat!—and cut down several bunches of berries. He cradled them in his arm as he carefully lowered himself back to the saddle, muttering, "What shall I do with these?"

"I doubt not their use shall become apparent, Magnus. The road leads upward. Are you settled?"

"As well as I may be," Magnus grumbled. He gripped the

horse's side with his knees and caught the reins with his free hand. "Away, Fess."

Up they rode, higher and higher. There was water somewhere, certainly; they passed small rills, purling across the path at intervals. They even passed a small marsh, where several of the streamlets pooled, and went by the dried stalks of rushes that rattled in the breeze. Then mist closed about them, chill and clammy. Magnus clung to the horse. "Canst thou tell thy way by radar, Fess?"

"Yes, Magnus, but I must go slowly. There is a limit to both range and definition; I cannot be certain of the condition of the path."

Then rock walls closed about them; even through the mist, Magnus could tell he was surrounded by stone, from the echoing of Fess's hoofbeats. "We are come into the pass, are we not?"

"We are, Magnus. And the signs of erosion are there—this was indeed a river's channel once."

The mist lightened, and thinned; Magnus could see the layers of rock to either side, glinting with flecks of mica—and the mouth of the pass before them. "Where there was a river, there may be a lake, may there not?"

"Yes, Magnus. Of more importance is that a former channel may indicate the river's course has changed—which would produce the oxbow lake your father spoke of."

"Even so." Magnus nodded. "Let us see what lies beyond the pass."

They came out into the false dawn, the whole land half-lit by the eerie, sourceless light—and the land fell away before them, sloping down to a flat yet restless surface: the curving lake, ruffled by the wind.

Magnus felt tension bring him to full alertness. "What shall I do now?"

"Use the mistletoe," Fess suggested.

"In what manner?"

The robot was silent, searching its memory, correlating. "The ancients who used mistletoe in their worship threw gifts to their gods in their forms as objects of nature. Think of this Green Witch as a river spirit; your gift is the mistletoe."

Magnus nodded and slipped out of the saddle. "Bide thee here, then, for I must pace down to the water's edge."

"I shall—but I shall come quickly if you call, Magnus."

"Do, I prithee." The young warlock hefted his rowan shield, cupping the berries in the crook of his arm, and broke off a bunch. He marched slowly down to the bank, then threw the mistletoe into the water, crying, "Maid of the Lake, I cry thy mercy!"

The water lay still.

Magnus was just beginning to think he had failed, and to see the whole night's ride as a senseless charade, when . . .

Water burst upward into a fountain, and a woman rose from the lake. Magnus stared, for this was not the crabbed old crone he had expected, nor even a woman in the fullness of maturity, but a girl younger than he, at least to the eye, clad only in the long, dark hair that fell about her shoulders, past her breasts and down her hips. He felt a pain within him, a sudden wrenching; her beauty took his breath.

Then she was out of the water, speeding across the waves to the shore, plunging away from him into the night. Magnus, jolted from his trance, cried, "Fess!"

"Here, Magnus." The great black horse was beside him in an instant.

Magnus dropped the mistletoe and leaped astride. "Chase her, Fess! I have come too far, have waited too long, am too sorely in need to be denied!"

Fess bolted off after the fleeing form, rejoicing that Magnus seemed once again fully alive.

For a wonder, she ran more quickly than the horse. Or perhaps no wonder, after all—she was a magic worker. Magnus rode entranced by the sight of the long, perfect legs flashing in the moonlight, of the glorious mane that swirled about her as she ran, cloaking her far better than a gown. Magnus focused his thoughts in a summons. "Fox and eagle! Falcon! I cry thine aid, in return for mine! Turn this woman from her path!"

And they were there, so quickly that they must have been following, the eagle and falcon flying straight at the lass's face, the fox leaping up to yap at her ankles. She faltered, halted, trying to fend them off—and Fess caught up to her. She turned, alarmed, as the horse swerved around in front of her, and her hair billowed about her, cloaking her in night. Magnus felt his heart seize up and his breath choke off at the perfection of her form, the curve of paleness that showed beneath her hair. He was not even aware that the eagle, falcon, and fox had melted away as suddenly as they had come.

The maid retreated a step. "Sir, wherefore comest thou so unseemly upon me?"

Breath came again, and Magnus protested, "Maiden, I would not impose upon thee for the world—but my heart's blood doth drain within me, and only thou canst aid me." Somehow, though, the pain of his heart already seemed lessened.

She stared, wide-eyed, then made a sudden gesture as though she were spreading a veil over herself, and she stood before him in a gown of rich crimson, a golden chain lying about her hips to form a Y, its long end hanging down before her. "Nay, good sir, there is no need for that sword that hangs at thine hip, nor for the shield of rowan that hides thee!"

"The shield, milady, wards my heart."

"If thou dost hope for cure from me, thou must needs let

that sundered organ ope to me." She advanced a step, holding out a hand. "Come, lay down thy shield."

Somehow, Magnus found himself standing on the ground; dimly, he remembered dismounting. Her hand seemed to wield the strength of a giant; he let the shield swing down by his side and drop from nerveless fingers.

"Come, then." She stretched out her hand, and he caught it. Slowly, step by step, they went back down to the water, where she took up the bunches of mistletoe he had brought. "Thine offering, kind sir—and thy cure." She took him by the hand and led him into the lake. "Trust in me," she said softly, "or I can avail thee naught."

Eyes fixed on her, he followed with mechanical steps; he did not think he could have resisted if he had tried. The waters closed over his head.

Fess watched, waiting, poised to dash in and pull a drowning man from the lake—but before the three-minute limit had passed, he saw, by the pre-dawn light, the maiden and the youth climbing up from the water onto an island that stood well out from shore, with a small hill on it. The woman turned to the hill, and a door opened in its side. She led the wounded warlock in, and closed the door behind.

Fess dropped his systems into standby mode, satisfied that his master's son was temporarily safe, at least physically. He could only await developments now.

The developments, to Magnus, were delightful and wondrous. The Maid of the Lake took his doublet from him, then made a poultice of the mistletoe and bound it round his chest, over the left nipple. Then she conducted him to a downy feather bed, an acre wide it seemed, that lay in another chamber, lit by the fire in a grate. "Lay thee down, sir knight," she murmured, and helped him, supporting him enough so that his fall was controlled, and his body unhurt as his mind drifted into oblivion. He was dimly aware of gentle hands pulling off the rest of his clothing, then of nothing else.

He dreamed—of nothing concrete, of no pictures or signs, with only fleeting images that blew through his mind, commanding attention for a few moments, then gone: the milkmaid who had tried to bind him under her spell, the wenches of the Floating World, the witch in the tower, the beautiful woman who had left him to mourn by the lakeside. With each there was pain, at first poignant, then eased; and with each memory, the pain became sharper. At thought of the merciless beauty, the pain seemed almost unbearable, then subsided, then was, miraculously, gone. Her face receded into a shifting, swirling series of colors and amorphous forms; delightful aromas that filled his head, constantly changing; the most delightful of sensations against his skin, so pleasant they seemed almost sinful—but that could not be, for there could be no sin in dreams. They came, after all, without his will, even in spite of his will. So there was no sin in treasuring the delicate sensations, the exquisite pleasures, the waves of delight that built and built to a shuddering ecstasy . . .

And the long, silken slide into velvet oblivion.

Sunlight touched his eyelids; scarlet enveloped him. He opened his eyes and found that he lay in the huge feather bed, with sunlight streaming in through a high window, almost directly overhead. He lay still, musing and remembering. . . .

He turned, startled.

She lay beside him, the most beautiful face he had ever beheld, full lips curving sweetly, huge eyes watching him with merriment—and beneath it, concern. "Art thou well, wizard?"

At her words, the wariness left him; he went limp with

relief—and realized that he felt whole and filled, far more healthy than he had been in an age. "Aye, milady. More well than ever I have been in my life."

"I am pleased to hear it," she murmured, and levered herself up, moving closer, lips covering his in a long, lingering, and loving kiss. She took her head away, looking at him with a secretive smile, then laughed and rolled away, gathering a robe about her as she rose, and stepped away through an archway. "Come, sir! The day is full, and thou art sound."

With amazement, Magnus realized it was true. The faerie child was only a memory now, with the reflection of pain; his humiliation by the hag in the tower seemed inconsequential. Joy welled up within him, and a feeling of wonderful, immense freedom. "I shall not die after all! I can never thank thee enough, maid!"

But she had gone out where she could not hear him, leaving him to dress, and to ponder how she could have healed him so thoroughly and with such ecstasy, and still be the Maid of the Lake.

Fess was glad to see him, but tactful enough not to say anything while the maid was present. "Mount," she instructed, and Magnus swung up into the saddle. She saw the question in his eyes, and lifted a finger to press against his lips, forestalling the words. "Thou mayest not stay by me, nor ever come hither again, unless thou art so badly wounded as thou wast but now—and that thou'lt not be, for I've taught thy heart, and the deepest part of thy mind, how to heal themselves, if they will."

"Can I find no way to thank thee?" Magnus protested.

"Thou art a warlock, and a puissant one, I wot. Thou knowest now the manner of healing I've given thee. If thou wouldst show me thanks, do thou to other wounded souls as

I have done to thee, healing and mending the hurts that none can see."

"Why, so I shall," he whispered.

"Go, now," she commanded, "and go without fear or doubt—for as I've taught thee to mend thine heart, I've taught thee to mend thy body also. If thou art wounded, thou wilt tell the smallest parts of thy body to cleave to one another; thou canst bid thy blood to cease to bleed, thy wounds to close. Nay, thou mayest yet be killed in a single blow, thou canst feel grievous pain—but thou shalt live, no matter what wounds are given thee, so long as thou dost wish to."

"Why, I shall wish so, now." Magnus reached out to touch her. "I shall wish to live, if for naught but the chance that I might someday see thee again."

But she caught his hand, though she kissed the fingers. "Why, then, court danger, in defense of others—and when thou hast given so much of thyself that thou hast naught left to give, find me again, and I'll replenish thee."

"I shall." She had just given him reason to kill himself trying to help other people.

She looked into his eyes, a merry roguish glance, then commanded, "Go!"

Fess turned and moved off. Magnus kept his eyes on her as long as he could, till his body's turning forced him to look away. Even then, he looked back once, to see her, a slender form in crimson velvet, hand upraised in farewell. Then a cloud crossed the sun, a shadow glided past, and she was gone.

13

While Gwen slept, Rod called Fess, via radio, and asked for a progress report; the robot told him that Magnus had found the healer and gone into her dwelling. When Gwen waked, Rod duly informed her, and they settled down for their anxious vigil.

They didn't have long to wait, though, before Fess assured them that Magnus was leaving the lake, alive and well—and looking far more cheerful than he had for quite some time. Half an hour later, Magnus's thoughts touched them briefly: *I am well, my parents. Prithee, await me by the lake where thou didst find me.*

May we not come to thee? Gwen asked.

Magnus considered, then thought, *At home, then. I shall teleport thence, and Fess will come as he may. . . . He is agreeable.*

I think I may be able to care for myself, the robot concurred.

Rod nodded, relieved. *At home, then.* He took his wife's hand. "Come fly with me!"

Gwen smiled, and summoned her broomstick with a thought. It came arrowing to her; she reclined sidesaddle, and rose into the air. Rod concentrated on being beside her, and caught up.

They landed in the courtyard—to find Magnus coming out of the keep with a backpack. Gwen threw her arms about him. "Praise Heaven, my son! That thou art well!"

"Thank also the Maid of the Lake." Magnus disengaged her with a gentle smile, stepping back.

Rod caught his arm and clasped his hand. "We were worried."

"Thou hadst need," Magnus said gravely, "but Mother did direct me well. I am healed."

"And off again?" Gwen glanced at the pack. "How is this, my son! Whither dost thou wander?"

"Away," Magnus said gravely. "Far, far away. I can no longer stay on Gramarye, Mother."

She cried out in protest, grasping him by the shoulders, searching his eyes—and his mind—but met only surface thoughts, and a stern resolve. She stepped back, composing her face. "So that is the way of it, then." She braced herself for Rod's fury.

But it didn't come. Watching Magnus, she saw that he was braced, too, and just as surprised. They turned to Rod, and found him grave and sad, but nodding. "Yes. You do have to go, son—as I had to leave my father's home. Only my father's eldest had to stay—and I wouldn't force that on a dog." He sighed and reached up to clasp the young giant by the shoulder. "I've known it had to come some day, so I'm prepared. Well, at least the apprehension is over."

Gwen and Magnus both stared at him, amazed.

Rod smiled, amused. "Go well—and write home often."

Fess came trotting into the clearing.

Rod turned. "You came fast enough!"

"I can move more quickly without a human to protect," the robot explained.

"And probably started another dozen local pouka legends, while you were at it. Good thing you hurried—we need your services."

"In what way, Rod?"

"It's time, Fess. Magnus has to leave the planet."

"Ah." The horse sounded sad. "The *Wanderjahr.* Well, I shall be honored to accompany him."

Gwen cried out in protest; so did Magnus. "My father! I could not deprive thee of thy boon companion!"

"How did you think you were going to get off-planet?" Rod turned, with a sardonic smile. "Fly? You're good, son, but I don't think you could achieve lightspeed—and I would be very surprised to discover you could shift into H-space." He frowned. "Or maybe *not* surprised, come to think of it— but I'd rather you had a ship around you, in any event. And my ship doesn't fly without Fess to run it."

Magnus was still, trying to correlate all the factors, trying to find another way. There wasn't any. Slowly, he nodded. "I thank thee, then, my father. And thou, Fess—though I regret the inconvenience."

"It will be no inconvenience, Magnus."

"You can send him back when you buy your own ship," Rod added. "You don't have to, though."

"I shall, my father."

"Come." Gwen set a hand on his arm. "There are some to whom thou must needs say farewell." She called by mind: *Cordelia! Geoffrey! Gregory!*

Twin explosions signalled the arrival of the young men; Cordelia came out of the keep, frowning. "Aye, Mother?"

"Thy brother is bound away, for a space of years," Gwen said, in tones that brooked no disagreement. "Tell him farewell."

With a wordless cry, Cordelia threw herself into her brother's arms. He held her gently, looking down at the crown of her head, stroking her back, his face carefully impassive.

Rod left them to it, and led Fess around behind the keep. He knew there was plenty of time—Brom O'Berin would have to be summoned, and Puck, and Toby and Alain and Diarmid, maybe even Their Majesties. Whether he wanted it or not, Magnus was going to get a farewell party, however impromptu.

Rod opened the hatch in Fess's side, took out the silver basketball, and disconnected its cable. The black horse body stood stock-still.

Handle with Care, Fess's voice said behind Rod's ear.

"I always do. You don't really think I'd drop you just to keep Magnus home, do you?"

Would I do you so grave an injustice?

"I don't like the way you say 'grave.' "

Rod took Fess's "brain" down into the dungeons. There, he plucked a torch from a sconce, thought at it until it lit, and went down to the end of the passage. There, he set the torch in a sconce, pressed the third stone block from the right in the fifth row down, and stood back as a section of the wall grated open. It left a doorway that was a little lower and a little narrower than most, but was still quite usable. Rod took down the torch and stepped through, leaning against the door to push it closed. Then he set off down the tunnel.

The elves had dug it for him, right after the family had decided to move in permanently. Rod had flown his spaceship in by night, telling Fess to make it bury itself in the meadow just across the moat, and the elves had covered it over with dirt. The locals had thought the bare dirt circle that was left was a fairy ring, and they hadn't been too far off.

It was very convenient—there were times when Rod needed the ship's lab and library facilities. More importantly, though, his escape route was handy, if he ever needed it in a hurry. Not that he ever had—but ten years as a secret agent had left him with a very cautious set of mind.

At the end of the tunnel was the rugged exterior of the spaceship. Rod pressed his thumb against the silver patch in the midst of the pocks and craters, and a larger-than-average crater swung out as a hatch. Rod stepped in, went to the control room, and connected the silver basketball to its cable in a niche. He clamped it in position and closed the panel. "Remember, now—you want to make an Appearance."

"My sense of the dramatic has not suffered from close association with you, Rod."

"Great." Rod smiled. "Take good care of the boy, huh?"

"I will, Rod. I have, for twenty years."

"True, Chiron. And see that he writes home a lot, okay?"

"If he does not, Rod, I will. You should rejoin the party, now."

When Rod came back, he found that there were at least two dozen people circulating around Magnus, hugging him, shaking his hand, and wishing him well. There was at least as much weeping as there was laughter—and, sure enough, Their Majesties had somehow managed to drop what they were doing and come in time. Elves circulated with trays of food and drink, and whenever people left Magnus alone for a moment, Puck was cuffing his knee and detailing all the marvels and wonders he would encounter.

Rod joined them, keeping his smile carefully fixed in place.

Suddenly, a deep thundering made the earth begin to shake. Everyone fell silent, turning in awe, and had just begun to think about screaming, when a fanfare of a hundred trumpets blared, followed by the theme from *The Ride of Koschei the Deathless*, as a huge, rugged spheroid rose into view above the walls. It was cratered and pitted from encounters with a hundred meteorites; it was an asteroid, come to ground. It glided over the courtyard and lowered itself gently to the ground. A final fanfare sounded as the hatchway opened and swung down to form a boarding ramp.

"Very good, Fess," Rod muttered. "Thank you."

The crowd was silent. Magnus glanced quickly at Rod; his father nodded. The young warlock turned to the crowd and said, softly, "I thank thee, my friends. I shall never forget thee, nor my delight in thy farewell." He looked around at them, then saw the tears on his sister's cheeks and caught her to him for one more brief hug, then stepped back and forced a smile for all his friends. "God be with thee."

"And with thee, Magnus!"

"Farewell, young warlock!"

"Farewell!"

"Yet hold." King Tuan stepped forth, face suddenly grave, and drew his sword. "There is a ceremony overdue thee by many years. I have long awaited thy petition, but it hath not come, so I cannot now accord thee the Vigil and the Bath—but I may still give thee the accolade. Kneel, Magnus Gallowglass d'Armand."

Everyone was silent, knowing the significance of his use of Magnus's true family name.

Magnus stepped forward and knelt before his king.

Tuan laid the flat of his sword on each shoulder, saying, "I, King of this Isle of Gramarye, dub thee Knight of the Realm, and charge thee ever to defend the weak and smite the wicked, wheresoever thou shalt go." He sheathed the sword, stepped forward, and struck Magnus on the cheek, saying, "Rise, Sir Magnus."

The crowd broke into wild cheering as Magnus rose and stood before his king. When the crowd could hear again, they heard Magnus saying softly, "I am thy man, henceforth and ever to be true to thee and thy queen, and the heirs of thy body, to defend thee in battle and serve thee in peace."

Then Prince Alain stepped forward to clasp his arm, and stepped aside for his brother Diarmid. At last, Queen Catharine stepped forward and offered her hand; Magnus bowed and kissed it.

Again the crowd cheered, and Tuan said, "Go now to thy father."

Magnus bowed and turned away. Gregory caught up his pack and ran to give it to him. Magnus took it and clasped his youngest brother on the shoulder. Gregory turned a shining face up to him and fell into step beside him, but Brom O'Berin caught his wrist and pulled him back gently, saying, "Nay. Let him go alone with thy parents for the moment."

And so he did, while the crowd melted as quickly as they had come, and Cordelia and her brothers welcomed the royal family into their home.

Magnus turned back at the foot of the ramp and said, "I shall come again, my father."

"I know." Rod clasped his shoulder, eyes shining. "Don't wait too long though, okay? We're not getting any younger." He raised his voice. "Fess!"

"Aye, Rod?"

"Here is your new master. Obey Magnus as you have obeyed me, until his life ends or he gives you leave."

Magnus's face suddenly drained of all expression as he heard the age-old formula.

"I shall, Rod."

"But remember what I said about making sure he writes home a lot."

Magnus smiled, looking down at his father with affection.

"I will, Rod."

Now, at last, Rod reached up and hauled the young giant down for an embrace. "Be careful, son, and always do your homework about customs and crooks before you make planetfall. There're a lot of mean ones out there."

"I shall, my father. Fare thee well!"

"But there are a lot of good ones, too." Rod stepped back, his smile still in place. "There will be times when you're tempted to forget that—so don't, eh?"

"Aye." Magnus smiled.

Gwen stepped forward for her embrace, murmuring, "Fare thee well, my son! Oh, fare thee well! And come back hale and whole to me, in heart as in body."

"As whole as when I left," Magnus promised. He kissed her cheek, then stepped back.

Fess gave him an out. "Traffic window assigned. Ship lifting."

They laughed, and Magnus stepped back inside the hatch, waving as the door rose and sealed itself, hiding him from view.

But Rod And Gwen kept waving, as the asteroid rose into the sky and dwindled, becoming a dot, a speck, a mere nothing.

Then Gwen turned and wept on Rod's shoulder. He held her tightly, his own eyes rather misty.

As they came back to the keep, Tuan and Catharine stepped forth. Without a word, Tuan embraced his vassal, and Catharine hugged Gwen, for the first time in their lives.

Aboard the ship, Magnus sank back into his couch, glad that the cessation of acceleration gave him a chance to go limp—and was suddenly aware of the huge ache of emptiness that rose up within him.

But as he sank rapidly down toward melancholia, a voice sounded in his mind. *Magnus!*

Magnus stilled, his face neutral. Then he answered. *Aye, Gregory. Canst thou speak mind-to-mind even off-planet, then?*

Aye, and we will now discover what range we have, shall we not?

Aye. Magnus smiled. *I thank thee, brother.*

And I thee. Only, Magnus . . .

Aye, my sib?

Wherefore must thou needs leave?

Magnus heaved a sigh and tried to frame the answer. *For that I cannot be fully myself whiles I do dwell within my father's shadow, Gregory. Canst thou comprehend that?*

Nay.

I hope thou never wilt. But let me offer one facet of the problem, yet only one. I do not believe 'tis right to sway a people to the form of government thou dost prefer.

I see, Gregory answered slowly. *And if thou dost stay on Gramarye, soon or late, thou must needs fight our father over that issue.*

Thou dost comprehend quickly—and therefore must I leave.

Aye. But, Magnus . . .

Aye?

Is that the sole reason?

Magnus was silent a second, then sent, *Thou art as acute as ever, my sib. Nay, 'tis not.*

There are others, then.

One other, at least. But all conjoin to this course of action.

Shall I have to follow thee, someday?

I cannot say—yet I think thou wilt not. Thou art the youngest, and hast ever found the world of the mind more real than the world of the senses. I think thou shalt find room enough to roam, though thou dost never leave our little Isle.

I trust not. Gregory sighed. *Well, fortune favor thee, my brother. Call me at need.*

I will, Magnus thought. *With thanks.*

Then Gregory was gone, and Magnus was alone again—but he did not feel quite so empty now.

"Thou shalt have need of stout warding for thine heart, where thou dost go," a voice said.

Magnus looked up, incredulous, and found the ragpicker sitting there in the second acceleration couch. "Thou? Even here, thou canst follow me?"

"Anywhere," the ragpicker confirmed, "for I am within thee, as I am within every man. What thou dost see is only the outward sign. Come, wilt thou have my warding for thine heart?"

Magnus just sat gazing at him for several minutes, evaluating the truth and validity of what the ragpicker had said. He could be a lying demon, of course—but was far more likely to be an hallucination. Magnus wondered what had gone wrong within his own mind, that he had begun to see apparitions so much sooner than his father had.

"A quarter of thee is truly of Gramarye," the ragpicker reminded him, "and thus doth incorporate what thou dost term 'witch-moss.'"

Magnus frowned. "Then, when we are far enough from Gramarye, thou shalt cease to manifest?"

"Mayhap. If 'tis so, thou must needs take my ward quickly, or not at all. Come, wilt thou have it?"

Magnus was silent, eyeing him and assessing. Then it occurred to him that the changes the Green Witch had made in his mind and body should protect him from any hurtful aspect of the ragpicker's "gift."

"Wilt thou have it?" the ragpicker pressed. "Wilt thou make thine heart invulnerable?"

"Aye," Magnus said at last, "I will."

The ragpicker's face broke into a grin. He clasped his hands, then parted them—and a translucent golden box rose from his cupped palms, with a large keyhole in its lid. Magnus stared at it, entranced, as it floated over to him, then suddenly plunged toward his chest. He cried out, and flinched away—but the box followed him, fading to a mere outline as it sank into his chest and disappeared. Magnus howled, clutching at his chest, expecting a stabbing pain—but there was only a mild sensation, as of something slightly shifting, then . . .

"Nothing," he whispered, looking up at the ragpicker with haunted eyes. "I feel no differently than ever before."

"Thou shalt know the benefit anon."

Suddenly, Magnus realized he might have done something irrevocable. "Yet what if I wish to be rid of it? Thou hast put mine heart in a box of golden; how shall I open it again?"

"The key is within thee," the ragpicker assured him.

"Where?"

The ragpicker grinned. "Ah, now. That is for thee to discover. Myself, even I know not."

"Fiend!" Magnus shouted.

The ragpicker disappeared on the instant, leaving only mocking laughter behind.

The hut was wattle-and-daub, like any other peasant hut, and like all the others around it; the anarchists did not wish to call attention to themselves. But under the wattle and daub was armor plate, and within the largest hut was a middle-aged man working at a wide desk under the light of a very modern lamp.

"Agent Finister is here to report," a voice said out of thin air.

The man looked up in surprise, then smiled with eagerness. "Show her in."

The inner door opened, and a slender woman entered the

room. There was a strange light to her eyes; she was slender, with an almost elfin grace.

"Sit down, sit down!" The man stood and went to pour two glasses from a dusty bottle. "Have some wine!" He handed her the goblet.

"Thank you, chief." She sat in the plain wooden chair in front of the desk, accepting the glass with a demure smile.

"Well! What news?" The chief bustled around to sit behind the desk. "I know the young warlock has left the planet—and that's good, very good, so far as it goes! But did you give him something to take with him?

"I think so," Finister said. "Of course, we can't be certain—but if the psychologists are right, I've given him a thorough distaste for sex in any form, which should last for the rest of his life."

"Barring psychotherapy, of course." The chief nodded vigorously. "Yes. But nothing is a sure bet, eh? Excellently done, Home Agent Finister! If we can't beat this second generation of warlocks, at least we can make sure there won't be a third. Splendid, splendid! Especially the eldest—he has the most powerful combination of psi genes of any human being yet born. If he reproduces . . ."

"But he won't," she said, with a very smug smile.

"Amazing! How did you do it?"

"I had the idea from an old witch he encountered, who lived in a tower and specialized in seducing young men to gain their vitality. It gave him a very unpleasant sexual experience, even if it wasn't complete, so I decided to continue the lesson. I disguised myself, of course, first as a nobleman's wife . . ."

"I wondered why you needed all those extra agents."

"I had to mock up a functioning court, in an abandoned castle. Agent Mortrain did a wonderful job as my aging, jealous husband, by the way. I might have been in trouble if Gallowglass had insisted on accompanying me right into my father's castle, but by the time we arrived there, he was only too eager to be done with me."

"And you gave him a negative sexual experience."

"Caught in the preliminaries to adultery? Very negative, I would say."

"Why just the preliminaries?" The chief frowned.

"I was afraid he would come down with an attack of conscience at the last minute. But it hit him hard; I eavesdropped on his thoughts, and found him communicating with his alter ego from Tir Chlis."

"The alternate universe we abducted his family to, when he was a child? I still can't figure out how they got away from that one." The Central Agent reflected that these home agents, Gramarye espers adopted as foundlings and reared to be loyal to SPITE, were very useful.

"The same—and the opportunity was too good to miss. I disguised myself as a faerie queen, blindsided him, and hypnotized him while his defenses were down. Then I gave him a very detailed dream. Not total—his little brother disrupted it at the last minute, with a couple of disguised images—but enough to shake him badly."

The Central Agent frowned. "Did the little brother know it was a dream?"

"I didn't probe his mind—he's only thirteen, but he would have known it in a second; Gregory is probably the most talented telepath among them. So I don't know, but I'm pretty sure he thought it was Tir Chlis, too. Then I showed up as an enchanted maiden"—she swept her own form with a gesture—"and hit him with every ounce of projected sex appeal I have."

The Central Agent sat very still, then slowly smiled. "I'm surprised he's still alive."

"He wouldn't be, if some meddling hussy in the lake

country hadn't interfered. I had him in a total depression, gave him a projected dream that convinced him he was doomed. He wouldn't have eaten a crumb, and would have pined away. But his parents jolted him into motion, and that confounded robot-horse found the Green Witch for him. We really should so something permanent about that healer, chief."

The Central Agent made a note. "We'll see to it. So she undid all your work?"

"Not all. She couldn't have. Oh, she brought him out of the depression well enough, and has him wanting to live again—but he's not sure why, and will have a massive distrust of women for the rest of his life. I don't think any psychiatrist could root that out of his mind. And he'll certainly have no interest in sex, except possibly as an intellectual pursuit."

"And intellectual pursuits don't cause children!" The Central Agent chuckled and rubbed his hands together. "Well done, Finister, well done! We must move you up to bigger things now, eh?"

"I would say that we should." Agent Finister rose and glided around behind the desk to touch the chief's cheek. "Very intimate things."

The chief's eyes kindled, and he smiled slowly. "Just what are you promoting, Agent Finister?"

"Myself." She touched his temple, and he suddenly lost all expression. With languid grace, she set down her goblet and touched his other temple. Slowly, his eyes filled with awe and deep, deep desire. "I would like to be Central Agent some day," she murmured.

The chief nodded and started writing. She didn't take her hands away until he was done, then stood behind him with a secretive smile.

"Agent Worely," the chief said into his invisible intercom, hunger hollowing his voice.

"Yes, chief?"

"Come in, please."

The door opened, and a young man came in with a frown. "What is it, chief?"

"You're my witness," the chief said. "If I die in the line of duty, Agent Finister will become chief in my place."

The younger man stared, looking from one to another. Finister gave him only a small, gloating smile. He reddened and turned away. "As you say, chief." The door closed behind him.

"Now," Finister purred, reaching down.

Almost mechanically, the chief rose and followed her, his eyes burning. She led him through an inner door, into his own suite.

The next morning, they held his funeral. It was very sumptuous, by Gramarye standards—Central Agent Finister made sure of that. It wouldn't do to undermine respect for the office.